That Girl Is Poison

D0063560

That Girl Is Poison

Tia Hines

www.urbanbooks.net

Urban Books, LLC
78 East Industry Court
Deer Park, NY 11729

That Girl Is Poison Copyright © 2012 Tia Hines

ISBN 13: 978-1-60162-517-5
ISBN 10: 1-60162-517-0

First Printing August 2012
Printed in the United States of America

10 9 8 7 6 5 4 3 2 1

This is a work of fiction. Any references or similarities to actual events, real people, living, or dead, or to real locales are intended to give the novel a sense of reality. Any similarity in other names, characters, places, and incidents is entirely coincidental.

Distributed by Kensington Publishing Corp.
Submit Wholesale Orders to:
Kensington Publishing Corp.
C/O Penguin Group (USA) Inc.
Attention: Order Processing
405 Murray Hill Parkway
East Rutherford, NJ 07073-2316
Phone: 1-800-526-0275
Fax: 1-800-227-9604

That Girl Is Poison

by

Tia Hines

Prologue

"Ouch!"

"Just be quiet! I'm almost done, I think."

"You're hurting me! It hurts!"

"It's supposed to hurt. Now shut up!"

I closed my eyes, wishing this nightmare would soon come to an end. The pain beyond pleasure, it was horrific! My pelvis pulsed, and my vagina screamed. I tried to lock my legs to take away the pain, but it wasn't working. I was too scared to yell, as his threat of making this more painful had frightened me.

"Don't move! Stop moving! Shit!" he whispered unpleasantly in my ear.

"Oooouch!"

He slapped me across my mouth to literally shut me up. The palm of his hand had the stench of a musty skunk, and it made me nauseous. I tried to make myself throw up, but I couldn't concentrate hard enough.

He kept forcing himself inside of me as I lay there lifeless, sobbing, my tears soaking his pillow. I wanted to close my eyes but in the weirdest way I thought if I did my life would be over. I thought I was going to die. So I watched my rapist take control of me, all the while anticipating when this violation would be over.

I watched as he closed his eyes, enjoying himself at my expense, while I lay there helpless, a stranger to this world of intercourse.

Then the pain. Oh, the pain. It increased as this child of a man began to ram his short stump-of-a-pencil penis in my other hole, where I was sure pleasure didn't lie. He started going crazy like he was having a seizure, while I lay there, eyes all bugged out, in pain and scared.

All of a sudden the pressure eased up. Then I felt moisture as he withdrew himself from me, still covering my mouth and now gripping my neck with his other hand.

"You better not tell anybody about this, because I swear I'll get you! You better not tell! This is our secret, understand?"

I responded quickly, shaking my head up and down slowly, hoping not to piss him off any further. He released my throat, uncovering my mouth, leaving me on the bottom bunk like a crushed can unfit to be recycled for a measly five cents.

I lay in a nasty wet puddle that, after a while, became a dried-up dirty stain on the sheet. My virgin temple had been violated on all grounds by a boy twice my size and three years older. He left me with soiled panties and a secret never to tell.

That wasn't the first time a man-boy predator, or whatever "Godly" creation of the human race, put his hands on me. My first time experiencing what I knew was supposed to be a loving, passionate, intimate feeling was the worst, and the second time didn't make it any better, because I had caught an STD. It was nothing big though, just syphilis, which cleared up in a few weeks.

The third time I had sex, I got hit with genital warts. Damn! No doctor could cure that! Yeah, go ahead and say it, "Damn! Either she is a dirty bitch, or she is messing with some dirty nuccas," because all of the above is correct.

Yup, that fourth time of sexual healing, I got pregnant, and the prince charming that knocked me up gave me HIV. Yeah, that's right, HIV that causes AIDS, the deadly, incurable disease. I'm still standing though. No deadly turns over here. Not yet, at least. And, hopefully, not until I infect some people.

That's right. I'm handing down the virus to the young, dumb, and stupid. What? You think something's wrong with that? Gimme a break! If the cigarette companies can legally kill people with their deadly ingredients, then passing on something that was given to me is perfectly permissible.

It ain't my fault that people are too naïve and not health conscious. Bet you can't even remember the last time you had a checkup or, better yet, an HIV test. Got you thinking, huh?

Oh yeah, by the way, my name is Desire, and I'm a sixteen-year-old on the grind, about to take you on a journey. I suggest you buckle up because you're going on a serious roller coaster. This is my story, my song. My desire to burn.

Chapter 1

The evening after my sixth grade graduation, my mother decided she didn't want me anymore. How nice, huh. I was devastated that day, which I remember very clearly.

Graduation commenced, and everyone went back to my uncle's house. My mother had told me she would be leaving me for an hour or two to set up this big surprise for me at home. I was anxious and excited.

I quickly came down from that high. I got a surprise all right. The surprise of her not coming back. I practically stayed up all night waiting for her to come get me, but she never showed. Uncle Frank had to break the bad news.

He wheeled in the living room as I sat up on the couch, anxiously flipping from channel to channel, thinking what my big surprise could possibly be.

"Desire, I have something to tell you."

I directed my attention to Uncle Frank. Hearing a tremble in his voice, I had a strong feeling that whatever he was about to say was going to be bad.

"Your mom . . . she's . . . she, ah . . ."

My eyes quickly watered, and my first thought was death. I thought my mother was dead, y'all. I had a horrific picture of her being killed in a car crash or something. I don't know why I thought the worst, but I did. The image disappeared quickly though when my uncle got his words out.

"Desire, your mother is not coming back for you."

"What about my surprise?"

"There is no surprise, baby. Your mother lied."

I sat there not really processing what was being told to me, stuck on the "no surprise." "So there's no surprise?"

"I'm sorry, Desire."

I sat mute for a bit, looking down at the floor. Then I looked up at Uncle Frank.

He must've noticed the confused look on my face. "Desire—"

"Why'd she lie? I didn't ask for the surprise. She just told me she had one."

"I know, baby, but—"

"Just forget the surprise. When is she coming to get me?"

"Desire, that's what I'm trying to tell you. She's not coming back to get you. You're going to live here now."

My eyes teared up. "She's not coming to get me?" I whispered aloud.

"No, honey, I'm afraid not."

Teardrops hit my cheeks. "I'm—I'm going to live here?"

"Yes, your mother left town."

"And when she comes back, I'm going home, right?"

"Desire, she's not coming back."

There it was. The moment of truth that nearly knocked me to my knees. My mother had skipped town and left me behind.

I didn't mind much because I loved my uncle and his wife, especially his wife. Both of them treated me like a princess. Every time my mother and I went to visit, Aunt Linda always had something for me. She was the sweetest thing. Until I started to live there.

Uncle Frank remained the same, but my sweet ol' Aunt Linda turned into the bitch from hell. She was so mean to me, her gifts couldn't even be cherry-coated on Christmas. Why and how she did a 360, turning into the wicked witch overnight, was beyond me. It was bad, though. She put the *h* in hate.

Uncle Frank tried to make up for her wicked ways, but it wasn't enough to overcome her evilness. She needed to down some holy water from Jerusalem because, I swear, she was the Devil's daughter and I was her slave.

I was eleven and cleaning house like I owned a maid service minus the employees. I had to do everything. It was crazy. The lady was trippin'.

My Fridays were set out for me. I'd get up, go to school, come home, and literally become the live-in maid. I hated it. I mean, yes, I understood that chores teach responsibility and cleanliness, but there is a difference between being taught responsibility and being treated like a slave.

She can swear up and down she was preparing me for the real world and teaching me responsibility, but come on, who was she fooling? I mean, it doesn't take a rocket scientist to figure out that she was just being a mean old lady. Not saying that Auntie Linda wasn't smart because, no doubt, she was. She knew exactly what she was doing, and I say it was plain cruelty. She had strict rules, a nasty tongue, and a quick backhand.

But getting back to Friday, I had to sweep and hand-mop the kitchen floor, bathroom floor, and the living room floor. In addition to that, I had to dust the living room and everything in it, vacuum the four bedrooms, change the sheets on all beds, make sure the dishes were washed, and put away all the laundry. Can you imagine that happening every single Friday?

And, God forbid, I ask to do something without doing my chores. All hell would break loose. I barely could go anywhere anyway, so what was the point? Most of the time I was a homebody. I was allowed to go outside in the front yard but not outside the gate.

Then there were times when I was allowed to hang out at Jen's house. It was mostly trying to get there on the weekend because, since it was summer time, Jen went to overnight camp during the week. I must say, though, it wasn't always hard getting to Jen's house. It just depended on Auntie Linda's mood, and you know most of the time, her mood was shot to shit.

I remember this one particular Friday night. I went downstairs all happy-go-lucky to ask Uncle Frank if I could go over Jen's house.

"Uncle Frank, I finished my chores. Can I stay the weekend over Jennifer's house?"

"Sure, I don't see why not."

"Well, I do, and the answer is *No!* You stayed over there last weekend."

"Naaw, that was two weekends ago."

"Two weekends, three weekends, it's the same thing. You ain't going. The answer is No!"

You don't know how bad I wanted to rip Auntie Linda's tongue out. Who told her to mind my business? I wanted to curse her out, but I remained respectful and stayed in a child's place. I did not follow up the conversation with a why-I-couldn't-go, or pop an attitude. I simply went into my bedroom, laid on the bed and cried. It was one of those hurtful cries too. You know, the one where you're shaking and you take the quick three breaths, and then exhale slowly. Yeah, it was that type of cry.

I lay there sobbing for about ten minutes, thinking, maybe if they heard me going at it that long, they would change their minds and let me go. My plan didn't work though. I was left up in my room to drown in my own tears. Oh well, I got over it quickly.

I built up a few courage balls and worked up enough nerve to go back downstairs to ask again. I was being bold now, 'cause, usually, once my aunt said no, that was that. There was no asking again. But, for some reason, I failed to take no for an answer that night. I guess I wanted to go that bad. Shoot, for what happens when I get over there though, I should have stayed my ass at home.

But, anyway, when I went back downstairs, my aunt was in the kitchen. My uncle was in the living room by himself.

"Uncle Frank," I begged, in almost a whisper, making sure Auntie Linda couldn't hear, "can I please go over Jennifer's house?"

"What did Linda tell you, Desire?" Uncle Frank asked in a you-know-better tone.

"She said no but—"

"But nothing! You know when she says no, I cannot go over her head. You know better than that."

"I know, but please, Uncle Frank . . . I did all of my chores."

"No, Desire!"

"Pleeeeeeeease, Uncle Frank? What did I do?" I begged, questioned and cried at the same time.

"You didn't do anything."

"Then why can't I go? She's supposed to be having a sleepover this weekend, and I'm going to be the only one not there." Jennifer wasn't having a sleepover, but I had to say anything to get over there. I needed a breather from that hellhole I was in.

My uncle looked at me and sucked his teeth while I gave him the sad puppy-dog face.

"All right, go pack your bag. Hurry up!"

"Thank you, Uncle Frank," I exclaimed, joyously hugging and kissing him.

"Yeah, yeah." He smiled, just as happy as I was.

That was my Uncle Frank. Got to love that man. He did have my back sometimes. I wish he could have had it all the time, but you know that was impossible with his devilish wife and her hellish ways. Ugh, she stirs up anger every time I think about her.

But, anyway, I ran up the stairs to my room. My bag was already packed. All I had to do was grab my tooth-brush, slip on my sneakers, throw on my coat, and lug my stuff downstairs. I was too happy to get out of the house. I pranced down the stairs with my overnight bag in hand.

"Where you think you going?"

Oh yes, Auntie Linda was on my tail, but don't worry, it didn't blow my high. "I'm going to Jennifer's house," I answered proudly.

"Says who?"

"Uncle Frank," I replied with a smile.

Auntie Linda stormed into the living room. "Frankie, you told this girl she could go over that fast-ass girl's house after I already said no?"

Uncle Frank put his head down, sighed aloud, and there went the arguing.

Arguing was the theme of the house, and guess who it was over? Me. It drove me crazy with all the yelling and screaming and this-and-that, going back and forth. No wonder I was damn near insane at the time. It was like there was no end to an argument always starting because of me. It made me feel like such an outcast.

I contemplated running away plenty of times, but at eleven years old, it remained just that, a thought. I had nowhere to go anyway, and even if I did have somewhere to go, I had no money. So what was the point? Besides, I didn't know the first steps of running away. All I knew was that Jen's house was my salvation, and I didn't want to do anything to mess that up.

Auntie Linda unwillingly dropped me off at Jennifer's house that night. You should have seen the look on her face. She was pissed, while I was smiling from ear to ear. She was so pissed, she didn't even wait for me to get in the house after she let me out of the car. I barely got my overnight bag out before she peeled off. It was cool with me, though. I was where I wanted to be, at my getaway spot, Jen's crib.

Let me tell you, Jen's house was the peace spot. The atmosphere there was refreshing. There was no cleanup, no attitudes, no frustration, no nothing. Her mother was a single parent raising only Jen and her fourteen-year-old brother. She was a charming lady to get acquainted with. I think that's why I loved it over there so much.

Her mother kind of reminded me of the good times me and my mom had when she was around. She often made me miss my mom, but then again, she made me want to forget her too. The memory was too painful. So Jen's mom ended up being the replacement.

I got to Jen's house that night around nine o'clock, the time I would have been forced to be in bed at home. As soon as I stepped foot in the door, my nose caught the aroma of brownies in the air. Oh, her mother's baking was the bomb. She sure did know how to treat a sweet tooth.

I threw my bag down and embraced Jen's mom like she was my own. Then I made my way to Jennifer's room to greet her. I caught her in the middle of playing dress up, and of course I joined in. Her mother was good for letting us mess in her clothes and dabble in her makeup. We pranced around that night as if we were America's next top models. To add to the excitement, we stuffed our faces with brownies, baked chocolate chip cookies, cheese Doritos, and drank pitchers of red Kool-Aid until our stomachs could handle no more. My stomach ached so bad, that night I could hardly sleep.

I woke up the next morning sick as a dog. I was vomiting, and I had the "runs." Jen's mom gave me something to settle my stomach, while I vowed never to eat junk food again. I stayed 'sleep for pretty much the entire morning, until Jen's mom enforced shower time. There was no question about getting up then. I needed a good shower anyway, since I had been doing number three all morning.

I was first up for the shower while Jen did the routine wake-up thing—the brushing of the teeth and the washing of the face. I'd skipped that step, since I was first up for the shower. I figured I'd get my face in the shower and brush my teeth after. Nothing was wrong with that, right? I was still going to get what I needed done.

I slipped off my nightgown and pulled my underwear off. Embarrassment set in. I quickly hid from Jen's view and examined the seat of my underwear. Can you believe my eleven-year-old ass had shit stains in my underwear. Yes, disgusting I know, and the sight for me was worse, but hey, it's the truth. I thought I'd wiped myself good but apparently not. It was no big deal though. I discretely balled up my stained undies, tossed them in the corner, and threw my nightgown over them.

I hopped in the shower like it was nothing and was in there for about thirty minutes. That was probably the best shower in my life. Seriously, I ain't joking. At home, Auntie Linda was on that one-minute-shower rule. Have you ever heard of a one-minute shower? How the hell was I supposed to get clean on a time restraint that short? She was trippin', but it was another rule I had to abide by. I would get in, count to sixty while doing my do, and get out. But at Jen's house it was a different story. I took advantage of the fact that I could stay in the steamer longer, until Jen's mom threatened to make me pay the water bill. I got my black ass out of there after that. I didn't waste any time getting dressed neither.

I didn't dry off good. I didn't lotion. I didn't do anything but hurry 'cause I was trying to get out of the bathroom before Jen came in. I was not trying to let her see my nasty underwear. Oh no! I was ready just in time too. She came walking in the bathroom just as I was coming out. We crossed paths, and I hauled my things to the room.

In the midst of my actions, I got this sudden urge to take a piss. I don't know where the hell it came from, but it felt like I had been holding it for a minute. I had to drop my stuff in the middle of Jen's floor and run back to the bathroom. Jen was just stepping into the shower when I invaded her privacy.

"Dang, Desire!"

"Sorry. I gotta pee."

"Oh, you better hurry up then."

"I know. I know." I quickly pulled my pants down as Jen made her way in the shower.

After I relieved myself, I felt embarrassment. Yes, yes, yes, there it was again—the shit stains on my new, clean underwear. All I kept thinking was, how is this possible? I'd just washed up in the shower for a long-ass time. I was nearly about to have a heart attack because my eleven-year-old ass was shitting on myself.

What kind of mess is that? I literally yelled at myself out loud.

Jen thought I was talking to her. She peeked through the shower curtain. "You called me?"

I covered up my doo-doo undies with my hands as discreetly as I could. "Ahhhh no."

"What's wrong?"

"Huh?"

"What's wrong? You're acting like something is wrong."

"Oh no, nothing. Nothing is wrong!"

"I hope you ain't doing number two while I'm in the shower," she joked, closing the shower curtain back.

I thought, *Too late. I already did it in my pants.* "No." I laughed, playing it off. "I'm done. It was number one."

Good thing she'd closed the curtain, 'cause that was my chance to make a quick getaway. I was on guard, making sure Jen wasn't trying to slip in a peek through the curtain, while I grabbed tissue to wipe myself. It was the strangest thing too because, as I wiped, nothing was on the tissue. I stared at the tissue like, *What the hell?* I was too puzzled.

When Jen turned the shower off, I had to snap out of it quick. I needed to make a break for it before she saw me. I left out of the bathroom with my underwear pulled halfway up, sitting just below my butt. I crept to her room, so her mother or brother would not get the privilege of seeing me naked from the waist down. How inappropriate a sight, seeing I was a guest in their home.

I made it to the room safe and sound and rambled through my bag for some clean underwear. But guess what? I was fresh out. You know I was just done at this point. I had gone through three pairs of underwear already after spending only one night out.

Yes, I violated the panty-sharing rule. You can borrow clothes but never share the panties, right? Hey, I had to do what I had to do. I couldn't walk around pantyless. That would be just nasty. Then again, come to think of it, sharing panties and being pantyless are both nasty. I probably would have been better off being pantyless, but oh well.

I rambled through Jen's underwear drawer trying to scoop a pair of her undies before she got out of the shower. Don't ask me why I didn't just grab any pair as opposed to being picky, 'cause she walked in on me and caught me red-handed.

"What are you doing?"

"Huh?"

"What are you doing?"

"I was—"

"Eww, you're putting on my underwear?"

"No, I'm not!"

"Yes, you are!"

"No, I'm not!"

"Then why do you have my underwear in your hand?"

I let the underwear drop back inside the drawer. "Oh, I thought these were mine."

"No, you didn't. Yours are right here."

She walked over to my brown-stained underwear on the floor, and I ran to grab them before she could get a good look.

"Eww, what's that in your underwear?"

"I don't know," I answered, embarrassed. "I think I keep doo-dooing on myself."

"That's dumb! Can't you feel when you have to go to the bathroom?" Jen laughed.

I stood there wanting to respond but couldn't. How could I? I had no comeback, and I didn't have a reason to give her as to why I was shitting on myself. Then something red and warm trickled down my thigh.

Jen started jumping up and down, excited. "You're getting your period. That's what it is."

"What? I'm getting what?"

I looked down at my legs. I had no idea what she was talking about. My period? The only period I knew about was the one you put at the end of a sentence. I was puzzled. I almost freaked out seeing the blood dripping down my leg. I thought I was dying, and Jen was like super happy. She couldn't be serious.

"A period is something that all women get, you know, going through poverty."

"But I'm not a woman. I'm a little girl. Do you think it was because we were acting like grown-ups last night?"

"What's wrong with you? No one ever talked to you about poverty?"

"Noooooo. What's that?"

"It means you can do the nasty now. Oh, and your breasts are going to get bigger."

"Do the nasty? Bigger breasts?" I shouted, freaking out more.

At that time, of course, doing the nasty was a thought that occurred to me. I had seen it on television one time or two and this lady was screaming out of control. I thought she was going to die, until I figured out what they were doing. Shoot, I was traumatized. If doing the nasty was going to hurt like how that lady was scream-ing, then I wanted nothing to do with it.

Yeah, so, anyway, as the blood ran down my leg, I was like, *What is this poverty thing?* You think I would have tried to wipe myself or something, but I stood there doing what I did best—look stupid.

"So you're not happy?"

"About what? I'm bleeding."

"I told you, it's your period."

"Yeah, I know, but what is that?"

"When you bleed every month, get bigger breasts, oh and your butt gets bigger too."

The idea that I was going to bleed every month didn't settle well with me. Oh my goodness, the thoughts I was having. I was like, *Dang, I'm going to have to change my underwear every five minutes. What if blood gets on my clothes?*

"Let me get my mom."

"No, no." I stopped her before she could leave out the room to let the secret out.

"Why?"

"Because . . . just don't!"

"But she needs to know."

"Nooooo, Jen, please." I really wasn't looking forward to being embarrassed anymore than I was.

"Okay, okay, I won't tell her." She pouted, stomping away.

I stood there feeling like crap because I had just made my best friend in the whole wide world mad. She sensed the feeling too.

"I'm not mad at you, Desire."

I was so relieved to hear that. That was something I didn't get too often.

"Here, wipe yourself with this towel. And go ahead. Take a pair of my underwear. I have some new ones in there that I haven't worn yet. Hurry up, though, 'cause I gotta show you what to do."

Boy, wasn't that a day to remember.

After finding the clean underwear and getting ourselves dressed, Jen became "Dr. Watson." We went into her office—the bathroom—and had our way. I think we went through like seven pads before we actually figured out how to put one on. Who said instructions with demonstrations were helpful? I think it confused us more. I mean, knowing how to put a pad on now, let's just say me and Jen were both idiots then. We were young, stumped, and stupid.

We managed though. We finally figured out how to get the pad to stick to the seat of the underwear and not me. Ha, that was funny! I thought I was too grown then.

We got back to Jen's room and overdosed on boy talk.

"Ain't Jeff coming to our school next year?" she said.

"I think you should go out with him."

"Why?"

"You don't think he's cute?"

"No, he looks like a monkey." I giggled.

"No, he doesn't. He's cute."

"Not really."

"Well, I think he is. You should talk to him. He's gonna like you anyway, once he sees your big titties." Jen laughed.

I looked down at my chest. It was sure enough getting to that stage. It kind of made feel out of place too, knowing that the girls my age probably didn't have breasts anywhere close to my size. What could I do? Nothing. I was eleven years old with a bra size of thirty-four C. I had to face the facts that this was puberty. Can you imagine that? Jen was the same age and barely fit a training bra! What was up with that?

"See, you already have big titties. All the boys are going to like you. I'm jealous."

"Well, when are you going to get yours?"

"I don't know."

"How can you find out?"

"I don't know, but forget about me. Let's talk about this new thing. Now that you got your period, are you scared about doing the nasty?"

"A little bit."

"You know what to do, right?"

"I think so, but shouldn't I change my pad now?"

"How long has it been?"

"Like fifteen minutes. I think you're supposed to change it every fifteen minutes."

"Okay let's go change it."

Our conversation continued, as we went into the bathroom.

"What part am I supposed to stick up there? It can't be this hard part."

"I think it is."

"I think y'all done lost y'all minds," Jen's mother said, out of the blue.

We looked at each other like, *Oh shit!*

I was hoping Jen's mother had only just walked up on us and hadn't heard our entire conversation about boys, sex, and periods. I was so scared and embarrassed. I didn't know what to expect. I thought we were going to get a good whuppin', as my aunt called it, but to my advantage, Jen didn't get beatings. Luckily, from her mother hearing the conversation, she knew we weren't just fooling around. I had valid reason to be checking out the tampons.

Jen's mom gave me pointers on what to do and told me the truth about going through *puberty*, not *poverty*. Glad I found out the correct name 'cause people would have been clownin' me. I'm mad I didn't know it was the wrong word in the first place. Had my deadbeat mother not run out on me, I probably would have been more knowledgeable when it came to hitting that puberty stage. That damn lady, I tell you. The memory of her makes me sick to my stomach.

Jen's mom told me tampons weren't for little girls, but I went ahead and used them anyway. She gave me a ton of pads to use, but my grown, hardheaded behind preferred to use a tampon. I think it was like some weird mental thing where wearing a tampon made me feel like I was grown and in control, as opposed to a smelly pad that I had to change every hour, like a baby wearing diapers. I didn't like that feeling.

I had already developed low self-esteem from my mother leaving and my abusive aunt. I needed something to boost me up, and wearing a tampon was the key. Weird, right? I know. My first period, using a tampon. Insane! I should have stuck with the pad though 'cause I do regret the day of taking on the idea of wearing a tampon. To this day, I don't wear them, and I will never wear them. Not after what happened to me.

Chapter 2

I woke up the next morning at Jen's house ready to go. I didn't want to shower, eat, or get my last-minute play in. I just wanted to get the hell out of dodge and go home. I got on the phone at five forty-five in the morning and begged to get picked up.

"Uncle Frank?"

"No, Linda. What you want?"

"Can you please come get me? I want to come home."

"Oh no, you don't!"

"Please, Auntie Linda, I want to come home now."

"It is five o'clock. Are you out of your mind?"

"Please, I want to come home," I cried.

"Girl, take your behind back to bed."

"Auntie, I'm scared!"

"You begged to go over there, so you better get over your fear." *Click.*

Just like that, she ended the conversation. I was about to call again, but Jen's mother woke up and startled me. I told her I wanted to go home, but she made me go back to bed, saying she'd take me home later. She asked me what was wrong, and all I could say was, I wanted to go home.

She came to the conclusion that I was a bit homesick and a little shook up over my period. I wasn't going to tell her the truth 'cause I didn't want to change her mind. I simply got back in the bed as she requested, sat up for three hours straight and cried. Jen never skipped a snore in her sleep, nor did her mother come back in to check on me.

No one cared that something was deeply wrong. I was the only one who cared about me. My aunt, that bitch. She didn't care about what was going on with me. I was crying out for help, and she pushed me away. All she had to do was let me speak to my uncle. That's all I wanted, but she had to go and make things complicated.

I couldn't sit on the bottom bunk anymore. *To hell with Jen's mother.* I was calling home again. I went in the living room to make the phone call, hoping my uncle would answer, but my aunt did.

"A-u-n-t-i-e," I stuttered, barely getting it out.

"Chile, if you don't stop calling here . . . "

"But I want to come home now," I cried out. "Please come get me."

"I am not coming to get you."

"Can I talk to Uncle Frank?"

"He's 'sleep, and he doesn't need to be bothered with you."

I was quickly going to change that thought. It was time to act a fool then. I screamed into the phone numerous times that I wanted to go home. That sure did wake Jen and her mom up.

"What's the problem, honey?"

"I want to go home," I screamed hysterically.

Jen just stood there staring at me. Her mom tried to take the phone from me, but I wouldn't give it to her. I wanted to make the arrangements.

"Auntie, please come get me! Are you coming?"

"No. Now stop with this foolishness." *Click.*

The bitch hung up the phone again. I was in dying need of being rescued, and she shut me out. *Damn! She doesn't care about me.* I'd never cried wolf before, so

I couldn't figure out why she was ignoring my plea for help. I tell you, that aunt of mine was wicked. It hurt like hell when she hung up the phone again.

I dialed the house right back. Oh, I was determined to make her care. As soon as she answered, I picked up where I left off.

"I want to come home now," I said firmly.

"Well, I'm not coming to get you. You better find your own way here, calling with that ruckus."

Click!

That was it. She got hung up on this time. I was through with the talking. She gave me the go-ahead to find my own way home. Shoot, she hadn't said anything but a word.

I ran in the room, grabbed my stuff, put my sneakers on, and made my way to the door. Jen's mom was trying to grab her keys to take me home, but I couldn't wait for her. I was ready, and when I'm ready and determined, there is no stopping me. I ran all the way home without looking back. I didn't even know if Jen's mom was trying to follow me or what. I was out.

I reached home quicker than ever, thanks to my Jackie Joyner running skills. Yeah, I was quick with the feet, and Lord knows I thank Him for that. I needed top speed that day. I wanted to get home in a jiffy. It was like getting rid of a ton of weight when I stepped foot onto my doorstep.

In my mind, I was safe again; out of harm's way, but that feeling didn't last for long. I was quickly reminded that I had run back to the place that I had constantly yearned to escape. Auntie Linda greeted me at the door with a brown leather belt in her hand.

I couldn't believe it. I had run from trouble, just to get into it anyway. I couldn't win for losing. I didn't even have time to catch my breath before I was snatched up, thrown in the house, and beat like a runaway slave. I had welts all over my body. She had gone ballistic on me.

"You think you grown, huh? You think you somebody? You ain't nobody. You ain't shit! You think you can do what you want? Not in my house. Not under my roof. I pay the bills here. You ain't grown, little heffa."

It was always the same ol' song—I ain't grown, she pays the bills, and I ain't shit! And I had no other choice but to take it. I took it all right and cried my eyes out after every episode.

On that particular day though, when I ran from Jen's house, I shed my tears in the bathroom on the toilet top. I stayed there crying for like fifteen minutes, until I noticed blood on my pants. My heart started to race as I thought something was terribly wrong with me. I thought I was dying, and the only thing that came to mind was the terrible beating I had just gotten. I kept thinking that Auntie Linda had beaten me so bad that she'd made me bleed. I didn't know how it could have been possible, but that was what I was thinking. I know, silly me, but what do you expect? I was eleven, and my mind was boggled from my traumatic morning.

I took my pants off in a panic and saw blood running down my leg. I was so zoned from the morning, I had completely forgotten about the whole period thing. I pulled my underwear down to check my pad but noticed that I didn't have one on. I was about to flip out, because I remembered that I'd used a tampon. Oh no, that was it!

I looked down to pull the string, and it wasn't there. You know a trillion things ran through my mind at that time. I started to cry harder. The damn tampon was pushed all the way up inside of me. I had to get it. Who else was going to do it?

I put my left leg up on the toilet top, put my two fingers inside my swollen vagina, and closed my eyes. There was a rush of pain, but I had to take it for the moment. I felt where the tampon was, and it was pretty deep. I kept trying to get a grip on it to pull it down.

In the midst, Auntie Linda walked in. "What are you doing? Are you playing with yourself?"

"No, I'm trying to get the tampon," I whined.

"Why you messing in my tampons? This is why you wanted to come home? To meddle with my stuff?"

"No, no. When . . . when he stuck his thing in me, he pushed it all the way up."

"What? What are you talking about?"

"Jen's brother. When he . . . "

Auntie Linda walked out of the bathroom before I could even repeat myself. I heard her yell to my uncle that he needed to come check on me 'cause I was going crazy.

My uncle came to the rescue. "What's wrong, Desire?"

At the same moment he asked that question, I had gotten a hold of the tampon and pulled it out. Boy, was I a happy camper.

"Desire, what the devil are you doing?"

"Uncle Frank, Jen's brother put his thing inside of me, and this got stuck." I dangled the bloody tampon in the air.

Uncle Frank didn't pay any attention to it. He was so caught up in what I had just told him. "He . . . who . . . what?"

Next thing you know, he wheeled away, yelling for my aunt to come see about me while he went to load his single-barrel shotgun. Uncle Frank was ready to get down and dirty. I almost want to say he didn't play when it came to me, but you know that would halfway be the truth. I mean, he did what he had to do in moments of need, but of course you already know going up against his wife, the Big Bad Wolf, called for a back-down. I wish he could have been more for me all around, no matter what the barrier was, be it his wife or not.

I know I wasn't supposed to mention anything about what happened, but it didn't go down that way. Uncle Frank nearly pulled a nutty. Then, surprisingly, my aunt, showing a little concern, came in the bathroom and asked what happened.

I blurted the story out in one piece. "Jen's brother stuck his thing in me when everyone was 'sleep, and he told me this is supposed to happen when a girl gets her period."

Auntie Linda stood there looking at me like I had two heads. She sucked her teeth. "What you know about a period?"

"I got mine yesterday," I informed her.

"How you know?"

I stood there confused. *Am I really supposed to answer that? And, if so, what do I say?* I couldn't tell her the whole stupid doo-doo story.

"I asked you a question. How you know?"

"Because Jen's mom talked to me."

"Mmm-hmm. And this boy you talking about, did you like him?"

Uncle Frank shut her down. "What the hell kind of question is that?"

"You know what? Every time I try to help you, you intervene like I'm some kind of dummy and I don't know what I'm doing."

"But, Linda, why—"

"Why nothing. Don't you dare question me. You ask for my help, and I was giving it. Now you got a problem with how I'm handling it. Suit yourself. Do it on your own. This is your problem, so you deal with it. You're the one who let her go over there anyway. If she didn't go, then we wouldn't be going through this mess." She pushed his wheelchair out of the way and stormed down the stairs.

Uncle Frank looked at Aunt Linda as she walked away and shook his head. He looked so angry, I thought he was going to shoot her. Then again, maybe that's just what I wanted.

Shooooot, something needed to be done with her. Just think, if she wasn't around, then half the drama I went through would have never occurred. Damn, that lady put a hole in my soul!

Uncle Frank made Auntie Linda take me to the hospital after they argued for a good twenty minutes. She didn't want to take me because she thought I was lying. I wasn't surprised. Of course, she would think I was lying. Uncle Frank had my back though. He argued that I wasn't.

Then it boiled down to, "Okay, fine. Let the doctor prove it."

Boy, did I not want it to go down like that.

I hated the clinic, and really didn't care if Auntie Linda believed me or not. I knew I wasn't lying, but Uncle Frank was determined to prove that I was telling the truth.

I tried to cry my way out of it, but that didn't work. In fact, it kind of egged Auntie Linda on to find out if indeed I was really lying. I think, for a moment too, that Uncle Frank kind of felt I might have been. I had no reason to lie though. I mean, come on. Who in their right mind wants to lie about being raped?

***

The doctors showed no empathy, all the while sticking cold metal utensils up in me as if it were nothing. I felt like I was being raped all over again. The hospital visit was stupid, and all to conclude, *Ding, ding, ding!*—I was raped!

You don't know how relieved I was when that hospital visit was over. There were no more questions, no more touching, and no more waiting. Surprisingly, my aunt stayed the entire visit. She had threatened my uncle with just dropping us off, leaving him to handle the mess he'd shitted and stepped in. But I was actually happy she'd stayed. It showed she cared somewhat, but that feeling didn't last too long.

As soon as she pulled into the driveway, she had a few choice words for me. "This hospital business was nonsense. Your mother knew you were going to be a problem child. That's why she gave you away. I tell you one thing—You better not ever step foot in this house saying you're pregnant because you will not be welcomed. The doors will be bolted shut, and you will be put out, point blank."

Yeah, she gave it to me raw just like that. It didn't hurt my feelings though 'cause I knew better. Me pregnant? Please. I was too scared to get next to a boy, let alone have him touching me. She was beat on that note 'cause I wasn't coming home pregnant.

Don't get me wrong though. Her statement did strike a nerve. I didn't just shun it off all like that, especially the part about my mother not wanting me. I didn't know how much of it was true, but it hurt to hear it.

It was no big deal as usual. Life went on, and all I could do was cope. I had Uncle Frank to get me through somewhat, for whatever it was worth, but he was just as miserable as me. His witch would stop at nothing.

You should have seen the look my uncle gave her when she made that "pregnant" statement to me. It had death written all over it. He was about to comment, but just as quickly as his mouth opened, she was out of the car.

Bam! The door slammed right in his face. Then she told him to find his own way in the house. She knew he needed help getting into his wheelchair.

That hurt my heart when she did that. I accepted her being cruel to me but not to my uncle. He was nothing but sweet to her, despite her ways. I started crying on that note.

"Desire, baby, please don't cry. Pay no attention to your aunt. She loves you. She really does. She's just bitter right now. It has nothing to do with you."

I thought differently. I figured it had everything to do with me.

Uncle Frank put his head down then turned and looked at me in the backseat. A tear rolled down his cheek as he cleared his throat.

"Desire, I love that woman very much, and Lord knows, I couldn't do anything without her. She takes good care of me, you know. With my MS kicking in overtime and keeping me permanently in this wheel-chair, I don't know what I would do without her. She used to be the sweetest woman I know, but I don't know what happened. I can't understand why she is so mean. It hurts me to see her treat you like this. But don't you for one second think that this was your fault. That boy should have never put his hands on you. Oh, God held me back because He knows what I was thinking wasn't right."

I wanted to console my uncle, but I didn't know how.

"Come give me some love, and hug my neck."

I climbed over the front seat and embraced my uncle with all my might. That was love right there, and as we hugged, I vowed that, from that day forth, he would be the only man I ever let touch me.

"Don't you worry about a thing. I am always by your side, no matter what. I just ask that you bear with me in dealing with my wife. She's a mean old lady right now, but I need her. We both need her."

I didn't respond. I just kissed his cheek. We both didn't need her. He needed her, and I was just there, in the way, getting treated like a stepchild.

Uncle Frank said, "One more thing. Here, take this." He handed me a business card that read "WoodSteel Stock Inc., James Taylor." "That is your father's company. If you feel you want to call him, then do so. If not, then that's okay too. Just remember that you always have someone."

I glanced at the card, not really paying it too much attention, and stuffed it in my back pocket. I hadn't thought about my father ever. I didn't have reason to. I had never met him. My mother had never mentioned anything about his existence, and I had never cared to ask. I didn't have to ask. Of course, he did cross my mind from time to time, but the thought of him wasn't strong enough to dwell on.

As I helped Uncle Frank out of the car, my aunt was watching from the window. You'd think she would have made an attempt to help, seeing that we were struggling, but she didn't. She just peeked out and watched. I took it personal the way she stared at us, especially me. I wanted to ask Uncle Frank why his wife despised me, but it definitely was not the time. Plus, I knew my place as a child.

Auntie Linda hated that my uncle had so much love for me. It made her feel like his love for her had diminished, especially since she couldn't have any children of her own. See, from what I knew, she and my uncle wanted children, but due to her having a health issue, she was unable to conceive. When I came to live with them, not being of her own flesh and blood, she felt as if I was intruding, like I had stolen her husband from her or something. After all, they were always a household of two, and there I was making it three. Yes, she wanted children, but she wanted her own, not me. And every chance she got, she let it be known that I was not what she wanted.

Chapter 3

After the incident at Jen's house, I was not allowed to go back over there, which was more than fine by me. What hurt though was that I had never heard from or spoke to Jen again. I wasn't allowed to contact her, but I thought she would have at least attempted to call me and find out what happened.

I knew she had an idea of what happened because my uncle had called and spoke to her mom. I don't know what the outcome was on Jen's side, but for me, their house was off-limits. I figured, since she didn't call, they didn't think I was telling the truth. I missed her, indeed, but I had to manage to get along by myself.

Seventh grade year, I started a new school, Boston Latin Academy. Me and Jen were supposed to be walking through that door together. From first to sixth grade, she and I were inseparable. We always attended the same school and ended up in the same class. I had never thought in a million years that she would become a dead memory with a painful afterthought. You may think I'm babbling too much or being too sensitive about the situation, but not having Jen around really hurt.

The thought of what her brother did to me was a solid memory on my mind, and somewhere along the line, I began to blame her. What her brother did wasn't her fault, but she was his sister—guilt by association.

My first day of school, I walked into the lunch room with my Goodwill outfit on and penny loafer shoes, looking like a reject from the '70s. I swear that aunt of mine made me wear that outfit on purpose. No other kid looked as cheap as me. It seemed like everybody had on the hottest gear, from the latest Jordan to the hottest Guess suit.

I stood for a minute and looked to see if I saw anyone I knew. Nope, not one familiar face whatsoever. So after accepting being alone, I found a spot in the corner, next to some kid who looked just as nervous and lonely as me. The only difference was, he had on name-brand everything.

I took a seat, got settled, and bit into my stale taco shell stuffed with undrained ground beef, soggy tomatoes, and brown, watery lettuce. I was ready to regurgitate every bite. I almost did too when this kid with bad breath got up in my face, pressing me with questions.

"What's your name? Desire, right? Can I get the hookup too?"

First of all, I had never seen the boy ever in my life. Second of all, how did he know my name? Third of all, what hookup? And last but not least, he needed to shove a few Altoids in his mouth before he continued to talk because, I swear, my eyes were watering.

I looked at him like he was crazy. "What are you talking about? And how do you know my name?"

"You know what I'm talkin' 'bout. Ya girl told me how you let her brother hit it. I wanna know how can I be down?"

I turned around to see who my so-called girl was, but I saw no familiar faces. "I don't know what you're talking about."

Everyone around me started snickering. A few people yelled out I was lying. I had no idea who these people were or where they came from. I looked around again, on the verge of tears, but this time, not from his hot breath. Guess who I spotted as the dirty culprit? Jennifer Watson.

My ex-best friend was now my confirmed enemy. Seeing her brought up memories of what her brother had done to me. Tears trickled down my face. I went from flashbacks of being violated to the whorish statements of every loud and obnoxious kid in the lunch room.

For a moment, I didn't know where I was. I sat confused, trying to come to terms with being embarrassed in front of more than half of the seventh grade class. The provocative name-calling didn't stop either. I had to get away.

I got up and power-walked through the upperclassmen cafeteria. I had no idea where I was going, but I had to leave. It didn't really make a difference though, because a crowd followed me. I could have slit every one of their throats. Jen's especially, since she lied. Me and her brother did not have consensual sex. How could she do that to me?

I ran out of the upperclassmen lunch room, and some kid dashed behind me.

"Hey, what's wrong? Jada only said you were cool and that you give it up easy 'cause her brother already hit it."

I cried even harder. Can you believe that bastard had the audacity to come chastise me about what that bitch Jen said? On top of that, the dummy didn't even say her name correctly.

I was so caught up in trying to get away from the "hackers," I didn't realize my bag was open and most of my stuff had fallen out. I stopped to pick up my belongings, my vision blurry from the tears in my eyes. I spotted another hand going for my stuff, and I was just like, *Whatever. Take it.* I just wanted to get away.

Then someone tapped me on the shoulder. I flinched, scared.

"It's okay," he said.

I looked up, and there stood this tall, brown skin, husky boy with long braids down to his shoulder.

"Here." He handed me one of my books along with some pens and my calculator.

I snatched my stuff out of his hand and jammed it in my bag. I wiped my eyes and then stood up.

He handed me some tissue. "Are you okay?"

I didn't answer him. I wanted to know why, of all people, was he helping me and not joining in on the teasing.

"I understand if you don't want to say anything to me but—"

"You tryin'a get fresh meat too, *G!*"

"Scram, Ant!" my new friend said to the same idiot that had come up to me in the lunch room. "And have some respect for the beautiful young lady."

Besides my uncle, no one had ever stuck up for me. It made me crack a smile inside.

"My fault, man. I didn't know you knew her."

"Whatever. Leave her alone."

Anthony scatted quickly, and I started walking away too, impressed.

"Hey, a thank-you would be nice."

"Thank you," I mumbled shyly.

"First days of school are hard."

"I guess."

"My name is Greg."

I shook my head in acknowledgment.

"And your name is?"

"Desire," I said softly, still trying to make my getaway.

He picked up his pace to keep up with me. "*Desire*—I like it. Who named you?"

"I don't know. My mother, I guess."

"You guess? Girl, you need to stop guessing and know something." Greg laughed.

I didn't even crack a smile.

"Dag, Desire. Lighten up. It can't be that bad."

Oh, you'll soon find out.

"I hope you don't let them get to you, because they're all immature jerks."

"I see."

"You know what class you're going to now?"

"I guess."

I laughed at my response.

"Uh-huh, see. There goes that pretty smile. I got it out of you."

I blushed.

"Look at your schedule."

I pulled out my schedule and looked at it, confused.

"Here, let me help you out, Desire."

He loved to say my name. That was my Greg.

From that day forth, Greg was my new best friend. He was the only other man, at the time, besides my uncle, that I let into my heart. He tutored me in the subjects that I lacked proficiency in and made it a point to keep me focused. He was the big brother I never had, while I was the little sister he always wanted. Our relationship was just dynamite.

We talked about any and everything. I wasn't afraid to let him in either. I even broke down and told him about what happened with Jen's brother. You should have seen his face when he heard the story. His empathy for me was very sincere. It was amazing how he seemed to feel my pain. I think that's what really drew me into him. Shoooot, I talked about him so much, it nearly drove my uncle and aunt crazy. I was on a Greg rampage—Greg this, Greg that!

Auntie Linda didn't like it one bit either. She disliked him off the rip. She wouldn't even allow him to call the house. Her excuse was that he was too old, and that he only wanted one thing from me—sex. She kept throwing the rape incident in my face, saying that Greg was going to do the same thing, especially if I didn't just give it to him.

She was dead wrong though. He wasn't like that; he was different from the rest. He cared about me. He wasn't trying to get into my pants. He was my big brother from another mother. He had my back, and I wanted Auntie Linda to understand that, but she didn't. I wouldn't let her come between us though.

Greg was the highlight of my seventh grade year. I breezed through that grade with him as my only real friend. It's sad to say, but he was. I had other friends, but Greg warned me that they all weren't true. Some of them were actually cool people, while others were just trying to get close to him, since he was a star athlete and all. He was very popular, which meant everybody wanted to be his friend. Everybody. And if that meant going through me to get to him, then that's how low people stooped.

People came up to me constantly, out of the blue, trying to spark conversation. At first, I was naïve, but then I caught on. I shut them kind of folk down real quick. No problem ever surfaced from me doing that either. I only had one rock in my way—my enemy, Jen.

When we passed each other, we didn't utter a word. All we did was stare one another down. It didn't bother me at first, but as time went on, I felt as if she was taunting me, and it bothered the hell out of me. I wanted to fuck her up. Oh, and you know I did too, right in front of everybody at a damn funeral.

Chapter 4

By the beginning of eighth grade year, I was one of the most popular girls in school and too hot to trot. It was crazy how fully developed I was at age thirteen. I was five four, a size six, and wearing a thirty-six-DD bra. Not to brag or anything, but my body was shaped like Serena Williams'. No lie. I had no shame in flaunting all of it either. The boys loved it. What can I say? Well, not all the boys, 'cause Greg wasn't too keen on that idea at all.

Yes, my popularity went to my head, and I was in the midst of all drama, which gave me first dibs on all the new gossip. Greg couldn't stand it. He despised being the center of attention as well as the he said-she said stuff. He made it clear that if I was to hang around with him, then there was going to be a change.

I got involved with extracurricular activities, which led to track becoming my new best friend. Running track became a passion of mine. I was happy Greg had introduced me to it. It kept me grounded, and I loved that it was a stress reliever, something I definitely needed in my life of horror.

Nonetheless, I didn't lose all my popularity ties, especially being a track star. Yup, I was burning rubber in my spikes. And guess who hated it with a passion? Jen. At least that was the word around school. I didn't care though. She was only mad that I had defeated her at her own game. She thought she was going to win popularity when she told those guys that I was easy and that I had slept with her brother. Wrong! I taught her a lesson—God don't like ugly. Our staring battles created so much tension between us that the entire school knew we had it out for each other.

Greg told me to let it ride though. He had a strict rule for unnecessary fighting, saying, "There's fighting for defense, and then there's the fight that is just not worth it." In his theory, unnecessary fighting proved and solved nothing; it was just violence that served no purpose whatsoever. I didn't agree, but the majority of the time, he was right. I mean, an eighth grader versus a senior—who had more sense? I should have listened though, but you know I had to learn the hard way.

One night, after attending a track meet, I decided to take public transportation home. I was supposed to get on the free yellow bus that took the team back to the school, but I took a detour. My friends had pumped me up to fight Jen, and I didn't want to look like a punk, but I really did want to fight Jen. I lied to Greg, but he didn't believe my story, of course, about going to Ruggles to get beef patties. He was no fool. He knew those girls I was hanging with had been pumping my head up to fight Jen. That's why he told me to get my behind on that yellow bus, but I ignored him and went about my business.

Me and my new friends got to Ruggles Station and waited for Jen. After we waited for the broad for about thirty minutes, we concluded she was going to be a no-show. I wanted to wait a few more minutes, but my homies were ready to bail. So, that was that. We parted and went to our separate bus stops.

I was standing alone waiting for my bus to come, and next thing you know, I was hemmed up in a choke hold by some dude. Then these girls from my school who called themselves "Molly's Crew" appeared out of nowhere and started punching and kicking me, getting some good licks in. I tried to fight back, but dude had me on lock. I screamed for help, kicking and punching the air, hoping someone would come to my rescue. I mean, it was only but a million people, grown folk at that, waiting on buses. They saw I was getting my ass beat and just stood there.

The torture kept coming too. I noticed the girls that had come to Ruggles with me were standing around watching. Can you believe that? Then Jennifer, who I originally went to the station for, showed up and joined in.

My lips swelled instantly, and my right eye was already black and blue. You don't know how badly I wanted to break out of that choke hold and whup some ass. All of a sudden, Greg appeared out of nowhere and tackled dude to the ground. Then finally I was released. Of course, they started fighting, and Molly and her crew made their getaway, with Jen tagging behind.

I watched out of one eye as Greg and the dude tussled. I didn't know what to do. To be honest, I couldn't do anything. I wanted to break up the fight, but Greg was handling his. Dude was getting a good ass-whuppin'. Blood flew from his mouth with every blow Greg socked him with. I thought Greg was going to break dude's jaw, until some older guys intervened and pulled Greg off the dude.

"Chill out, chill out, youngblood."

"Nah, fuck that! Don't no bitch nucca sucker punch me," the dude rambled, trying to come at Greg.

"Sucker punch? Come on now, it was fair game. You got your ass beat. Take it like a man."

"Nah, this ain't over."

"Come on, youngblood, he's right. Take your whuppin' like a man and keep it moving. You can't win every fight."

"Nah, ain't no bitch nucca gonna sucker punch me and think he won."

"A'ight, you know what? Hit me. Hit me, and I'll fall to the ground. You take the win, and this is squashed."

"Fuck you!"

"I don't have time for this ignorance." Greg shook his head and began walking away.

"Yeah, turn your back bitch!"

Greg stopped, turned around and began walking back toward the dude. He stood directly in his face. He was so close to the dude, their lips almost kissed.

"You're the bitch, holding my sister down so them little chickenhead girls can jump her."

Homeboy jumped at Greg, but Greg didn't flinch. He stood there eyeing down dude. Then Greg broke the stare and walked over to my aid as I was hunched over, holding my stomach.

"Yeah, nucca, walk yo' bitch ass away."

Greg turned back around like he was irritated and walked back over to the dude. "Listen, I ain't the one for all this fighting mess. Let's just squash this, man. I didn't mean any harm. I was just defending my little sister, a'ight."

Dude sucked his teeth, reached in his jeans, and pulled out a black steel 9 mm.

"Fuck a squash! I ain't squashing shit!" The dude pointed the gun at Greg's third eye.

"Come on, youngblood, he's right. This ain't the way you solve things. Put that gun away."

"Nah, fuck that! He should have never put his hands on me. That's where he made his mistake."

Greg stood still, no expression on his face. "Man, put that gun away. We ain't even gotta go there," he said, a little throttle in his voice.

"We'll see." Homeboy laughed, tucking the gun away back inside his pants. "I'll see you," he said, running away.

Greg just stood there for a minute without saying anything or moving an inch. I guess he was in shock and angry. I knew for sure though, he was furious with me. This was the first time ever too. That's what happens when you're a hardheaded fool like me. You get people who care about you upset, and boy, was Greg upset.

"Come on, Desire."

He began walking as I limped beside him. He flagged down a cabbie, who was reluctant to stop at first, but Greg assured the driver he was just trying to get me home safely. The driver understood and took us on our merry way. We sat in silence almost the entire ride. I wanted to say something, but I was too scared, especially since Greg hadn't spoken two words to me. He was really heated, and I couldn't blame him. I'd lied to him, and it resulted in a beat-down for me and a threat toward him.

"Desire, I am so mad at you right now, you don't even know the half."

"I'm sorry," I expressed sadly.

"Sorry? That's it?" he yelled. "Those girls could have done worse to you, and this knucklehead had the opportunity to shoot me right then and there. Aw man . . . that was . . . nothing like that has ever happened to me before. I told you! I told you! Why do you like finding out things the hard way?"

"I didn't know I was going to get jumped."

"Nobody knows when they are going to get jumped, Desire. Gosh, look at you. No female should look like this." He moved in closer to me. "You feel okay?" he asked, toning down his anger.

"Yeah, I guess."

"Of course, you guess." He laughed.

I cracked a smile and scooted closer to him.

He gently hugged me, as I cried in his arms, ashamed that I had disappointed him. Of all people, I had failed Greg, the one person who hadn't failed me.

"Don't cry, Desire. Just listen to me, please. I will never steer you wrong. When I tell you things, trust that what I'm telling you is for your own good. Okay?"

"Yes."

We arrived at my house, and when I walked in the door, Uncle Frank quickly wheeled to my aid.

"Oh my goodness! What happened to you?"

"I was supposed to—"

"She got jumped by some girls at Ruggles Station."

"Some girls? Why? What were you doing at Ruggles Station?"

I looked at Greg, and he gave me that you-owe-me-one look.

"What's going on in here?" Auntie Linda asked, appearing from the kitchen.

"Some girls jumped on Desire," Uncle Frank answered.

"I'm sorry, Mr. and Mrs. Jones. It was my fault because I asked Desire to wait for me at the station, but unfortunately while she was waiting, some girls jumped on her. I'm extremely sorry."

Uncle Frank sat there with a look of disbelief on his face. I think he had a hunch Greg was covering for me.

"Thank you, ah . . . "

"Greg. My name's Greg."

"Oh Greg. I kind of figured. Finally we meet in person." Uncle Frank shook Greg's hand.

"Sorry under these circumstances," Greg apologized.

"Oh no. I appreciate you bringing her home."

"No problem, sir."

"Oh, cut the shit! This is your fault, Greg. Don't think because my husband is thanking you that you ain't the blame. What you got a little girl waiting for you for at this time of night by herself? You probably had something to do with this mess."

"Ma'am, I assure you I had nothing to do with what happened to Desire. It's my fault, yes, because I asked her to wait for me, and I apologize. But I would never plan for something like this to happen to her. She's like my—"

"Like your what? Guinea pig? Get out of my house and stay away from Desire!"

"Yes, ma'am."

"It's not his fault. It's my—"

"Girl, you better hush up before you get popped again in your busted lip."

"Linda, please . . . the young man brought her home safely. He didn't have to do that."

"Like hell he didn't!"

"Linda, you're talking crazy now. This boy—"

"It's okay, sir. I'm leaving. You all, have a good night."

Can you believe my aunt? She never wanted to see me happy. And Uncle Frank, man, I wish he had a backbone to shut his wife down. I wanted to take a stand myself and give my aunt a good cursing out, but I wasn't stupid. My ass knew better. Disrespecting your elders was a no-no. That was grounds for a good whuppin'.

In some kind of way though, I needed her. I didn't like knowing this, but it was true. And Uncle Frank could only do so much for me. She was the bread of the household, Uncle Frank was the edges, and I was the crumbs. Yeah, that's exactly how I saw it. Pitiful, right?

I got my war wounds cleaned up by whom else, Auntie Linda. She put her old-school doctor skills to work. She even talked regular to me, as if she was a paramedic, advising me on how I was going to feel in the morning and what to continue to do.

See, that was the caring Auntie Linda, the one I grew up knowing. I guess it was good times while it lasted. What can I say? I enjoyed the moment.

But then she shattered my world with a quick Greg alert. "You listen to me, Desire, and you listen to me good. You stay away from that Greg boy. I'm keeping you out of school for a couple of days until your face clears up, but when you return, Greg is off-limits. He already can't call here, and now you are not allowed to be anywhere near him. I'm going to call the school and let them know. He ain't nothing but trouble. Do you understand?"

"But, Auntie—"

"Do you understand?"

"Yes."

"Come again."

"Yes, ma'am." *I hate you so much right now.*

Auntie Linda left me with a feeling that burned a hole inside of me. I couldn't even form into words what it felt like to hear her say, "No more Greg." Was she buggin', or was she on crack? My Gregory wasn't trouble, she was the trouble. Greg took care of me. That was my bro right there. Why was she hatin'? And you know what sucked? As much as I hated her, I still had to abide by her rules. It was hard, but I did it, to a certain extent.

See, when it came to Greg, I pretty much disobeyed every rule in Auntie Linda's book. She couldn't keep me away from him. Nobody could. Only one person stood between us, and that person, later on, did see to it that our relationship came to an end. And it all happened in the blink of an eye too.

Chapter 5

Greg and I walked the long way home after an early dismissal. Ever since the incident though, he would only walk me to the corner of my street. My aunt was still on some stay-away stuff, and he didn't want to give her any reason to go ballistic on me. He knew the situation at home, and he wanted my life to be drama-free.

"You like Malik, don't you?"

I knew that question was coming sooner or later. I just didn't know when. He always knew when I was interested in someone or something. He never missed a beat, and I couldn't hide the fact that I was in love with his best friend Malik. He was sexual chocolate on a stick.

Let me school you on Malik. He was one those fine brothers that any man or woman would drop their drawers for. He reminded me of the ex quarterback for the Atlanta Falcons, Michael Vick. They both shared that dark complexion and that cute baby face. But what he had over Vick was his light brown eyes. He stood about five eight—four inches above me—was muscular, fine, and bowlegged, with a tight ass. He maintained a sharp, low Caesar with deep waves, and he had those just-right LL Cool J lips that were to die for. Whoa! I must say that boy was a beauty. Man, I can see his face now . . . just drop-dead gorgeous.

"I know you heard me ask you a question."

"Yeah. And what made you ask me that question?"

"Don't try to avoid it. Just answer it."

"I just asked why."

"Forget why. Better yet, forget the question. I'm going to tell you straight up. I know you like Malik; it's written all over your face. But I'm warning you—stay away from him. He may be my best friend, but he is bad news."

"Whatever." I laughed.

"I'm serious, Desire. I'm not playin'."

"How can you say that about your friend? Your own best friend?"

"Because I know the truth. Trust me on this. I really don't want you around him. I see him flirting with you, and it makes me sick to my stomach. He knows better, but he's hardheaded. You, on the other hand, are no dummy. You're hardheaded too, but you tend to make wise decisions. I schooled you well."

"Yeah, I know, but he is soooooooo cute."

"Don't let the baby face fool you. Beauty is skin-deep. Besides, he's too old for you anyway."

I knew Malik was too old for me, but he was cute. That's all that mattered. Plus, he liked me, and I liked him back. It wasn't a crime. We weren't sexually involved. Well, at least not yet.

Anyway, we stopped at the corner, and I noticed that my aunt and uncle weren't home. It was around that time when Auntie Linda had to take Uncle Frank to his regularly scheduled doctor's appointment.

"You wanna come inside?"

"Oh no. I'm good with your house, Dee."

"My aunt and uncle are gone. Pleeeeeeease?"

"Your aunt will kill you if she catches me in the house."

"Just for a few minutes. They won't be back for a while."

He thought about it for a second, and then sighed and looked at me.

"A'ight," he sighed.

"Just for a few minutes. Then I'm out. I ain't tryin'a get you in trouble."

I was too excited to chauffeur him into my palace, the room I had described to him numerous times over the phone. I can see him now clear as day as he glanced around my room with his bright eyes bulging out and his long eyelashes. He scoped every wall. He burst out laughing, clownin' me of course, because I had framed posters of Tupac plastered everywhere. I was crazy about Tupac.

"I knew you were a Tupac fan, but dang! I didn't know you were sweating him like this. Can the brother breathe? You got him all framed-up on the wall like you knew him personally," he joked.

I playfully hit him. "Shut up! You want something to drink?"

"You got a Heineken?"

"A what?"

"Ha! Ha! Nah, I'm just joking. I'm cool. Thanks for asking."

"Gotta be courteous."

"I taught you well."

"Indeed you did." I laughed.

"Sooooo, this is the room that you lock yourself in to be away from the rest of the danger zone."

"Yup! This is my cozy comfort getaway palace."

"I really hope things get better for you here."

"It's been okay lately."

"Remember though . . . "

"It will only get better," we said at the same time.

"Yeah, yeah, yeah. But how soon?"

"In time."

"Well, it needs to speed up."

"Patience is a virtue."

"In the eyes of who?"

"Who you think?"

"I don't know."

"Let me ask you something. If you could live any-where in this world, then where would it be?"

"Ah, I would have to say in L.A. with Tupac."

"Get out of here." Greg laughed.

I laughed too.

"I'm serious, Desire."

"I don't know, Greg."

"Well, next time someone asks you, know the an-swer—Always have dreams."

"I'll keep that in mind."

"Yes, please do. Did you think about calling your fa-ther like we discussed?"

"Yeah, but I don't want to."

"It may help sort out some of your feelings."

"I know, but . . . "

"Hey, no sweat. You can't rush sensitive situations like that. My fault. When you're ready, just let me know. I'll be here to lend a hand."

"Thanks."

"You're welcome. Have you written anything lately?"

"I started two poems that I didn't get to finish. I'll let you read them tomorrow. I have a finished one you can read now though."

I handed him the piece of paper, and he began read-ing it aloud.

"Heroin. Deliver us from evil, this world is a living hell, the system is so corrupt, drug dealers are settling well. Mothers are killing their babies, thieves are getting three to five, crooked cops get suspended with pay; it's a deep blue sea of crime. But dirty laundry hits the fan, welfare frauds are beyond, fathers are donating sperm; babies are air born. It is so contagious; this madness here on earth, you can't depict a lifetime, contraceptives don't work. Crack cocaine gets you ten, a rapist; I'll cut you a deal. Murder, if you know Johnnie Cochran you'll be a'ight, Chill! Just be aware of severe life sentences; state time leads to federal crime, a pregnant girl is having contractions, thirteen on her second child, man we don't love them hoes, but you sleeping with ya best friend's girl. Let's rebuild our cities, instead of jails for our upcoming males. Thugs are turned into playboys, newborns can smell the corrosions. A blind eye can see through glass, a bullet can spell out a name, murder is on another level, can't you see it's all a game? Pollution is turned to destruction. HEROIN! HOT DAMN! IT KILLS! He Even Runs Outside Infants Nerves. Addicted to what? HEROIN! Yeah, yeah, it's ill. Nicotine gets you hooked. Snort, sniff, or smoke can string you out. No prescription is needed for HEROIN, it's in our lives on different routes."

He applauded me. "Damn, girl, this is deep. You got skills."

"Thank you. I have one more too."

He started to read another one aloud: "Full of shit, muthafucka," but then he immediately stopped after a few lines.

I guess the profanity was a bit too much for him to continue to read aloud. So he read it silently then commended me on a good job once again.

"See, I told you. You ain't stupid. You know the game these dudes be out here runnin'. I like this one. Yeah, this is the jump-off right here."

"You think so?"

"Yeah!"

"It's just a bunch of words and sentences to me."

"No. What you have written is poetic. This is talent right here."

"Mmmm. I guess."

"Don't guess, know. You got potential right here. This is major." He looked at his watch. "But we'll talk about this later. My minute is up, and I gotta get going."

He got up to leave while taking another peek around the room. I glanced around too and almost broke my neck to cover up the open condom I spotted on my nightstand. I ran to pick it up, but it was too late. Greg's tunnel vision had spotted it already.

"What the hell is that?" He pointed as he moved closer to it.

"What is what?" I asked, pretending to have no clue as I stood right next to the evidence.

He grabbed my arm. "Don't play stupid with me. Are you having sex?"

He stood so close to me, yelling in my face, that I could smell the green apple Now and Later he was eating on the walk to my house.

"No."

I was getting scared then. It was the look. He had the same look Jen's brother had when he'd forced himself on me. I started crying because it was like, here we go again. Auntie was right.

"My fault, I'm sorry. I'm overreacting," he softly spoke as he wiped my tears. "You know I love you like a sister, right?"

"Y-yes," I stuttered, not knowing what to expect next. I was hoping he was not about to come on to me, 'cause we were close enough to kiss.

"And you know I care about you?"

"Mmm-hmm."

"Okay, now, don't take this the wrong way when I tell you this."

My heart was racing. I felt like I was about to be violated. I took a tiny step back and started to quiver.

"Dee, don't be scared. I know I was trippin' out a minute ago, but I'm cool now. I just want to have a heart-to-heart with you. Let's sit down over there."

We made our way over to sit on my bed.

"You are in eighth grade, and I'm graduating this year. You are maturing and physically developing faster than most females your age. Boys are going to be at you harder than they are now."

"I know." I sighed, indicating I didn't have time for a speech.

"Just listen. I have told you before that your body is your temple. You make the choice of whether you are ready to be intimate or not. A guy will pressure you into trying to do things. Don't do anything you don't want to. The tight clothing and stuff you wear needs to be at a minimum. These guys in school are flying out of their jeans to get you in the bed. Don't fall for it. And, last but not least, stay away from Malik. You will be in high school next year. Stay away from these nasty little boys. Keep your head in your books. And now, with that said, explain to me why you had an open condom on your nightstand."

"I wanted to see what it looked like."

"Desire, don't play me."

"I'm serious. I was curious, so I opened it."

"Where you get it from?"

"I don't know."

"Desire, this is me you're talking to."

"All right. I got it from Malik."

"From who? What? What the hell for?"

He got up as if he was about to hit me, and I flinched, but he punched double jabs in the air. "Desire, I mean what I say. He may be my best friend, but he's bad news. Stay the hell away from him."

"Ookayyy, Greg," I pleaded.

"I gotta go."

Just as he started to walk down the stairs, I heard keys rattling in the door. I pulled him back upstairs.

"Oh shit!" I whispered. "They're back."

"I knew I shouldn't have come in. Damn!"

"Quick, hide in my closet." I shoved him in my closet as I heard my aunt heading toward my room. I squeezed the closet door shut and then realized I still had the open condom balled up in my hand.

I quickly opened the closet door and threw the condom in with Greg. I hated that he had to be jammed up in my pint-sized closet, but there was nowhere else for him to hide.

"What you doing in my house this early?"

"I had a half a day."

"And what you looking for in that closet?"

"Uhh, I was looking for . . . my, my cleats," I stuttered.

"Your cleats, huh. Let me see what your lying ass is talking about."

"Why do you always think I'm lying? I'm sick of this! You never believe me, and you are always accusing me of something. I'm tired of this shit!"

I got bold. It was the only way to stir her attention away from the closet.

"Have you lost your mind? No, I know you lost your mind. Who the hell do you think you're talking to like that? You better come correct!"

Then it happened. Greg's cell phone rang. *Oh shit! That's it. I'm caught!* The phone rang for a split second. I knew she'd heard it. I thought my life was over.

My aunt looked around like, *What was that noise?* She walked toward me while I was standing in front of the closet.

I told myself, "Whatever you do, don't let her in that closet."

"Don't come near me!"

"Who do you think you're talking to?"

"I'm talking to you, that's who! You!"

I was stepping way over my boundaries. My aunt could have knocked me silly at any given moment, with her Mike Tyson power and her Nell Carter build. That's right. Mrs. Linda Jones was no scrawny woman.

She came at me full force, charging with her fist. I tried to run but like a Flintstone, but my feet didn't pick up fast enough. She grabbed my shirt from behind, twisted the collar, and got me in a choke hold. I thought I was about to die. I don't think my blood was circulating at all. I struggled to get her off of me, but it was no use. I was about to be 'sleep, as tight as she was squeezing my neck.

And Greg, poor Greg, I always had him caught up in something. He couldn't resist helping. He had to do something. She was damned near about to kill me. I guess my silent struggle gave it away.

He rushed out of the closet and tried to muscle my aunt off of me. She let me go, turned and punched him in the face. Greg took the punch like a man and backed out of the way.

I jetted out of the room, almost tripping down the stairs. I didn't know my aunt could run that fast. She caught up to me as soon as I took the leap from the second-to-last stair. Then you know what happened next. I lost my balance as I came down from the jump, and *Splat!* My face made friends with the floor.

This gave my aunt the opportunity to get at me. She scooped me up, locked a hold of both my arms, and shook the shit out of me.

Greg must have thought I was going to break in two because he came out of nowhere and tackled my aunt to the floor. Now that was a Kodak moment. He should have gotten an award for tackle of the year for that move. Boy, was that a funny sight.

Greg, of course, was not too happy about what he did. You could tell from his facial expression that he didn't mean to do it. "Oh my. Ma'am, ma'am, I'm sorry! I didn't mean to I'm so sorry." He tried to help her up, but she resisted. And even though he insisted, she kept shunting him aside.

Then, before you knew it, Auntie Linda had grabbed the closest object near her—the broom. Greg moved out of the way as she swung at his legs, going for the kill.

I told him to run out the back door. He took my advice and made a dash for it. I was going with him. I didn't care. I wanted out too. He unlocked the door in a hurry and let himself out, and I followed behind him.

"Desire, where are you going?"

"With you. I wanna go with you."

"You can't. You know you can't go with me."

"I don't wanna stay here. Please, just let me come with you."

Then, out of nowhere, my aunt snatched me up and threw me on the ground. Greg stared, hurt displayed all over his face.

"Ouch!" I cried.

"Please, Miss, can you just let her up? I'm sorry for what I did."

"Get off my property! And don't tell me what to do with this here floozy."

Greg started walking away.

"Get off of me! I wanna go with Greg. Let me go with Greg. Greg, help me! Get her off of me!"

As the side of my face lay in the grass, I saw for the first time tears come to Greg's eyes.

"Desire, I—I can't. I'm sorry. I'm sorry."

"Get your sorry ass off my property before I call the police!"

"Desire, I gotta go."

"Greg, noooooo! Don't leave me!" I cried, struggling to get up.

Greg didn't move, listening to my plea, tears seeping from his eyes. I had him caught up for real this time. I didn't mean to get him involved, but who else could I run to? I hated that he had to witness what really went on with my aunt behind closed doors.

"I'm not going to tell you again. Get off my property!"

"Yes, ma'am. I'm leaving, and I'm sorry for everything. Just please, I promise I will never talk to Desire again if you just—"

"I'm calling the police."

"No, that's not necessary. I'm going. I promise, miss. You won't see me again."

Greg wiped his eyes, gave me a good-bye look, and left. His last words stayed with me. Greg was my world, y'all. He did right by me, and then he just left me. It was my fault though. I started this mess with a stupid plan that backfired.

When my uncle got home about an hour later, he was furious with me. It was understandable, you know, since I broke the rules. But he failed to see that his wife was out of control. He wouldn't even listen to my version of the story, and Lord knows, he was the last person I wanted to think ill of me. In both their eyes at that point, I was disobedient, disrespectful, and un-trustworthy.

It wasn't all me though. My aunt failed to mention that she almost killed me, taking discipline to the level of abuse. But I guess none of that mattered. And it wasn't right for Uncle Frank to give me the silent treatment. I mean, he did say a few words to me, but they were discouraging and hurtful. How helpful was that?

I mean, geez, I'd only apologized more than a million times, taking responsibility for my actions. Apparently, it wasn't good enough. Uncle Frank still gave me the cold shoulder, which hurt, but not as much as not knowing whether I'd be able to communicate with Greg again.

I didn't cry though. I didn't shed a tear. I wanted to, but I'd been hurt so much and cried so many times, I just couldn't cry anymore.

I had no phone or TV privileges. And to ensure that I had no easy access to them, both were taken out of my room. My aunt wanted to make sure I had nothing. She even tried to take it as far as not letting me run track. Surprisingly, Uncle Frank had me on that one, but he did agree with the other changes.

Chapter 6

Around 2:00 A.M., while everyone was asleep, I snuck out of my room, went to the kitchen, and grabbed the cordless phone. I tiptoed back into my room with the phone, got deep under my covers, and started to dial Greg's number. I pressed the six, and the loud tone of the button startled me. I paused for a minute, thinking, *Damn, I'm caught!* I let three minutes pass, but nothing. Whoa! Can we say close call? I couldn't afford to get caught, but I was determined to make that phone call.

I went to dial again, remembering to put my palm over the earpiece to silence the tone of the buttons. The phone rang, rang, and rang until the answering machine picked up. I tried Greg back two more times, and it was the same thing. No answer. Something wasn't right. Greg almost never ignored my phone calls.

I waited a few minutes and dialed him again, one last time. There was still no answer. I was puzzled at that point and couldn't help but think the worst. It was official. Greg hated me. That's what kept going through my mind. I was thinking, *Did my aunt get to him? Is he really not going to talk to me again?* Obsessed and overly anxious, I called him one more time, but to no avail. My mind started racing. *He's probably sitting by the phone knowing it's me and just watching it ring because he hates me.*

I placed the phone on the bed, contemplating if I was going to sneak out and go to his house. Later for that thought. All of a sudden, I felt some metal hit my leg.

I snatched the covers from over my head and my aunt had a brown oversized leather belt in her hand lashing it at me through my comforter. I tried to move out of the way, and the buckle side swiped my face, leaving a long slanted welt across my left cheek.

"Sneaky little bitch! On the phone, huh! And you were having sex in my house?"

"No," I cried, trying to duck and move, but there wasn't too much moving I could do in the bed.

She dragged me out of the bed. "You lying hussy!"

"I swear, I didn't!" I stressed at the top of my lungs.

"Shut your trap before you wake Frankie."

I was about to scream again, but I knew yelling would get me nothing but a cursing-out and an ass-whupping. I just continued to beg and plead, but it was no use. She wouldn't believe me. Why would she? She'd found the empty condom wrapper in my closet. I don't know what possessed her to go into my closet at that time in the morning, but she did.

"You were having sex with that boy in my house?"

"No, I was—"

"And steady lying! He's going to jail. You hear me? Your little molester friend is going to jail."

"No, he didn't—"

"Shut up! Just shut your mouth! Say one more word, and I'll knock your teeth out!."

I remained silent, trying to calm my nerves from crying.

"When the police get here, you tell them what that boy forced you to do. Even if he didn't, you tell them he did."

"No, I won't," I whispered.

"I said shut up! And, yes, you will. You know what? Matter of fact, you ain't gotta say nothing. I can fix this. I'll tell them I caught you two nuccas in the bed in my house. Yeah, you ain't gotta say nothing."

I looked at her like she was crazy. Can you believe her? My aunt had lost her damn mind.

The doorbell rang, and it was the police. Before my aunt let them in, she came charging upstairs into my room, snatched me up, threw me on the bed face first, and tied my hands behind my back. At first, I didn't know what she was doing, but I quickly figured it out. I started hollering. Until she covered my mouth with gray tape. She even tied my ankles together, where I couldn't move at all.

Then the doorbell rang again. She rushed out of my room, leaving me tied up.

My aunt was really trippin' on some mafia-type status. I listened in agony to the mixed-up story she was telling the police. I couldn't believe my ears. She told them that I was so distraught and upset that I cried myself to sleep, and that waking me up would really not be a good idea. And they bought it too.

I was fighting to get loose, so I could set the record straight. I fought so hard, it caused me to tumble to the floor. I think at that point the police had to be on their way out the door because, within seconds of my hitting the floor, Auntie Linda came barging into my room, her lethal weapon in hand, the infamous thick brown leather belt.

"You wanna be causing a ruckus while I was downstairs speaking to the law? Huh? This is for your own good," she ranted as she whupped me. "You almost got me busted. You get on my nerves, little hussy!"

I rolled around on the floor like I was on fire.

"Stay still, li'l heiffa! Rolling around here like you in a jungle or something. Keep yo' ass still!"

I kept rolling as if I didn't hear anything she said. She was crazy, if she thought I was gonna lie still while she burned my legs with that leather.

"Keep rolling . . . 'cause the more you do it, the longer I'm going to beat you."

What type of ultimatum was that? Could I lie still while she beat my ass? I couldn't win for losing. So you already know what I had to do. Yes, take it like a champ, plain and simple.

After giving me what she would call "a good ass-whuppin'", I sat on the floor balled up in a knot. Every scene from that day replayed in my mind. I wanted my aunt to go to hell for what she had done to me, and for lying on Greg to the police. That was the day my hate for her became permanent.

Chapter 7

Boy, was I eager to get to school the next morning. The anxiety was a true adrenaline rush for me. I literally shut my eyes three hours before it was time for me to get up. I kept saying to myself, *You gotta get to Greg. You gotta get to Greg. You gotta get to Greg.*

Yeah, I was on some real junkie status, but I couldn't help it. It was imperative that I talk to him. I had to clear my name. I didn't want him to think that I'd lied on him, especially if the police had gotten to him first.

I rushed into school with three minutes to find Greg before homeroom period started. As soon as I stepped foot in the door, all eyes were on me. That was the sign, y'all. My life was over. They knew. The kids knew. They knew I had cried rape, but it wasn't true.

I contemplated skipping homeroom because Greg was definitely the priority, but getting marked absent was only going to lead to more trouble. So I had to go to homeroom and wait it out. I tapped my foot impatiently, staring at the round analog clock. The period was almost over, and right before the bell was about to ring, the damn principal delayed it for an announcement. I was about to lose my mind with all the setbacks.

"Excuse me, students," he said. "We have a very important announcement, a sad one. Last night, if you all didn't hear on the news, Gregory Little died after he was shot in the neck during an altercation with another teenager. Ah . . . bereavement counselors are—oh, this is hard for me. I'm sorry—they are available all day if any student needs them. Thank you."

I thought, *Oh my God! That's why people were pointing and staring at me. They knew Greg was gone.*

My world immediately shut down. I lost sight and focus. My heart was beating triple times its normal rate, like I was running a fifty-yard hurdle. I couldn't move. My legs stiffened, and my mind went blank. I cursed God out from the moment I was wheeled from homeroom to the guidance office. How could He? Every safety net I treasured and cherished, He took them away from me.

Words can't explain the pain I felt at that time. My best friend, my only friend, was taken away from me, and I didn't even blame the murderer. I blamed my aunt and God.

I blamed my aunt because, who knows how Greg felt when he left my house that night? Then I blame God because He let Greg, a humble person, get shot and die. To this day, I still ask why? I don't know though. All I can say is Greg's death took a toll on me, and my entire world remained shattered.

Later on that day after school, Uncle Frank was surprised to see me arrive home early.

"You skipped practice today?"

"No, it was cancelled."

"What's wrong with you? Don't come in here with an attitude. It was your fault you got yourself in trouble last night, young lady."

I sat on the sofa, tears forming in my eyes.

"Desire, I know how you feel, but you were wrong. And you're not going to be able to cry your way out of this one. You know what you pulled yesterday was irresponsible, disrespectful, and downright defiant. You had company without permission and—"

"He's dead, so you won't have to worry about me being irresponsible, disrespectful, and defiant."

"You watch your—Who's dead?"

"Greg. He's dead. He got shot. Somebody killed him. They announced it in school today." Tears streamed down my face.

"Oh, Desire, baby, come here!"

Just then my aunt walked through the living room. "What the hell is wrong with her now?"

"Her friend Greg was killed."

"Somebody got him before I did? Humph." She smirked.

Uncle Frank lifted his index finger. "Linda, now last night you went overboard. Don't you dare."

"I hate you, Auntie Linda!" I yelled. "It's all your fault anyway!" I ran to my room. I slammed my door and sat in the same place I'd hid Greg—the closet.

Uncle Frank came in some minutes later and found me. "Desire, come out of the closet for a second. I want to show you something."

I was reluctant at first, but this was Uncle Frank. There was no reason to be stubborn with him, even if he did give me the silent treatment sometimes.

I came out of the closet slowly and noticed he had a crisp black-and-white photo in his hand of two young boys with their arms around each other's neck. "Who's that?"

"That's me and your grandfather, my brother. He always thought he was the boss of me," Uncle Frank reminisced.

"Who's older?"

"Take a guess."

He handed me the photo, and I analyzed it. "He was the oldest," I said, pointing to my grandfather.

"Nope. He was three years younger than me, believe it or not."

"But he's so much bigger than you."

"I know. That's how he got his name Li'l Big Man. He got his height from Daddy, and I took after Mama."

"He's dead now, right?"

"Yes, your grandfather Eddie died some time ago, before you were born. It kills me to this day to even talk about it. It all happened right before my eyes too."

I thought he was about to cry, but he just balled up his fist and continued to talk.

"You know, he was always the courageous type. He always wanted to help somebody. Sort of like your friend Greg. Anyway, one afternoon he and I were walking home from work, and he noticed these teenage guys shoving this girl around. Before I could stop him, he got himself in the middle of it.

"It was about six guys, but he didn't care. I tried to talk him out of it. He was persistent though. He wanted to help this young lady. He always had a thing about protecting women. But, anyway, her clothes were ripped, and these guys were just tormenting her, and tossing her every which way within their circle.

"Eddie, being a macho man, spoke no words and went in, fists first. He knocked a couple of guys down, and I had no other choice but to jump in. We ran the boys off.

"I had run ahead of Eddie. I was always the faster one. But when I stopped to catch my breath, I turned around and noticed he was way behind me, moving funny. That instant, he fell to the ground. He was having one of his seizures again. I ran over to him, but there was nothing I could do. The seizure was too far along."

"What made him have seizures?"

"I don't know. But I tell you what I do know."

He blinked repeatedly. I guess, to hold back tears.

"I was sad for a while, 'cause it hit me hard. I was in his presence, and I was unable to save his life. I didn't let it stop me though. I didn't let it stop me from going on with my life. That stayed with me for a long time, but I had to let it go. I couldn't let being guilty for anything hold me down. I had to be strong, especially for your mom and the family. Your mother was just getting through college. She couldn't get anyone weak in her corner. I had to get it together. And I'm not saying you may not cry here and there, because you will. But try to think about the good times you all had. Laugh your cries away. It helps. Believe you me."

"Yeah, Greg was a joker." I laughed, picturing him being silly.

"See, there you go. I wish I could have gotten better acquainted with him. I knew he was a good person, despite what I've heard."

"Yeah, he was like the big brother I never had and . . . and now he's gone," I cried.

The tears flowed, and Uncle Frank embraced me.

"Oh, I know it hurts, but you have to remember he's in a better place."

"But why?" I cried hysterically. "Why did he have to leave?"

"You know he didn't choose to leave, Desire. You know that. The Lord called on him to lead a different life. His work here has been done."

"Why couldn't he choose someone else?" I whispered.

"Desire, I can't answer that. I don't know. Only the Man above can give that answer. I do know that you need to stop crying, and laugh a little more. Think about the good times, like the time your track team went skating. What was that story you told me?"

I burst out laughing from the image in my mind.

"Oh yeah, you said he couldn't skate for nothing. You said he kept falling and every time he tried to get up, he'd end up right back on the floor."

"Yeah, that was funny." I laughed, wiping my eyes.

"We definitely had fun skating that day."

It felt good to think about the good times with Greg. It didn't help me cease the crying too much, but it did calm my nerves a bit. I was still hurt to my soul and damn near boohooed a river. What do you expect? I missed him, and the thought of not being able to hear his voice or see him again hurt my heart to the core.

For the rest of the week I skipped school and track practice. I spent my time in the library doing my work for my classes that had given me a syllabus in advance. I kept my head in whatever books I could get my hands on. I was doing me. I hadn't even thought about the fact that the school was going to call my house to report my absences. That's how gone I was, but reality hit quickly once Auntie Linda got the message that I had been absent from school for *x* amount of days. She was furious with me.

Shoot, Uncle Frank was flat-out disgusted. Once again, he didn't bother to utter a word to me. Not a single word. He ignored me for two days straight. And when he shut me out this time, I felt like I had nobody. Greg was gone, and now my uncle had me feeling like he didn't care about me. When he did decide to talk to me the day before the funeral, it didn't feel genuine.

It seemed like he was forcing himself to do something he really didn't want to do. I know I messed up. Okay, I knew that, but I was a young lost soul grieving. My aunt wouldn't let me stay home, and going to school just made me think of Greg even more, which caused me to lose focus in class. Obviously, skipping school wasn't the greatest choice in the world. But, hey, I was mourning. I thought at least my uncle would have understood that. He always understood me, but it seemed as if he no longer had empathy for me.

I don't know. I couldn't call it. Maybe I just missed Greg and was looking for my uncle to fill the space. You know, take away the pain and just be Greg, but that was impossible. I was asking for a miracle. That's what being distraught and confused can do to you. Greg was my backbone, my teacher, my friend, my big brother from another mother, and just like that, he was gone, leaving me alone, alone to fend for myself in this house of hurt and in this world of hate.

The day of the funeral my aunt wasn't trying to let me go, and Uncle Frank wasn't home to back me up.

"Where do you think you're going?"

"To Greg's funeral."

"Oh no, missy. If you can skip school, then you can skip the funeral."

"I can't miss the funeral, Auntie Linda."

"You should have thought about that before you decided to cut school."

"Can I please go to the funeral?"

"No. I said no."

I ran to my room crying. How can you compare cutting school to going to a funeral? It wasn't like I was trying to go to a party or something. I was going to a goddamn funeral, and I wasn't going to let her stop me. Oh yes, y'all, I got brave with it. I took matters into my own hands. I got my purse, put my shoes back on, grabbed my notebook, and walked down the stairs like I was grown. There was no stopping me.

"Desire, I don't have time for your shit today. Take your narrow behind back upstairs and pretend the funeral's in your room."

I ignored her and kept walking toward the door.

"Oh no, you don't!"

She reached for my purse, and I clutched it tightly against my side. She was not about to get a hold of me.

I dashed out the door. To hell with my aunt. Although she said no, I went to the funeral anyway.

The church was packed with people. I couldn't even sit down. I had to stand the entire service. It was cool though. I managed to stand tall, with heavy tears here and there. I didn't feel awkward or out of place. I just remember wishing the whole thing had never happened. I wanted it to be a dream; a dream that was never meant to come true. Shit was real. Greg was gone. Dead. Lying face up in a coffin ahead of me.

During the funeral, they allowed family and friends to get up and say a few words. I wanted to read a poem I had written for him, but I was scared. There were too many people in sight. I watched everyone else go up and speak. Then the pastor gave the final call, and I found myself walking to the podium. I don't know how I was able to walk up there, but I did. I ain't superstitious or nothing, nor do I believe in all that weird ghostly stuff, but seriously, it felt like Greg's spirit had taken over my body and made my fear disappear.

I stood up behind the podium with my head held high and recited a poem I wrote, titled "Until We Meet Again."

My school friend
My home friend
My phone friend
My best friend

My big brother
My shoulder to cry on
My listening ear
My safety zone

I wanna lie with you
Die with you
No longer want to cry for you

You left me alone
I no longer have a safety zone

Your mother
Your father
I wish we shared the same

No sisters
Nor brother
But I was your sister in vain

It's hard to say good-bye
When hello is always said
You were my comforter
My guidance
I wanna lie with you instead

Forgive those oh Lord
For they know not what good You have created

Ease the pain of broken hearts
Touch the lives of their souls

Lessen their burden of hate
Free the madness from their souls

So until we meet again
Let the good rest in peace
Why'd you leave me dear Greg
Again we shall meet

His father acknowledged that my poem was beautiful. Then he embraced me. My tears ran strong.

"It's okay. He's in a better place."

I dried my eyes as I listened to his words of comfort. I walked back to where I was standing while I listened to his father make his speech.

He said, "My son was one of the most humble young men you could ever meet. He surprised me sometimes with the things he did for people. He had a one-in-a-million heart, and I wish he was still here to share it. He was an excellent athlete and an honor roll student. I can't think of any sport that he didn't play or any subject that he couldn't master. He was one of those kids that didn't care about winning or losing either. He came up with his own concept that even if you lose, you are still a winner within yourself, because you tried, you gave your best. He was connected like that, you know. He gave more than he had to at everything."

"He was hoping to go to Georgia Tech next fall. He just mailed his early admissions application . . . the day . . . the day he was killed. He would have gone to college and taken over the family business. He had it all planned out. He used to ask me all the time, 'Dad, is it true that since I don't have your last name that means I can't take over the family business?' My brother would always tease Greg, saying, 'You ain't no Taylor!'"

"His last name may not have been Taylor, but he was a Taylor at heart. I miss him dearly. He was truly an angel here on earth. He touched many hearts, and I-I hate to see him . . . go."

After the funeral was over, I stood in line and embraced the family, feeling like I should have been standing up there with them. Listen to me; like I was blood. I felt like it though. I really did. That day was rough for me. My first time attending a funeral, and I had no support. I had no friends to comfort me. There was no one by my side. I had to walk in the church alone and walk out alone.

On my way out, things got a bit out of hand. It wasn't my fault though. I was provoked. For real! See, while I'm walking out, I spotted Jennifer staring at me. If she knew what was good for her, she would have stopped staring, but she didn't. I wasn't in the mood for her stupidity, especially not at a funeral. I was too emotional and deeply hurt. At any given moment, I could have exploded on anyone. One button pressed, and my welled-up anger was erupting in flames. And, sorry to say, but erupt I did. I know, I know. I was at a funeral. But she asked for it.

I was almost out the door, and she just had to stick up her middle finger. Why'd she do that, y'all? Why'd she do that? She just had to press that blinking red "Do Not Push" button.

She thought I was going to ignore her stupid ass too, but she was wrong. She probably figured, *Hey, we're at a funeral. She ain't gonna do nothing*.

Wrong!

I made a U-turn through the crowd of people and premeditated bashing her head into the wooden pews. I had to bust her ass.

Immediately, when she stood up, I was standing right in her grill, and *Bam!* I socked her with a mean blow to the dome.

I got about three good punches in before her friend Anthony intervened and pulled me off her. He carried me outside of the church as I kicked and cried for him to get off of me. He dropped me like a dirty towel on the concrete stairs. I lay on the ground hurt from the toss.

A crowd stood around nonchalantly, trying to see what was going on, looking like they didn't know whether to help or mind their own business.

Malik came out of nowhere and shoved Anthony to the ground. "What the hell is your problem?"

I got up and wiped my hands off. Anthony was about to get it. Who did he think he was, tossing me to the ground like that? Fuming, I charged at him, going right for his groin.

Malik snatched me up before I could get a good kick in. "Chill out, Dee!"

"Chill out" was not in my vocabulary at that moment. I saw an opportunity to give him a good ass-whuppin'.

Anthony was the kid that came up to me on the first day of school and ruined my day. That was the day I met Greg. Tears poured down my eyes as I thought about it. Greg was no longer around to save me.

I fell to the pavement distraught. People started looking at me.

"She's fine. The show is over," Malik announced.

"Desire, come on. Let me get you out of here." Malik had tears in his eyes.

"I want Greg," I shouted.

"I miss him too," he whispered.

"Why? Why is he gone? I can't believe he's gone. Who am I gonna talk to? Who's gonna . . . " The anxiety, the tears, the pain. I could no longer speak.

Malik knelt down beside me and caressed my face, wiping away my tears. "I know. I know what you mean. You can talk to me though. I'll be here for you. I know you feel lonely inside, but you will be okay. I'm gonna take care of you."

He leaned me over in his lap and caressed every strand on my head. It was soothing. I was digging his "comforting" skills. He earned an A for effort, but something was still missing. He just wasn't Greg.

So much for him not being Greg. Oh, man! The things I did. Greg had to be turning over in his grave. He'd told me to stay away from Malik, but he got me at a time when I was vulnerable and had no control over my feelings. I was hypnotized. I swear, I was. He got me.

I lost my virginity to Malik the same day of the funeral. I let him in just like that. He told me he loved me though. Didn't that count? Back then, those three words meant a lot to a new kid on the love scene. It was the best feeling in the world.

I lost my virginity in a way that every girl wanted to lose it. I was wined and dined. He told me he had always been in love with me, and that if I let him pleasure me with sex, it would ease my pain of missing Greg. Our one day together made me feel like I was in heaven, and I wanted that feeling to stick around. I felt like someone else did care.

I thought I was in good hands. I figured Malik was going to take good care of me, seeing I was his best friend's fake little sister and all. Hmmm, he took good care of me all right. How could I have been so naïve?

Greg's passing away was the worst thing that could have ever happened to me.

Chapter 8

I skipped school for another week after the funeral. I played it smart this time though. I went to homeroom in the morning, got marked present, and then left. Thinking back, I feel bad that I had convinced myself Greg was the reason I couldn't stay in school. I mean, I was still grieving, but I was mainly skipping school to be with Malik. Yes, I was sho' 'nuff being fast, nasty, and having sex.

Malik had convinced my dumb ass that he was my ticket to getting over Greg being gone, and the highlight of the whole getting over Greg was sex. Yeah, you heard right. Sex. How stupid was I? My gullible behind believed everything he told me. He was quite the conniver, I soon found out.

He did show me love though, which is why our relationship felt so real. And, at the time, that was all that mattered to me. I was lonely, and he filled the void. He opened my eyes to a whole new world. He served me breakfast in bed. He gave me full body massages. He treated me like I was his queen. I adored him. I guess that's why I was crazy in love.

Things had toned down at home. My aunt didn't really say much to me anymore. During that week I was leaving school, I stayed at Malik's house until it was time for school to let out. Then I would arrive home at the time I was supposed to, as if I had gone to school. I wasn't all the way stupid though. I did keep up with my studies. I made friends with at least one person in each of my classes, and they hooked me up with my assignments daily. So I handed in my assignments on time.

It was a lovely cut-week, but I couldn't take too much time out of school. I couldn't risk the news getting back to my aunt and uncle.

Before we returned to school, Malik made a few things clear. There was to be absolutely no kissing up on each other like we did at his house. And no hugging or cuddling or showing each other any type of affection whatsoever. Our relationship was to be shown as nothing. His reasoning—he didn't want anyone in our business, and with the rumors floating around, he didn't want people to talk more. It was crazy how people were calling his crib telling him that we were the latest topic in school.

Anyway, I rolled with it. I thought it made sense at the time, but looking back now, it was bullshit. The whole relationship was bullshit. Malik did me wrong on many occasions.

One time I was in homeroom longer than usual, and I think it was because we had activity period or something. But, anyway, Jen was the attendance girl for the eighth grade floor on this particular day. She came into my homeroom to get our attendance sheet, and she started running her trap to these nosy girls about me. The only reason I knew she was yappin' about me was because they started pointing at me. I couldn't believe my eyes.

Frankly, I was shocked. I thought the bitch had gotten enough from her beat-down at the funeral.

So she leaves out of the room after she says whatever, and this girl Stacey comes up to me like, "You got jumped after your brother's funeral?"

"Who told you that?" I asked, pretending like I had no clue.

"I heard that attendance chick tell Marissa and Crystal. She said that's why you were absent all last week, 'cause your face was all jacked up."

The bell rang before I had a chance to respond. Jen was a loose cannon definitely needing to slow her roll because she was not going to be saved from the next beat-down. I didn't have time to cater to stupid people. Huh, I really didn't. She was pushing me though. She was.

I went to my locker to get my books, and people were looking at me weird, laughing. Two seconds later, Jen walks pass my locker, grilling me. See, she was asking for it.

"What the fuck you looking at, bitch?" I questioned.

She turned her head, breaking our eye contact, and stuck up her middle finger.

I slammed my locker door shut. Then, just as I was about to get at Jen, somebody rolled up behind me and pinched my butt.

I turned around to see who else was going to get their ass beat, and in the process I was pulled into this dark closet. I let out a half scream before the person covered my mouth to shut me up. I panicked.

"Baby, it's me, Malik. Chill out. Calm down," he whispered.

I took a deep breath, relieved but still a little shaken up. "Sorry. I got scared."

"Oh, now you scared of me?"

"No, I didn't know it was you. How was I supposed to know it was you?"

The move was borderline rape. My mind wondered, thinking about Greg, hoping the thought of him would calm my nerves, because Malik's presence wasn't. "I miss Greg," I announced.

"Me too." He forced his tongue in my mouth.

We French-kissed. Then he stuck his tongue in my ear and whispered, "Why don't you give me a blowjob?"

"A what?"

"A blowjob."

"I have a class now."

"Real quick."

I stood there reluctant to do what he desired but afraid to say no.

"You said you miss Greg, right? It will only take your mind off of him, so you won't hurt anymore." He caressed my face.

I was a dummy, y'all. A true dummy.

"I never did it before. What do I do? "

"Get on your knees."

"My knees?"

"Yeah, your knees."

I got down as instructed.

"You know I love you girl, right?"

"Yeah." I blushed, feeling all mushy inside. Then, there my gullible behind went. I was on the floor, on my knees, about to do something a child had no business doing. How could I have been so stupid?

It was horrible, how I gripped his penis with my hands and then moved my mouth toward it. My nose got a whiff of a funny odor. I didn't know whether it came from his thing or what, but it didn't stop me though. I leaned forward, making the tip of his thing touch my lips.

He grabbed the back of my head. "Just lick it, baby."

I stuck my tongue out.

"Yeah, now circle that tongue around the tip. Yeah!"

I kept circling my tongue around, thinking this was all I had to do. Until he shoved his penis in my mouth. I gagged, and he pulled back a little.

"Loosen up. Suck it. Stop being scared."

I tried, but it was too hard, and my teeth kept getting in the way.

"Watch the teeth, baby. Okay. Yeah. There you go."

My jaws started to burn. Then he pushed his thing in deeper, keeping my head at a standstill, 'cause I kept pulling back. I gagged again and felt pressure at my throat. Next thing you know, I was throwing up.

He jumped back as vomit splashed everywhere. It didn't get on me, but it surely got on his new blue suede Tims. He was mad as hell. He didn't even say anything to me. He wiped off as much as he could with an old rag he found in the closet and then bolted just like that, leaving me in the closet all by myself.

I found some Kleenex in my purse and wiped my mouth. I felt bad. He had me feeling bad. All I could think about was, I'd messed up his brand-new Timbs. I was a loser for that, right? *Hello. He made me give him a blowjob, and my dumb ass is concerned about his brand-new Timbs?* I could slap me then.

Anyhow, I walked out of the closet twitching my mouth because my jaws were burning. Then what do you know? I spotted Malik all over this girl, his arm around her, playing in her hair and kissing her on the cheek and shit.

I run up behind him, feelings all hurt. "Malik! Malik!" I yell down the hall.

He ignores me.

"Malik!" I yell again.

The girl turns around and says, "Your little sister is calling you. Answer her."

I thought, *Little sister*. I was far from his little sister, unless we had some incest going on.

"Yo, I'm late for class. See me at lunch," he yelled to me down the hall.

What a jerk! Greg had warned me to stay away from him, but I just didn't listen. They say a hard head makes a soft ass.

Lunchtime came, and while I was in the cafeteria sitting with a few associates, someone snuck up behind me and covered my eyes. All the girls at my table started snickering and giggling. The only two people they would get that happy for were Greg and Malik. So you know who it was.

I pulled his hands off my eyes and got up from my table to move away from him. I was fronting like I was mad, but you know that lasted all of two seconds.

He put his arm around me and muscled me outside of the lunchroom. "Desire, baby, I'm sorry."

"Greg told me you were a jerk!"

"Don't get stupid. His words weren't too keen about you either."

"What?"

"Nothing. You're right, I am being a jerk. I'm sorry. I was just mad that you messed up my brand new Timbs." He got down on one knee. "You forgive me, baby?"

He got me, y'all. He got me again. Mr. Smooth-Talker got me.

"Yeah." I blushed, too amazed he was on one knee.

He hugged me then he kissed my forehead. "Meet me at my house after school. If I'm not there, just wait. Oh, and don't forget, only at my house we can . . . you know," he rambled, running ahead of me back inside of the lunchroom.

I smiled all the way back in behind him, feeling warm inside and madly in love. I scooped up my stuff, and of course nosy heffas were on me.

"Is that your boyfriend?"

"No, I'm her brother," Malik responded out of nowhere, before I could get a word out.

I had no idea he was near me. I was about to break our code of silence and answer yes. And then he had the nerve to wink his eye in the process. Of course, only I saw this. Yeah, yeah, I knew the drill. Everything had to be kept a damn secret.

I journeyed to my fifth period class that I had with Jen. I was really looking forward to this class, right? Yeah, sure I was.

Half the class was there by the time I arrived. Apparently, seats were assigned because, when I went to sit next to this kid, Aaron Nettles, who we called "Gay Aaron," Ms. Drimmer made me park it next to Jen. What possessed her to do that? I don't know, but I know I was pissed.

Putting me next to her was like a problem waiting to happen. Every five seconds the damn girl was staring at me. Next thing you know, during the middle of the class, Clayton, who was sitting in front of me, passed me this note.

I opened it up to read it, preparing myself for the worst, in case the note was about me.

> *Desire is a ho. She sucks dick and licks ass.*
> *The bitch is ugly too. Who would wanna hit that?*
> *Silly bitch, silly bitch, Desire's a silly bitch!*
> *A Genie in a bottle*

Even if Jen claimed to not have written the note, she was point five seconds away from an ass-whuppin'. I had anger written all over my face.

"Girlllll, what's wrong with you? Fix your beautiful face." Aaron smiled as he was passing out our worksheets.

I handed him the note.

He read it, and his mouth dropped. He threw the note back to me. "Jen was wrong for that, girl. She was dead wrong."

"Mr. Nettles, this is not social hour. Pass the work-sheets out quietly."

"Watch, wait until class is over," I mumbled.

"What was that, Miss Jones?"

I didn't answer.

"Excuse me, I'm talking to you, Miss Jones. You had a lot to say a minute ago. What's the problem?"

"Nothing."

"No, it's something. Bring that note up to me."

I brought the note up to her, threw it on her desk, and walked back to my seat.

In the process of me walking back to my seat, I hear the note being read aloud. "Desire is a ho. She sucks di—Okay, I will not continue to read this."

I was confused as to why she was reading it aloud anyway. What was up with that? Was the word *ho* not enough to stop her? How embarrassing?

"Who is responsible for this?"

No one raised their hand. What idiot would?

I was about to cry. I slouched down in my seat, no longer tough. The class was quiet, except for minor giggles, but all eyes were on me.

"I want to know who wrote this letter about what Desire does."

I wanted to make a quick getaway, but it would have been more idiotic for me to get up and run out of the class. I would have gotten clowned even more. I was saved by the bell though, Thank God. It rang right on time.

I jumped up out of my seat trying to make the get-away before my tears became active. Aaron, all in my face, saw my eyes watering. He put his arm around me to slow my pace as I was power-walking out of the classroom.

"The heffa is not worth it. Don't let her get to you. I heard you beat her up already anyway."

Aaron was right. She wasn't worth it. There was no need for me to waste energy on her again. I would have gotten suspended, sent home, yelled at when I got home, and then put on punishment. Yeah, she wasn't worth it.

I walked to my sixth-period class wishing the day would hurry up and be over. I made a detour to the bathroom to take a quick tinkle. I walked in on two girls talking about what had just happened during fifth period.

"That girl Jen wrote this nasty note about Desire."

"Who?"

"You know Desire? So-called Greg's sister."

"Oh, that chick? What did the note say?"

"Something about her sucking dick."

"Ooh! What? You read it?"

"No. Ms. Drimmer read it out loud."

"Are you serious?" The girl laughed.

Spare me the humiliation. I didn't even bother using the bathroom. I just walked out, pissed. Then I ran into "Mr. Piss Off" himself, Malik.

"What the hell is wrong with you?"

"I'm tired of this bitch Jen spreading rumors about me." I started crying.

"Stop crying and check her on it. Tell that bitch to stop spreading rumors, or you gonna whup her ass again."

I didn't say anything, but as I thought about what Malik had said, I was motivated. I forgot all about the advice Aaron had given me. It was like he'd said nothing, because I went searching for Jen.

I inquired through some people in the hallways what class she was in and made my way there. I walked into her class as if I belonged there, and with no shame in my game, I gave her a few choice words.

"You better stop spreading rumors about me, bitch, or I'm gonna bust your ass again."

"Desire, young lady, get out of my classroom!" the teacher yelled.

I walked out, obeying the command.

"Kiss my ass, bitch!" Jen yelled to me.

I did a U-turn. "Say it to my face."

"Do not step foot back into my classroom, Miss Jones. Go to your sixth period."

I did as I was told, pulled myself together, and made it to my last class late. I got in trouble, of course. I got sent to the office and was mandated to stay after school for a mediation session with Jennifer. You know I was pissed. The damn thing was going to be pointless. I was never going to be her friend again. She was practically the root of all my problems, and the situation that brought it about couldn't be mended.

After school I sat in the mediation room aggravated, waiting for Jen to show up. I had been waiting for at least fifteen minutes. I was getting impatient. She had one more minute, or I was out. My countdown started from sixty, and once I hit zero, I was headed toward the door.

My guidance counselor stopped me and made me sit back down. I tried to argue my way out of leaving, telling her that this was a waste of my time, and obviously Jennifer wasn't coming. Little did I know, Jen had already been there waiting in the office with her own guidance counselor. Somebody should have said something. Hello. Why have me waiting, thinking the girl wasn't showing up, when she was already there?

The other guidance counselor, Ms. Burgess, walked in the mediation room with Jen. "Hi, Desire. How are you?"

"Fine. Can we get this over with?" I rudely greeted.

"Sure can." She ushered Jen to sit down opposite of me.

Jen sat quietly staring down at her fingernails as if she was nervous. I sat tapping my feet and hands, waiting impatiently for this mediation bull to start.

"First, I need to know why you think there is a problem between yourself and Jennifer."

"I know there is a problem. The bitch—"

"Absolutely no profanity. It will not be tolerated."

"I won't tolerate her. I'm tired of her. She keeps spreading disgusting rumors about me. And I'm sick and tired of it. She's always staring at me, throwing up her middle finger."

"Is this true, Jennifer?"

"She be staring at me too and talking about me."

"Talking about you to who? Puh-lease! You ain't a topic of discussion."

"What?" she yelled and stood up.

I took a stand too.

"Wait, hold on. Let us keep our cool here. Take a seat, ladies."

"This is stupid. Can I please leave?" I asked.

"No, this mediation session is not over."

We both sat back down with our faces screwed up and mouths poked out.

"Now, ladies, I understand that you two used to be friends."

"Yeah, used to be . . . until her brother took what was mine."

"He did it to me too. What was I supposed to do?"

There was silence.

"Did what, ladies?"

Neither one of us answered.

"Can you guys fill me in here?"

We put our heads down.

"I didn't even tell my mother," Jen whispered.

"Tell your mother what?" the counselor asked.

"That my brother—"

"Was the one who stole this thing I got blamed for," I said, covering up for her.

Jennifer looked up at me and gave me that thank-you look. "Yeah, this diamond necklace that my mom had." Then she stood up. "I'm sorry."

"And what are you sorry for?" the counselor asked.

"I'm sorry for talking about her."

"Don't tell me. Tell her."

She turned to me. "I'm sorry for talking about you, Desire, and embarrassing you."

"Yeah, why'd you do that? You embarrassed me on the first day of school, and today with the rumors, and the notes. Why?" I got very emotional, wanting to make sure her apology was sincere.

"I don't know. I didn't know how to be your friend. I was so happy to see you that I didn't know what to do. I'm sorry."

Can you imagine that the dummy did all of that to be my friend? Wow! I didn't want to apologize, but what the hell, I had to. I wanted my best friend back. "I'm sorry too."

We hugged in tears. The mediator looked like she was about to shed a few tears herself. It was a beautiful thing.

As soon as we walked out of the mediation room, we picked up where we left off. It was like we'd never stopped being friends. She owed me anyway. She put me through a lot, and with us being back in the good graces of each other, I had planned to get as much as I could out of the relationship.

I did too. Oh boy, did I. I can't say it was sincere on my part either. All I can say is, Jen had it coming.

Chapter 9

Christmas rolled around, and it was just another day for me. Scrooge lived in my house for the holiday. There was no Christmas spirit whatsoever. I didn't get so much as a pot to piss in. I stayed locked up in my room for the entire winter break. I had phone privileges, thank the Lord, but it didn't really matter though. I felt depressed, not wanting to talk to anyone. I mean, come on. What did I have to brag about? Nothing. 'Cause I didn't get shit.

There was no jolly story for me to tell about getting new clothes or games or whatever other goodies kids get for Christmas. I knew whoever I talked to would run the conversation a mile a minute about how they got this, how they got that, and blah, blah, blah. Then it would be my turn to run down my gifts. So I spared myself the pain of talking to anyone. I couldn't even pull myself together to talk to Jen, who kept calling. I gave her some lame excuse about not feeling well. It was wrong, I know. She was someone I should have been able to talk to, but I just wasn't in the spirit.

The only person I really did want to talk to though was Malik. I cared less if he knew I got nothing. I just wanted to talk to him. I waited days to hear from him too, but he never called. I only called him like every hour on the hour, just to get none of my calls returned. I ended up not hearing from him or seeing him until I returned back to school from break.

The first day back to school, we met up in the bathroom, went in one of the stalls, and got busy. That's
when I ran into my first problem with him. He gave me
crabs.

I never confronted him though. I was too scared. I
was afraid he would have turned it around and blamed
it on me. I knew I didn't give it to him, but at the time,
my mind was playing tricks on me. I wasn't sure what
to expect because, the way the doctor put it, I could
have given it to him and vice versa. Anyway, I got rid
of them.

I used the shampoo the doctor prescribed, and it was
cleared up in minutes. Then, within an hour, shaved
coochie and all, I was back in bed with Malik. This
time, though, he left me burning. Oh my goodness!
That's a memory I'll never forget.

My vagina was itching so bad, I could hardly sleep. I
think it had to be about ten o'clock at night when I got
this horrible, itchy, shocking feeling. I was almost in
tears from the discomfort. I called up Jen, and she advised I should go to the emergency room. I didn't know
how she thought I was going to get there. I couldn't tell
my aunt my vagina was on fire. That would clearly let
her know my fast ass was having sex. *Serves me right.*

I got through it though, thanks to good ol' Jen. My
girl had my back. She held me down. She stole her
mother's car and picked me up at about one o'clock
that morning. I had my health insurance card in my
purse ready. Uncle Frank had given it to me about a
month prior, in case I was ever admitted to the hospital, or if I ever needed some emergency assistance. It
definitely came in handy that night, and I tell you, that
was damn sure an emergency.

Jen was whipping her mother's car like she had a
license for years. We were lucky not to get pulled over

from her self-taught driving. Whoa! That would have been a quick lockup.

Anyway, we got to Boston Medical around one thirty and didn't get out until five in the morning. It was all to conclude that I had syphilis. Yeah, you heard right, syphilis. This time, I was confronting him.

The doctor explained that he had to contract it from someone else and pass it to me. He had to have it for a while too. He also said I was lucky to catch it at the stage I did. I didn't know you could die from syphilis. Imagine that, a thirteen-year-old girl in junior high dead from syphilis. What a headline! The risks people take having unprotected sex. I was sure enough a dummy, but like I said, I confronted him this time.

He had no excuse with this one, and there was no way in the world he was going to talk his way out. There was no maybe I could have in this situation. Oh no, Malik was getting a good foot in his ass. I couldn't wait to get to school the next morning to confront him. It weighed on my mind too. I kept thinking get home, get up in about two hours, and dig a new asshole into that bastard Malik.

Coming back from the hospital, me and Jen pulled up to my house and saw both my aunt and Jen's mother sitting on the porch, just waiting. You know our faces dropped like, *Oh shit!* We were trying to figure out what we could say about where we had gone when they asked, not like it would've made a difference anyway. We were in trouble no matter what. I wasn't going to volunteer the truth though, and neither was Jen. The emergency room and STD thing would raise a bigger issue, a huge issue, so I was good with sticking to "cruising," as our story.

That was some night, boy. I got the whuppin' of a life time. Thing about it too, my aunt didn't even whup me. My uncle did the honors. Yup, I stood in one place while he lit my behind up with his black leather belt. My butt was sore. I was hurting too. Not so much from the whuppin' though, but for the simple fact that it was my uncle who gave me the licks. He had never before in his life beaten me. I guess there's a first time for everything, right?

Just like being on punishment for life. Yeah, Uncle Frank took it there. I was officially on punishment for life. Shoot, I thought I'd never see daylight again, let alone school. He gave me a good ass-whuppin', and it left my body hurting like hell. Between the welts and the red tender spots, I was all broke down.

The tears I cried showed the next morning. When I woke up, I could hardly see. My eyes were puffy and swollen. My body ached more, and I was dead tired. Yet, I had to rise and shine to go to school looking a wreck.

The bags under my eyes made me look like I hadn't slept for days. Everyone kept asking, "What's wrong?"

Jen didn't even show up for school. She had gotten a worse whuppin' than I did, and I'm not even trying to brag that mine wasn't that bad, 'cause it was. None of this stopped me from looking for Malik though. I still had to confront him. I had some fierce words for him.

I searched for him in school all day, but he was nowhere to be found. By the end of the day, I realized that there were no seniors in school. They were all gone on a two-week Black college tour. And, of course, Malik said nothing to me about the pre-planned trip. The bastard.

***

When he got back though, I chewed his ass out. I got bold. Yup, I grew a backbone. I walked right up to him, pulled him to the side and smacked the dog shit out of him. Jen had pumped me up, so my eagle was soaring sky-high.

"Girl, what the hell is wrong with you?" He smiled thinking I was playing.

I guess my slap wasn't hard enough. "This is what's wrong with me." I handed him the syphilis brochure the doctor had given me.

"Oh, baby, you mad?"

"What? Am I mad? Hell yeah! You burned me. The doctor said if I didn't catch it in time, I could have died."

"You still standing, right?"

"Oh, this is a joke, Malik?"

"Baby, calm down, okay. I didn't know."

"What you mean, you didn't know? How could you not know? Didn't it burn when you pissed?"

"Here you go."

"Here I go what?"

"Here you go acting crazy."

"I ain't acting—"

"Listen, just listen," he said, cutting me off.

"I'm listening!"

"Baby, I'm sorry, okay. I am truly sorry. I love you, and I didn't know this would happen. You know I wouldn't purposely do this. I love you too much. I love you, Desire. I love you."

He pulled me closer to him and caressed my cheek. He began French-kissing my bottom lip, and *voilà*. I met him at his house after school. It's sad how naïve I was when it came to Malik. He had so much power over me, it was ridiculous.

Remember now, the entire time he was on his trip, I was on heavy-duty punishment. He wasn't around to influence me, which made it easier for me to stick by the rules. How quickly that changed. In a matter of seconds, he smooth-talked me back into his bed, and I started lying to my aunt and uncle again.

Every day after school I'd go to his house or hang out with Jen downtown. I told my aunt and uncle that I had track practice. I made sure to come back at the time practice was normally over, or else they would have gotten suspicious.

One Wednesday night, I reached home later than usual. I had my track gear on, faking like I was exhausted. I had my lie all ready, about having missed the bus. When I unlocked the door and let myself in, my aunt greeted me with the infamous black leather spiked belt. I knew I was in trouble then. She snatched me up and went haywire.

I went haywire too. "Get off of me! You witch! I'm too old to get a beating!" I resisted.

Uncle Frank ordered her to stop, and Auntie Linda surprisingly listened.

"Where have you been, young lady?" Auntie Linda asked. "Because we know damn well you were not at track practice."

I stood there looking stupid, while Uncle Frank waited for my reply. They weren't going to get the truth out of me, so I came up with a bold-faced lie. I told them I went to the library after practice because I had to do research for a project. Then my uncle started asking me questions about exact times and all this other crap. It was a wrap for me. I couldn't give exact times 'cause I was lying, and frankly, I wasn't a good liar. Not yet.

I made them furious this time. My television had already been gone, and the only thing left for them to take out was the stereo. I could live with that, 'cause I often stayed in my room writing in silence anyway. That was too good to be true though. They hit me with the big one. I couldn't run track anymore.

How could they? I loved track. It was the only thing close to therapy I had to relieve my stresses. Between the pain of not having a real father and trying to continuously understand why my mother left me, I needed track. It kept my mind off the rape. It kept me from questioning why God took Greg away. Track was my world, and it was taken away from me right under my nose. Why couldn't Greg have stuck around longer? Things would have been much different. I wouldn't have been involved with half the things I was if he'd stayed around. But so be it. The decision was final. Auntie Linda got what she wanted. Uncle Frank backed her up too. You know what that meant. I had burned one too many bridges with my uncle, and he was all set with me.

That was cool though. It was just another hump to get over. When you break the rules, you have to suffer the consequences, right? I can't be mad at that, especially since the punishment didn't last too long. Oh no, Desire was getting the hell out of dodge.

That same night I had decided to runaway to Malik's house. I waited for my aunt to go to sleep, and I got my bike off the back porch and rode to the nearest pay phone. I called Malik, and he gave me the okay to come over. I rode my bike all the way to his house, which was about a half-an-hour ride. Not too much of a ride from Roxbury to his place in Dorchester. My track legs did me well.

Malik did me well too. As soon as I got in his house, we got down and dirty. We had sex about three times, three different ways, and as usual with no condom.

Then, you know, we concluded with cuddling and talking.

"I don't want to go back home, Malik."

"So stay with me."

"I can't stay with you."

"Yes, you can. Why not?"

"I mean, I never want to go back."

"And you can stay with me. I'll take care of you."

"Are you serious?"

"Of course, baby."

"What about your mother?"

"What about her? You're my girl. She ain't gonna say
nothing. You can stay right here with me. You know
daddy ain't gonna let nothing happen to you."

I looked up at Malik, and he had a big Kool-Aid smile
on his face as he leaned in to kiss me. Malik sounded so
sincere in his words, I just knew he cared.

We did it one more time and then fell asleep in each
other's arms.

Chapter 10

"Desire. Desire. Desire, wake up!"

"Huh? What?"

"Get up! You gotta go!"

I opened my eyes, and my vision was blurry. I sat up and slouched back down.

"Come on, you gotta go." He lifted me out of the bed and placed me on my feet.

I could hardly walk. My legs were shaking, and my eyes were heavy. For a minute I didn't know where I was.

I looked at the clock. "Malik, it's four in the morning. What's wrong with you?"

I tried to turn around and get back in the bed, but he stopped me in my tracks.

"Desire, you can't stay here. You gotta go." He picked up my sneakers and handed them to me.

"What? I thought you said—"

"Shhh! My mother is 'sleep." He led me to the kitchen. Then out the back door we went.

"I thought you said I could stay with you?"

"Desire, come on. You know I was playing."

I stood there looking pitiful.

Slam!

Just like that, he closed the door in my face. I got on my bike and began peddling home, trying to hold back tears. All I could think about was how Malik lied to me and how my black ass was going to get in trouble for sneaking out.

See, when Malik told me I could stay with him, it was like he'd lifted a burden off my shoulders. I just knew I wouldn't have to see or answer to my aunt and uncle anymore. There would be no getting in trouble for sneaking out or being yelled at constantly for no reason, or being treated like a piece of shit.

Malik made me think that all that was gonna be washed away. I was wrong though. He left me riding home trying to figure out what lie I was going to tell when I got caught for sneaking out. There was no way I was getting back in the house without being heard or seen.

Reality hit, y'all. I couldn't face my aunt and uncle. I came up with a plan though, and guess where it landed me? In the hospital.

Auntie Linda and Uncle Frank were once again fuming. They'd rushed to the hospital after hearing I had been hit by a car. I rode my bike in the middle of the street purposely to get hit by a car. It was stupid, but it worked. Luckily, I didn't get hit bad enough to break any bones. I only got knocked off my bike, and ended up with minor scrapes and bruises, and some aches and pains.

"Desire, what the hell were you doing at four thirty in the morning on your bike?" Uncle Frank asked.

"I was trying to kill myself."

"Trying to kill yourself?"

"My mother doesn't want me, and y'all don't want me. I thought I'd be doing y'all a favor."

"You ain't dead, and we got plenty of knives in the kitchen," Auntie Linda commented.

"Linda, please!"

"Shit! If she wants to kill herself because of what she thinks, then let her do it."

"It's not what I think. It's what I *know*." I turned on my side, pretending to be hurt, playing my role to the hilt.

Uncle Frank wheeled around to the other side of the bed. "Desire, we love you, and you know that. This was just stupid. You're not making us feel better by trying to kill yourself. This is nonsense. We love you dearly and would be crushed if you weren't around."

I tried to make myself cry as I lay there in silence, but it wasn't working. After all the crying I did, at that particular time, I couldn't fake it for nothing.

"Desire, baby girl, listen to me. We love you, and trying to commit suicide does not solve any problems. I know. I've been there. You think I like being in this wheelchair? If I had a choice, of course, I'd rather be walking, but I'm not, due to the bad decisions I've made in life. You gotta do better. You are a bright young lady. You have so much to achieve. Don't let that go."

Okay, I really was about to cry there. My uncle was reaching out to me. Damn, I love that man.

"Now, the doctor said you'll be able to come home tomorrow morning. We gonna leave you to yourself, but when you get home tomorrow, we are going to have some *us* time. We need to have a nice long talk, okay?"

I nodded my head up and down in agreement.

"Good. Get some rest and see you tomorrow."

He leaned over to me, and I leaned in to let him give me a kiss on the forehead. My aunt stood there like she was about to melt. I said nothing and continued to lie there in the bed with an awkward look on my face.

"You all right, kiddo?" Uncle Frank asked.

"Yes," I answered softly.

"Okay, we'll see you tomorrow, and you think about what I said."

That was that, and he went out the door with my aunt. It was a relief to know that my crazy plan had worked, a stupid one, might I add, but it worked.

I dozed off to sleep and was awakened from the phone ringing. I didn't even know I had a working phone in the room.

I picked it up in a daze. "Hello," I answered, puzzled.

"Desire, baby, are you okay? I heard about what happened to you."

"Who's this?"

"What you mean, who's this? Who else would be calling you?"

"Malik?"

"Yeah. You better know who it is. When you getting out of the hospital?"

"Tomorrow."

"Come see me tonight."

"Huh?"

"You heard me."

"Malik, I'm in the hospital," I reminded him.

"I know where you are. That's where I called, right?"

"Yeah."

"A'ight then. What's up? You comin' or what? I heard you didn't get hit that bad."

I didn't respond.

"Hello."

"Yeah," I answered.

"So you comin'?"

"Nope," I hesitantly answered, not wanting to hurt his feelings.

"What you mean, no?"

"I thought I couldn't stay with you?"

"That was last time. Tonight's a new night."

"I don't know."

"I'm coming to get you. Be ready."

"Wh—"

Click. He hung up the phone.

Before I knew it, I had snuck out of the hospital and hopped in the car with Malik. We got to his house, and I was introduced to weed for the first time. I watched him roll a Philly Blunt, filling it with marijuana. You know what happened after that. We got high as a kite. My amateur ass was choking and shit, but it was a good feeling. I think we smoked about three blunts together then we had sex multiple times. I didn't know what was going on half the time. I was not in my right mind. That weed did me in.

I went from dazing, to laughing, to depression. Then I got the munchies, and Malik only had enough junk food to feed himself. Stingy bastard. I watched him eat, got lightheaded, and eventually passed out.

I woke up in Malik's bed naked with no one lying next to me. I looked at his clock, and it was nine thirty in the morning. I hadn't planned on staying the night. I got up, grabbed my sneakers, and was headed to put my clothes on. Then I heard this lady singing, and her voice was getting closer. Malik's mom was heading toward his room.

I dashed to the bed, with my sneakers in hand, and crawled underneath.

She walked in the room and came straight over to his bed.

I moved in more, hoping not to get caught.

She stood there for a good three minutes. I don't know what she was doing, but next thing I knew, she was snatching his sheets off. She threw them down on the floor and left back out of the room.

I waited a little bit. As soon as I thought the coast was clear, I started easing my way out, but she came back into the room. I slid my leg back up under the bed.

She walked over to the bed and started putting new sheets on, mumbling to herself about how messy Malik was. She spotted my clothes, because she started talking about how he always got some girl in her house leaving their stuff around. She was saying she told him the next time she sees something out of place in her house, it's going in the trash. If I didn't feel humiliated to be under a bed with sneakers, stale bread, trash, and Lord knows what else, with no clothes on, and now his mother was talking about throwing my clothes away.

She left out of the room, and I eased out from under the bed, reactivating the aches and pains I had incurred from my accident. I looked around for my clothes, and they were nowhere in sight. They were gone. She wasn't playing. She really threw them away.

I sat on the bed naked, holding all I had left—my sneakers. I didn't know what I was going to do, and I was hoping while I was thinking about it that his mother didn't plan on coming back in the room. I wanted her to leave the house, so I could get the hell out of dodge. But where was I going with no clothes on?

That damn Malik. I was mad at him. *How the hell he gonna leave me in his house alone with his mama? Why would he do that?* He was a real son of bitch, I tell you. I hated myself for liking him.

Anyway, I waited and waited and waited. Between his mother's phone conversation and the shower and her cooking breakfast, I'd say I was stuck for about two hours just sitting on his bed naked and cold. I didn't want to make too much noise because I wasn't trying to get caught. Then I finally heard the door slam.

I walked to the window and watched as she walked to her car in a MBTA uniform. That was a good sign. That meant she was going to work. I waited for five minutes to make sure she was definitely gone.

I bombarded Malik's closet trying to find something to put on so I could leave. I really wanted to take a shower, but that would have been pushing it. I found a long T-shirt and a pair of gym shorts to throw on until I got to wherever I was going, of which I had no idea at the time. I think my hospital time had expired.

I knew my uncle and aunt would eventually be looking for me too, but I didn't really care. I was going to get in trouble anyway. All my privileges were gone anyway. What more could they take?

I went out the way I came in—the back door. I searched around for my bike but realized in less than two seconds that Malik had picked me up from the hospital. I panicked for a second not knowing what to do, shivering from the cold wind.

I strolled from the backyard to the front of the house, and lo and behold, a police officer stopped me. Apparently, there was an alarm system, and once his mom left, she'd activated it. He asked me what was the pass code and everything. Of course, I had no idea what he was talking about.

"So you don't live here?"

"No."

"Then what are you doing here?"

"I was looking for my bike."

"Why would your bike be here?"

"Because this is where I rode it to," I answered rudely.

"You're a smarty, huh? What's your name, young lady?"

I paused for a while, trying to think of a fake name.

"Your name, please."

"Betty." Why I chose that name, I have no idea.

"Betty, huh. Betty what?"

"Smith," I quickly said.

"You ever been to jail before, Miss Betty Smith?"

I got tense. "No."

"So I'm gonna ask you again. What's your name, young lady?"

"Desire."

"You think this is a joke, Desire?" he yelled. His deep Barry White voice intimidated me.

"No." The tears were about to come.

"Desire what? What is your last name?"

"Huh?"

"Desire what?"

"Jo—Jones," I stuttered.

He yelled, "Desire Jones, do you live here?"

"No."

"Then what are you doing here, Desire Jones?"

"My friend lives here."

"Oh, your friend lives here. And your friend is where?"

"I don't know."

"You don't know?"

"No, I don't know," I answered, getting agitated. I was crying by this time. His voice was too raw and rigid.

"Not too smart now, huh? What you crying for?"

I wiped my eyes.

"Do your parents know where you are? How old are you?"

"No. I mean, yes. I'm thirteen."

"So I can call them right now?"

"Yeah, but our phone is off."

"Desire, I've had enough with the fooling around. You're going to the station, so we can contact your parents."

Huh! Over my dead body! I kicked up dirt as I raced away from the officer.

He immediately bolted behind me.

I kept looking back to see how far behind he was, and he wasn't too far. I picked up the pace. If I'd had on my cleats, he would not have been as close as he was to me, cop or not. I looked back for the last time, and that was my downfall. He caught me.

My aunt had to come down to the police station to pick me up. I was in boiling hot water.

I didn't get in the door good enough before my uncle laid the leather to my behind. I could hardly sit down from the soreness of the welts on my butt.

"You try to kill yourself, and then you pull this mess. I'm starting to think you're playing me for a fool, Desire."

"I'm not, Uncle Frank. I just—"

"I didn't ask you to talk, and I definitely do not want an explanation. Here, take this piece of paper."

I took the sheet of paper from him. He made me write down everything that I did wrong and sign a contract of some sort. It was agreed that if I screwed up anymore, then I was to be sent away for good. It was a choice of boarding school, boot camp, or something to that effect.

"This is your last warning, little girl. Believe me, you will not get the same treatment anywhere else the way you do in this household. Those little boys you want to be chasing after can give two shits about you, Desire. We in this house love and care about you. We clothe you, shelter you, and feed you. Not everyone lives in a nice house, and not every child has their own room. So I'm telling you get your act together because, if you don't, you will no longer live under this roof, and mark my words when I tell you, there is no place like home."

My uncle was right, but it wasn't all my fault. What about Auntie Linda and her bipolar ways? All the stuff she did to me behind his back. I'll never forget how she tied me up, beat me with a belt buckle, and lied about me having sex with Greg. She was part of the reason I was acting out.

I know I did things that were over the top, but geez, give me a break. Could I just be a teenager without being criticized and brutalized? I mean, I must admit, it did become a habit of mine, learning things the hard way. I don't know why it had to be like that, but it just was. I couldn't control the demons inside of me. I wanted love elsewhere besides home. Why couldn't they understand that, or why couldn't I understand them?

I vowed to try mending my ways, but just as I was willing, something else came up.

Chapter 11

For a week straight I obeyed and abided by the rules. I felt weird not getting into trouble and not being able to do what I wanted, but I couldn't get Uncle Frank's heartbreaking expression out of my mind. He looked so hurt from my actions, as if a newborn had died. I had to do right by him. He loved me unconditionally and would do anything for me.

Malik and I hadn't been talking. I'd built up the courage to ignore him. I was still pissed with him for leaving me alone in his house. He was ignoring me as well, so it wasn't too much of a courage thing on my part. He'd see me and turn his cheek, and I'd do the same. I was hurting, but I was beginning to realize the jerk he was. It was like we hadn't even had a conversation a day in our lives. Can you believe that? Man, I wish I had known better. What's so bugged out too was, even though we weren't on speaking terms, he still managed to be a thorn in my side.

The day I was given permission to resume track, I woke up sick as a dog. Nothing I ate would stay down. Jen asked me, "When was the last time you had your period?" I had been running wild for so long, I couldn't recall. I had an irregular period anyway, so it was definitely going to be hard to tell.

Jen suggested I take a pregnancy test. What an idea that was. I didn't really want to, but I was peer pressured. I should have stuck with my gut feeling though, because getting a hold of that pregnancy test added another burden to my life.

After school, before track practice, me and Jen hit up the Walgreens drugstore down the street from the school. We wasted no time making our way down aisle six to grab a pregnancy test.

I picked up one and handed it to Jen. She picked up another and handed both to me. I looked at her like, *What are you doing?*

"Get two just in case."

"Okay, but here."

I tried to hand them to Jen, but she pushed my hand away. "What are you doing? Why you giving them to me?"

"I don't have any money," I said, handing them back to her.

She pushed my hand away. "I don't have any money either."

"So how we gonna get 'em?" I asked.

Jen gave me that "five-finger look." I was with it too, but it was damn sure going to be a team effort. I handed one back to her. Then, at the same time, we stuffed them in our coats and bolted out of the store.

We thought we had made a quick getaway, but oh no, the security officer saw our thievin' asses and was on us. My heart was racing. Boy, was I trying to get away. It was crazy. The adrenaline rush you get when you're in a sticky situation. The feeling is definitely not cool. The security guard chasing us was this sloppy, fat, nasty-looking guy, who should not have been running as fast as he was. He fooled us. He had speed. I didn't think he'd be right on us, but he was. I had to put more pep in my run. You know I wasn't trying to see another police station ever, especially for stealing a pregnancy test.

So while we were running, I turned my head to look behind me, which gave Jen a good lead. She was smart. She never looked back. Me, on the other hand, I got caught up. I tripped on my own two feet and hit the pavement.

Jen was straight. She got away. She stopped when I fell, but I told her to keep running. I didn't want her to get caught up over me. She took my advice without hesitation too. She was out.

The security guard snatched me up from off the ground and dragged me back to Walgreens by the hood of my jacket. I was trying to pull loose, but I would have only strangled myself. I wished I had a detachable hood. It would have definitely come in handy, but too bad. I was shit out of luck. Big man had me, and all I kept thinking was, *If I didn't trip, then I would have gotten my ass away. Damn!*

After we got back inside the store, he took me to this secluded room behind the photo area. The way the door looked and where the room was located, you wouldn't even know it existed. When we got in the room, he wasted no time in searching me. He patted me down like he was getting a free feel.

At first I wasn't really paying attention to it, but when the whole pat-down process seemed more like fondling than a pat-down, I shoved his hands off me.

"Is there a problem?" he yelled in my face.

"Yeah. You're feeling all over me like I stole something!" I yelled back. "I didn't steal nothing."

"Yes, you did, and it's on you somewhere."

"Nothing's on me. I didn't take nothing."

Lucky for me, the pregnancy test had dropped while I was running.

"Strip to your underwear. I don't have time for games."

"What?" I asked, confused.

"Listen, I don't have all day. Either you strip so I can confirm that you didn't take anything, or I call the police and they come down and lock you up. Simple as that. You make the decision, but I ain't got all day."

I thought about my choices. Notifying the police was definitely out of the question. If a strip search had to be down to avoid me being locked up, then I was going for that.

I started taking off my clothes slowly.

"How old are you, by the way?"

"Thirteen."

"Thirteen?"

"Yeah."

"You ain't thirteen. Don't lie to me."

"Yes, I am."

"What grade are you in?"

"Eighth," I responded, taking off my last bit of clothes. I was down to my bra and panties.

"You done?"

I looked at him like he was crazy, as if I wasn't two articles shy of being naked.

He giggled. "Excuse the question. I'll search your clothes first."

I watched him as he bent down and went through my clothes.

"You must have ditched what you stole."

"I told you I didn't steal nothing."

"Please, don't spare me the truth," he commented as he stood up. "Spread your legs and put your arms out," he demanded angrily.

You know he wasn't right for doing this to me. What was he going to find on me, seeing that I was half-naked. He definitely had another agenda, but I was too scared to question it.

"And you did steal something. I saw you take it." He nonchalantly slid his index finger through the seat of my underwear.

I jumped, feeling funny.

Then he proceeded to pat my legs down. How much more patting of me did he need to do? I practically had no clothes on.

"Almost done," he said. He walked behind me, patted my arms, unhooked my bra, and gently squeezed on my breasts.

I took a deep breath, and tears came to my eyes. He was fondling me, y'all, and I was too scared to do anything about it. So I just stood there.

He ran his hand down my sides, caressing my waist. Then he slipped his hands inside my panties and gripped both my ass cheeks. "All right, you're free to go. You're clean."

I stood there in awe like, *What just happened?*

"You don't wanna leave? You want another patdown? I'll be glad to give it to you," he joked.

I didn't think anything was funny. He had just violated me. I was dumbfounded and didn't really know what to do.

"You need help putting your clothes on?"

I shook my head no and started putting on my clothes. I couldn't believe it. He had just gotten a cheap feel. In Walgreens. *Pervert!* I hurried to get my stuff on. I had just zipped my pants when the door opened.

"What we got here?"

"A thief."

"Age?"

"Thirteen."

"What she take?"

"I don't know. I couldn't find it. I think she ditched it when I was chasing her."

"Did you see her ditch it?"

"No."

"Well, let her go. There's nothing we can do. You know we can't search minors anyway."

I swung on my coat, took one last mental picture of the predator, and hauled ass. I pushed my way through the man standing in the doorway, got outside of Walgreens, and burst out into tears.

I was in a daze. I was thinking about my aunt and the way she treated me. Malik and the way he screwed me over. My mom ditching me. Greg being swooped away by God. All that came to the forefront of my mind. I thought I was about to lose it. I couldn't think of anything good about myself or anything good that someone had done for me. I felt as if I had "Violate Me" written all over my forehead. I began to hate people more, and I was beginning to hate life. I needed a change quick.

I managed to pull myself together to go back up to school, where Jen was out front socializing.

When she noticed me, she ran over my way. "Oh my God! I was so scared. I was just telling Clayton what happened. I didn't tell him about what we stole though. How did you get away? What happened?"

A mental picture of the violation came to mind.

"Whatever. Nothing. You got the test?" I asked softly.

"What's wrong?"

"Nothing!"

"Something's wrong. What happened?"

"Nothing! Do you have the test?" I yelled, agitated.

"Yeah, right here. Calm down."

I started crying.

"What happened, Desire?"

"That man . . . the man . . . "

"Who?"

"The security guy . . . he made me take my clothes off."

"He made you take your clothes off?"

I nodded my head up and down as I wiped my eyes.

"Did he do something to you?"

More tears fell.

Jen embraced me. "Oh no, Desire."

"He didn't like rape me or anything. He just like felt all over me," I cried. "He was a fucking pervert."

"It's okay. Calm down," Jen soothed.

"I hate people!"

"No, you don't. You just feel like that now. It's okay. Everything's gonna be all right."

I wiped my eyes as Jen's words soothed me.

"Come on, let's go inside the school."

I pulled myself together as we walked inside the school. We headed straight for the bathroom. It was that time, y'all!

Jen reached in her pocket and handed me the test. We stared at each other like, *This is it.*

I went into the stall, followed the instructions, and came out to wait. I handed the test to Jen, so she could spill the results.

While we waited, I prayed to God that if he made my results negative, I would never have sex again in my life. Ever. I told Him I'd become a nun, sacrifice myself to Him, and all this crap. I should have known better though. You can't negotiate with God. Who was I fooling? Whatever He wanted to go down, it did, and that's how it went.

Jen confirmed a plus sign. I was now pregnant with Malik's baby.

Chapter 12

Pregnant, pregnant, pregnant! I couldn't bring myself to believe it though, so I told myself I wasn't. Yup, I went right ahead and took my pregnant behind to track practice. Jen tagged along because she was trying out. She thought I was stone crazy to go on as if it was nothing. It didn't matter to me though 'cause, like I said, I didn't want to believe it. So I didn't.

I got into practice with a clear mind, geared up, ready to run. I did my laps and exercises, no problem. Then it was time to get busy. My specialty in track was running the fifty, so my main practice consisted of sprinting. I was holding up for a while, but as soon as the coach blew the whistle, memories surfaced, and that was it. I lost it. I couldn't stay focused.

I kept thinking and thinking and thinking. It was like a live nightmare. My thoughts wouldn't go away. I was hearing cries, seeing Greg lying in his coffin, and Malik giving me the finger. I was freaking out. And it showed in my running too.

Coach immediately became unhappy. I was already on his shit list for the trouble I was getting into, and now I was fucking up his practice. He lashed out at me, leaving spit on my face and all. And he kicked me out of practice.

I didn't mean to mess up. I had tried to stay focused. I really did, but my burdens were too heavy. I was only thirteen, y'all, and carrying half the world on my shoulders.

After I got kicked out of practice, I stuck around in school to wait on Jen. In the meantime, I used the last bit of money I had to try to get in contact with Malik. I called him from the pay phone at school. He picked up but told me to call him back.

I waited for about fifteen minutes and rang him back. Again, he said call him back in ten minutes. I wasn't trying to kick it with him over the phone. I was just trying to tell him what was up.

I gave him his ten minutes and called back, but of course you know the bastard didn't answer. I couldn't even call him back, since I had used up my last bit of change. I waited like thirty more minutes before Jen was let out of practice.

"Oh, I didn't know you were going to wait for me," she said.

"Might as well," I responded, feeling depressed.

Jen rubbed my back. "Desire, it's okay."

I was pregnant at thirteen, y'all. Eighth grade. What the hell was okay about that?

"Did you call Malik to tell him? You need to tell him, because you should not be dealing with this on your own."

"I called him like three times, and he kept telling me to call him back. And just now he didn't pick up the phone. I was trying to tell him, but he never gave me a chance to get a word in."

"He's trying to avoid you. Go to that nucca's house."

"I'm not going over there."

"You go over there to have sex with him, but you can't go over there to tell him that you're pregnant?"

"I'm scared."

"Desire, this is no time to be scared. This is serious. You got a baby up in there. Go to his house and tell him. He can't avoid you face to face."

"You gonna come with me?"

"I can't. I gotta be home by four thirty. I'm on punishment, remember?"

I took a deep breath and thought, *Just go ahead over there and get it over with.* I couldn't wait until school the next day to tell him because I wasn't trying to put my business out there like that. I didn't want to chance a bad reaction from him in front of an audience.

I had an hour before I had to be home, which was enough time to make the trip. I got my bus pass out and hopped on the bus. It took me about twenty minutes to get to his house. The walk from the bus stop was all of two minutes, if so much.

When I got to his doorstep, I saw this girl crying hysterically. It startled me.

Before I could turn around to be on my merry way, Malik came out of his house. He went to touch the girl to comfort her, I guess, and she yelled out, "Don't fucking touch me, you HIV-infested bastard!"

I remembered that three-letter STD from a pamphlet I got at the clinic. HIV was the one that couldn't be cured. Now, as I stood there and remembered this stuff, nothing dawned on me like it should have. My mind was scrambled. I just stared at Malik and the girl in a daze. I snapped out of it quickly though when Malik yelled out at me. I didn't even know he had seen me.

"What the fuck are you doing here?"

I looked at him in awe. I don't know why, because I did know him to be an ignorant bastard.

The girl glanced over at me. She jumped up in Malik's face, pointing her finger at me. "Oh, is that one of the little bitches you were fucking while I was away at college? Huh, Malik?"

Homegirl started to mimic Malik, while screaming at the top of her lungs, "*Baby, why you so worried about what I'm doing? You know you my only girl. I should be worried about you away at college.* And all this time you were the one fucking around!"

Before he could respond, she hauled off and smacked the living daylights out of him, causing his head to snap to one side, and they started fist-fighting.

I couldn't believe what I was seeing. He had actually hit her back. They were like two boxers in a ring, no lie.

I got out of there. I couldn't watch anymore. He didn't want me there anyway, so sticking around would have only made matters worse. The girl probably would have tried to fight me, and I wasn't about to be the next in line to get rumbled on. On top of that, imagine if I'd told her why I was there. Yeah, we all would have definitely been fighting. Shoot, I probably would have gotten double-teamed, and I wanted to avoid all unnecessary drama. I turned right around and walked my black ass away like I had no business being at his house.

During my bus ride home, I thought about what I was going to do. Memories flashed back about my aunt telling me to never step foot in her house pregnant. I was a flat-out disgrace. Someone had a curse on me, I swear.

I had to make a decision though, and my mind was made up. I wasn't going to cause my uncle any more hardship. By 2:00 A.M. that morning, I was planning to be gone. My bags were going to be packed, my Dear John letter was going to be written, and I would be out of their hair.

As soon as I arrived home, I went straight upstairs to my room and started packing a runaway bag. While I was in the process, my aunt wanted me to go to the gro-

cery store for her to get some things she needed right
away. She didn't have any cash on her, so she gave me
her bank card to get some money out of the teller. That
was a shocker. She was trusting me, the liar and the no-
good niece, with her bank card. *Wow!*

She was a bit hesitant at first, but I assured her I'd
be right back. I wanted to get her what she needed, so I
could come back and finish packing.

I got to the store and bought what my aunt needed.
On the walk back home, I thought long and hard about
the whole pregnancy thing and where I was going to
stay once I left home. I thought about the essentials:
money, clothes, food. I was thinking, *How am I going
to do this? Am I going to live on the street and out of
my bag until the baby is born? What am I going to do?*

I made it halfway home then I realized that I couldn't
go back. I turned right back around and began my
journey as a runaway. Auntie Linda wasn't getting her
groceries that night, or her ATM card.

Chapter 13

I wanted to call Jen and fill her in on my new plans to run away, but then I decided against it. I didn't want any type of leads to my whereabouts. I roamed the neighborhood for a while just walking and thinking, not knowing what the hell I was going to do. As it got late, I hopped on the bus to Ruggles Station and got on the Orange Line.

I rode the train all the way to its last stop, Oak Grove. I stayed on as it rode right back to where I had started. I had no idea where I was going, what I was going to do, or how I was going to survive. Then I remembered I had Auntie Linda's bank card, which meant I had access to money. So, of course, I thought about getting a room.

I got off the train at Back Bay Station. I figured that would be the best area for finding a hotel. There were mad hotels in that vicinity. I stopped at the ATM in the train station to take out more money. I didn't know how much a room would cost, but I figured three hundred would be more than enough. I felt bad about taking my aunt's money, but that feeling quickly sailed away after I thought about all the shit she'd done to me. Shoot, she practically owed me.

It took me no time to browse the area and step inside the first appealing hotel, the Sheraton. I was amazed to walk inside of such an unspeakably beautiful hotel. I had never seen anything so richly decorated or delicate in appearance. What can I say? I had never been inside a hotel before, so I didn't know what to expect. I didn't know where to go, who to see, or what to do.

I saw people with luggage coming in, and I figured I'd just follow them. That led me to the reception desk. I stood in line to get a room, thinking the process was going to be easy.

"Hi. What can I do for you?"

"Ah . . . I need a room."

"Okay," she said, typing into the computer, and then glanced up at me. "Are you here alone? Do you have a guardian with you?"

"No, I'm getting the room for myself."

"How old are you?"

"Sixteen," I lied, and it still wasn't good enough.

"Honey, where are your parents?"

"I just need a room for the night. I have money." I pulled out my knot of twenties.

"Ah, young lady, no, this is not—"

"Please, I just need a room for the night. Don't you see I have money?"

"I'm sorry. You're not of age."

"I can pay for a room, please. I have nowhere else to sleep tonight." I gave her the sad puppy-dog face.

"I'm sorry, but there's nothing I can do. Why don't you try Tween Street Inn? It's a homeless shelter for teens. They can probably help you better."

I stepped out of the line to let the people behind me go next. It was sad that the damn receptionist didn't even care about where I was going to lay my head that night. She could have helped me out. She could have given me a room, instead of sending me to a damn teen shelter.

I ended up sleeping on one of the little couches they had in the lobby. I didn't intend to do this, but in the midst of my thinking, I'd dozed off.

"Miss! Excuse me, young lady!"

I opened my eyes as I felt someone tapping me.

"You cannot sleep here. Have you been here all night?"

I looked up and saw this tall, pale, skinny white man whose name tag said: Asst. Manager, Jacob. I jumped up. "No, no. I was waiting for my grandmother to come downstairs."

"What room is she in?"

"Huh? Oh, I'll just go get her."

"But I can call up to the room for you."

"No, no, I'll go back up. I just remembered I left something in the room anyway. Thanks."

I got up before he could ask me any more questions and got on the elevator to the tenth floor. I got off and walked down the hall, acting as if I was going into a room. He wasn't following me or nothing, but I was just trying to play it off, just in case.

I saw the maids in the hallway pushing their little buggies. Most of the room doors were open too. I peeped into one of the rooms they were cleaning. The room was spacious, and the bed looked awfully comfortable. It was calling my name. I wanted to just drop dead on it. I wasn't shy about asking to do so either.

"Excuse me. Can I lie down while you clean the room?"

"Ju make a resovation fo' dis room?" the Hispanic lady asked in broken English.

"They won't let me."

"¿Qué?"

"I tried to but—"

"I no speak English. *Lo siento. Yo no puedo ayud-arte.*"

"Huh?"

"I no help you. *Lo siento.*"

I just had to get the lady who didn't speak English well. The only option left was to talk money. I pulled out my knot of twenties.

She looked at me and looked around. She pulled me into the room. "You pay me." She held out her hand.

I put one twenty in her hand, and she kept it out. I put another twenty in her hand, and she still kept her hand out. For someone who didn't speak English, she sure was fluent in American currency. I placed another twenty in her hand, and she smiled, indicating that she was happy with sixty dollars. Immediately after that twenty dropped in her hand, I let my body fall across the bed.

"You leave *tres*, okay."

"Okay, thank you," I said.

"*Tres*," she firmly repeated, holding up three fingers.

"Yes, *tres*," I repeated, happy to know beginner's Spanish class did come in handy.

I slept until about one thirty that afternoon. I wanted to sleep longer, but the shower was calling me. I hadn't showered since the morning before I ran away. I needed to get my smell-good on quick.

I had no other clothes to put on, but I figured, until I hit a store, I could flip my underwear inside out and put back on the same clothes. Hey, I had to do what I had to do, you know what I'm saying.

I made the bed back up nice and neat, making it look like I hadn't even slept on it. I followed up with a steaming hot shower. Boy, was it a relief to feel so fresh and clean. I got out and wrapped myself in a crisp white towel.

I walked out of the bathroom as I dried off, watching the cartoon network. I was laughing enjoying the show like a two-year-old. Then, suddenly, my room door opened. I shuffled, wrapping my towel around me quickly.

This dark-skinned, short, bumpy-faced guy walked in. He had on the same uniform as the manager I had seen earlier. "This room is not reserved. How'd you get in here? Aren't you—didn't I see you in line last night?"

"Yeah, I mean, no. I'm leaving. Please don't call security." I started grabbing my stuff, and my towel fell off. I swooped it up, embarrassed.

"What's your situation? Are you homeless or something? You on the run?"

"No, no."

"Are you prostituting?"

"No, I just needed a place to take stay for a while, but it's cool. I'm leaving. Just let me get my stuff. I don't want any trouble."

"No trouble at all. Matter of fact, I might be able to help you."

I stopped gathering my things, interested in how he could help. "How?"

"Any chance you got money on you?"

"You take cash?" I fumbled with my jeans and reached in the back pocket. I pulled out my twenties. "How much do you want? I can get more."

He closed the door. "Nah, nah. Nothing like that. I like what I see, if you feel what I'm saying."

I didn't say anything at first, puzzled by his comment.

"How about you take your towel off."

"What?" I joggled with a screwed-up face.

"It's cool if you don't want to. You can take your stuff and leave. I'd have to report you first though."

Yeah, it was just my luck to be threatened with the police. I was hesitant, but I couldn't get reported. I didn't want to be found. I had to do what I had to do. I needed a place to stay. I took one for the team, y'all.

I tossed my towel on the floor as if the request was nothing new to me. As he stared at my amazingly over-developed body, a bulge rose in his pants.

Then I let him sleep with me. I had to do it. It was the only way to keep the room.

Chapter 14

I was living in a hotel free of charge for sleeping with one of the employees and, on occasion, giving head to a few of his friends. I couldn't do this for long though. Believe it or not, I really didn't like what I was doing. Plus, my stomach was slowly but surely getting swollen. Dude had no idea I was pregnant. Shoot, I sometimes forgot I was pregnant, with all the extracurricular activities I was getting involved in.

It was party time almost every night, and I was dishing out money like I was a rich girl. I'd withdraw hundreds of dollars at a time and give dude money to buy expensive dinners, liquor, and whatever expensive lingerie he wanted to see me in. That went down for no more than two weeks as the money only stretched so far from me misusing and abusing it. So of course, before I knew it, I blew it. The money was gone. I was on *E* and my funds were cut off.

I got the surprise notice when I went to make a withdrawal one night and the damn machine kept the card. Auntie Linda had finally reported it stolen, and I was flat out of luck broke. Not to mention, I only had three outfits to my name, with little to no underclothes. I was washing out underwear every day. That shit was crazy.

My uncle was right when he said there was no place like home. Every day I was wishing I was home or that I was dreaming. I wanted to wake up in my bed at home, saying, "I'm glad that wasn't real." But it was real. I was out in the real world struggling, on the grind.

I ate what I could when I could. My daily meals were something else. It got so bad, I used to get up early in the morning, go down to the free continental breakfast, and get enough food to stash for the rest of the day. For dinner, I usually went to the store and stole a couple of frozen dinners, microwaved them, and called it a day.

It got tired though. I was tired of stealing and running the streets. I wanted to go home, but I knew I couldn't.

I attempted to call a couple of times, but when my aunt answered, I hung up immediately. I was scared to speak, but more or less, scared to speak to her. Then one day I got very depressed, and I just called, willing to speak to anybody.

"Hello!"

"Hello!" the voice loudly repeated again.

"Ah, hello," I whispered.

"Desire!"

"Yes!"

"Where the hell are you?"

"Can I come home?"

"You shouldn't have left. You think you are so grown. You probably laid up with some nucca, and now he can't take care of you no more so you wanna come home."

"I'm not laid up with anybody."

"You can't fool me, Desire. I hope y'all had fun with my money."

"Can I speak to Uncle Frank?"

"Hell no! You had us worried all this time. You took my money and now you want sympathy. Oh no, you don't! You stay your narrow behind where you're at. Me and your uncle are sick of your shit. You stay right where you are and don't even think about coming back." *Click*. She hung up the phone.

I called back.

"What did I tell you?"

"Auntie, please, I will never call again if you just let me speak to Uncle Frank."

"Over my dead body!" *Click*.

I knew I had messed up, but damn, she didn't have to shut me out like that. I was a confused kid growing up. Gimme a break!

I was on the verge of a breakdown. I needed someone to talk to. I missed my good ol' friend Jen. She was my next phone call. I had her worried sick too 'cause I hadn't talked to her since I had run away.

"Desire, where have you been? Where are you?"

"I'm at a hotel."

"A hotel? Why?"

"Because I ran away."

"You ran away?"

"Yeah."

"I thought you were sick on the verge of dying with pneumonia, and you couldn't get visits, and no one was to know, not even the school and—"

"Who told you that?"

"Your aunt. She said you were—"

"She lied, Jen. I ain't been home in weeks."

"What? I've been sending you balloons and get-well cards. I can't believe her."

"Believe it," I said.

"I really thought you . . . your aunt is crazy," Jen blurted.

"That's nothing new."

"It's new to me. Well, I mean, I knew she was strict, but damn. She's gone over the top with this one. I have been really depressed, thinking you were going to die. I had no one to talk to either, because your aunt said I was to tell no one, not even my mother."

"I guess that's why no one came looking for me." I sobbed.

"So wait. Dang, you're in a hotel, by yourself?"

"Yeah," I huffed.

"You sound sad."

I started crying. "I'm scared."

"Scared? Scared of what? Why'd you run away?"

"I couldn't stay home being pregnant."

"Oh my gosh, Desire! What hotel are you at?"

"Downtown."

"Where downtown?"

"At the Sheraton down by Copley."

"The Sheraton! How you staying there? Ain't that an expensive hotel? I bet the room is nice though, huh?"

I blanked out for a minute as the pain of being a lonely, scared runaway hit home. My cry grew louder.

"Desire, don't cry."

"I wanna go back home. I don't have any more money. I don't have any clothes."

"It's okay. I'll bring you some clothes and money. What room are you in?"

"Ten twenty-three."

"I'll be there before you know it. I promise."

Jen came in a flash as she promised. I was so overwhelmed to see her that I didn't know what to do. We hugged, and hugged, and hugged. She was amazed at my hotel room. She didn't think there was any reason for me to want to go home, but she didn't know that living luxuriously was not all it was hyped up to be.

"You're crying to go home, and you are livin' large."

I looked at her like, *If only you knew what I was doing.*

"Girl, this place is nice," she said, falling backwards on the bed.

"How much does this place cost? How are you paying for it? Didn't I ask you that already?"

"It doesn't cost that much."

"Well, how much? Maybe I can have a hooky party here."

"I stole the money from my aunt," I informed her, not proud of my actions.

"What you looking all sad for? That bitch deserved it. She treats you foul."

"I hate myself!" I broke down in tears again.

"What? What's wrong? What are you talking about?"

"I hate myself. I want to go home, and I can't go home because I'm pregnant. My aunt wouldn't let me talk to my uncle. He hates me now. They don't even want me to come home."

"Desire, calm down. Don't cry. How many months are you?"

"I don't know!"

"What you mean, you don't know?"

"I don't know! I haven't gone to the clinic."

"Desire, you have to go. Are you keeping the baby? You can get rid of it, you know. Let me see your stomach. Are you showing?"

"No, I don't know! Stop asking so many questions. I don't know," I lashed out.

"Sorry, sorry. I didn't mean to ramble."

"It's okay. I'm just trippin'."

"Cool, no sweat. Here. Look at the clothes I brought you. I picked you up some underwear from the dollar store too. I had sixteen dollars to my name, so I spent three, got the rest for my train ride, and ten for you."

"Thanks. I appreciate it."

"Any time."

"I hate I'm in this predicament."

"You should really go to the clinic."

"I know. I know," I whispered.

"You want me to go with you?"

"No, I can go by myself."

"Are you coming back to school? Oh yeah. That's what else I got for you. I brought all of your work you missed. I even got you a fake doctor's note."

"I ain't going back to school."

"What? Why?"

"How can I?"

"Just go. I told you I got the notes to excuse your absence. It's not like your aunt is telling the truth about why you're not in school. She didn't say anything to them. It's like you're just a dropout. You gotta come back."

"I'll think about it."

"What is there to think about?"

"I don't know. I just gotta think."

"Okay, suit yourself. Think about it, but I gotta go. I'm supposed to meet my mom at her job. Make sure you call me, okay?"

"All right," I sadly said.

I hated to see her go. I wish she could have stayed with me, or I stay with her, but nah. My stay with her definitely wouldn't work. Just picturing her house ran a chill through my spine. I couldn't go back there. My mental would not allow it. I had to stay where I was. What else could I have done?

My uncle was done with me, and my aunt was done from the start. Jen did give me a little something to think about though, abortion. At the time, I didn't really know the full details of what it was, but I surely found out.

I went to the clinic to have my first checkup. My doctor was surprised to learn that I was pregnant. I was surprised to learn how far along I was and that I might have contracted another fucking STD—genital warts. That damn Malik. It had to be him. He was the only one I was sleeping unprotected with. Damn!

On top of that, I definitely had a yeast infection. If it wasn't something from one man, then it was something from the next.

My doctor told me I couldn't even get the abortion without consent from a parent or guardian. We know that wasn't happening 'cause, duh, my guardians knew nothing about my pregnancy.

The doctor explained she couldn't tell them but tried to convince me to do so. She was funny. There was no way and no how I was spilling my pregnancy to anyone. Shoot, Jen was lucky to know, okay. I did not need anyone else in my business.

All I needed was that abortion. Straight up. I was too young to be knocked up, and abortion was the only way out for me. The only problem with that was, I had to tell my aunt and uncle, which meant there went that option.

I did get put on to another way out though. It was promising too, and the best thing about it was that my guardians would not have to know whatsoever.

See, if I didn't want to spill the beans and ruin my life forever, not like I wasn't heading down that path anyway, I would have had to go in front of a judge. He would have had to grant me permission to get the abortion as if he were my guardian. This meant that I had to go back to school and talk to a guidance counselor, which I wasn't doing. I couldn't do that. How could I have done that? I had not been to school in God knows when, and duh, I was a runaway. So if I was reported, shit would hit the fan, and it would be just like me telling my aunt and uncle I was pregnant. It was just too risky. So I decided to just wing it out. Yup, the abortion option was out the door.

I left the clinic disappointed and worried. I didn't know what I was going to do next. I kept peeking at my stomach that didn't really seem big enough to be a week shy of four months. Then, glancing at my surroundings, I saw the health van advertising free HIV testing.

My doctor had asked me if I wanted to take the test, and I told her no. I ensured her that there was absolutely no reason why I should. But who was I fooling? I'd had nightmares about what that girl had said to Malik. I kept seeing a picture of her face and the replay of her smack. That whole incident weighed on my mind heavy all the time, but I'd constantly shunted it off. Then it got to the point where I just blocked it out completely.

It didn't really hit me that I was a victim of Malik's STD giveaway, until that doctor's visit. That's why I was staring at the HIV truck, but that passed too. I did the usual. I cast off the subject as if it was nothing. I had other problems to worry about, and at that time, it was getting my prescription filled.

I get to the pharmacy and I can't even purchase the damn medicine. I thought it was going to be free, but it was twenty-five dollars. Twenty more than what I had. I called Jen to see if she could get me some more money.

"I told you all that I had was what I gave you. You can't steal it?"

"No, it's behind the counter."

"Just get some yogurt and put it up your vagina."

"What? I'm not doing that!"

"Okay, suit yourself. I'm just trying to help you out."

I wanted to go behind the counter and steal the damn thing after Jen put the idea in my head. I would have never gotten away with it though. It would have been impossible to climb over the counter, grab the bag, and jet. It was just not happening. There was no way I was going to be able to do that. I had to just say forget it and be on my merry way.

Had I known any better though, I could have stolen a generic over-the-counter medicine. Silly me, I didn't know. I'd never had a yeast infection before. It wasn't like it was something that was common among teenagers. I guess, unless you're sexually active.

Anyway, as I was walking out of the store, I thought about Jen's suggestion. It was a silly one, but guess what? I stole some yogurt, y'all. Yup!

I went back to that family van too and took the test. It was weighing on my mind too heavy. Plus, that little man on my shoulder said, *"Just do it."*

They told me I could have the results in three days. I was scared as hell, but all I could do was wait.

Chapter 15

The night before I could get my test results back, I was shitting bricks. I couldn't sleep for nothing, and I had no one to ease my troubles, because this test was between me, myself, and I. The more I worried, the more I felt sick. It wasn't any better with yogurt up my vagina either. I did what Jen said and at first I thought it was silly, but it really worked. I had been stealing plain yogurt for the past two days praising Jen's suggestion. I vowed to never eat it again though.

The day had come. I trooped my way back over near the clinic to get my results. The health van was in the same spot I left it when I had taken the test in the first place. I knocked on the door, they let me in, and there I got it.

Don't ask me why I was shocked when the results came back positive. I guess I made myself think that my fear was a joke, and I was going to get good news. The staff on the family van tried to offer additional services, but I declined. I didn't want anything from anyone. I ran out of that van numb all over. I felt like I was marinating in a tub of ice cubes. I was distraught, like how could this be? Why me? I just kept telling myself my life was over.

I roamed the streets for hours before I decided to go back to the hotel and off with my head. Yes, I made the decision to kill myself. I was going to find the sharpest tool in sight and jam it into my neck, right at my jugular vein. It was time to take myself out of my misery.

I walked in my hotel room with my hair all over the place. My clothes were everywhere, not fully covering my body.

A crowd of men stared at me, yelling, "The stripper's here!"

I had no idea what was going on. I looked around for a stripper because I knew I wasn't one.

Then Chuck pulls me in the bathroom. "I need you to strip for my man's bachelor party."

I didn't answer.

"You all right? You look like somebody just died."

"I'm fine," I lied.

"Cool. I need you to strip."

"I don't strip."

"Listen, put this on and go on out there and shake ya tail feather. Do you have makeup or something you can put on? 'Cause you can't go out there looking like that."

"No."

"Oh well, it doesn't matter. Just put this on. They don't care about how you look anyway. They just want to see some ass."

"I'm not doing it," I said, firmly handing him back the skimpy outfit he gave me.

"If I say you're doing it, then that's what it's going to be. Remember, I hooked you up with this room."

He was right, and I had nothing to say.

I was too frightened to speak anyway. I was alone in a room full of guys. Guys I didn't know. They could have ganged up on me and done anything. Quite frankly, that was not a chance I was willing to take. I needed my place of shelter. I had to do what I was told, so I shook my tail feather.

I danced with no joy or excitement in what I was doing. I wasn't taking my clothes off either. I refused.

Until I saw a dollar bill go in the air.

A few more followed, and that was enough.

They may have only been dollars, but I needed them desperately. That was my motivation to pretend to enjoy what I was doing. I started getting into the music. I was shaking it and dropping it like it was hot. I was letting them know I was working with something, ya heard!

I couldn't believe I had actually stripped and got paid for it. I got fifty-three dollars for showing my breast and letting some horny nuccas see my ass. For the rest of that week, Chuck had me doing strip parties.

It wasn't too long after that Chuck had me doing regular after-hour hotel joints. I was showing everything then and getting paid more. Well, not a lot more.

I was making like two hundred each gig, but of course, I didn't see all the money. Chuck kept a big chunk, leaving me with less than half of the money, saying it was his rent for letting me stay in the hotel. I couldn't dispute it. The rooms were like a hundred and something a night.

But if I was smart enough at the time, I would have known that he was playing me and pocketing the money. For the hotel, my ass! He worked there, which meant he got a discount. What a dummy I was.

Anyways, all in two weeks, I got accustomed to making fast money. I was smoking, drinking, and wilding out. Forgetting entirely that I was pregnant. I couldn't forget it too long though. I was definitely starting to show, and my metabolism was getting low.

It got to the point where I wasn't able to get it anymore or shake it fast. Shit, I used to get down with my individual lap dances, flipping over backwards, popping my pussy in their faces. Whoa! Those were the days. Now I was constantly tired, and my body just gave out.

Chuck was kind of getting pissed when I began to slow down in my gigs too. He didn't like how I was showing less of my body. He started making comments about me being lazy and getting fat, saying that was the reason why I couldn't dance the way I used to. I prayed his comments remained comments, and he wouldn't get the bright idea that I was pregnant.

"We're going to the gym today."

"Who?"

"Me and you. We gotta get your strength up and tone that body 'cause I'm losing money with you being lazy and not wanting to show shit. You think you slick, stripping in those shirts that have holes at the nipples. I know you putting on weight, and you don't want to show your stomach, but you gotta get naked, boo."

"I've been working out."

"Baby, picking up a cheeseburger and muscling it to your mouth is not working out. You need to hit the gym. You eat like you're pregnant or something, or like you got a tapeworm."

I had a sour look on my face, hoping he wouldn't ask if I was pregnant, and thank goodness, he didn't. I knew sooner or later though, I was going to have to pull out on this stripping thing before he figured out I was pregnant. I didn't know how I was going to do it, but I had to come up with something and risk the chance of being a real homeless person with no where to lay my head.

I danced for another week without any plans of how I was going to get away from the atmosphere. I knew I could have probably just left out one day and never came back, but I was scared. I don't know why, 'cause dude probably wasn't gonna find me once I bolted, but I don't know. I guess you can say I was being the stupid, scary person I was. I had nowhere to go though.

On top of that, I needed money. So, there, that was a good reason to stay, right?

It didn't matter though, 'cause I got put out anyway. Yeah. Me and dude parted on bad terms.

See, I was doing this party, and I had been dancing for like over an hour. I was dead tired, exhausted, and damn near on the verge of passing out. The perverts I was dancing for didn't want me to stop dancing, and Chuck was granting them their wish.

They had reason to try and get whatever out of me because frankly I was slacking that striptease. I hardly showed anything. I wasn't really dancing.

But they were getting some feels on me. Yeah, I let them touch my titties and squeeze my ass. I let one guy go so far as touch my clit. Then he had me feeling his hard-on. Not so much of a striptease, now that I think about it. I'd say more like a freak fest.

I went from low-budget dancing to cheap feels. I guess that's why they were so into the so-called striptease. I was only letting them feel though, because I thought it would speed up the process of them leaving, but I should have known better. It only made them want more, and Chuck was on some ol' give-them-what-they-want.

I, on the other hand, was ready to just drop dead. I came up with a plan to make that happen too. I put an end to that bootleg striptease quick. I thought of the nastiest thing you could ever imagine and made myself throw up. Ugh, it was disgusting!

You should have seen their faces. They were mad as hell. They wanted all of their money back, but Chuck wasn't having it. He kicked them out and went off on me. He gave me a good cursing out while he chased me into the bathroom, calling me every sleazy name you could think of.

I was scared because I had never seen him that furious. I locked myself in the bathroom afraid of what he was going to do to me. He kept pressuring me to come out, but I wasn't hearing it. I cleaned myself up while he was on the other side of the door yelling.

I had just taken my soiled shirt off when he kicked the door in. For the first time in months, he got a close-up on my stomach.

His eyes bulged out as he got a good look. "No, no. I know you ain't fucking pregnant. Are you fucking pregnant?"

Before I could answer him, he rambled on. "You stripping and fucking, and you having my baby? Wait, is that my baby? No, that ain't my baby. Wait a minute. Are you pregnant?"

I hesitantly answered yes.

He grabbed me by my neck and threw me up against the wall. "Bitch, are you serious?"

I didn't say anything.

"You fucking ho! Get your shit and get the fuck out!"

Without putting up a fight, I gathered what I could in a hurry and hauled ass. Moving so fast, I didn't even grab my little stash. I thought about taking the money I had just made, but I dared not. I got the hell out of dodge while I could and added myself to the midnight homeless bunch on the street.

I walked the streets lifeless until my body and swollen feet said stop. My legs were giving out. I had made it as far as a park bench by Boston Common. And guess what? That was my hotel room for the night. I put my bags behind me, placed my hood on, stringed it tight, laid down, and called it a night. I was hella scared, hoping no one would bother me or try to touch me, but at the same time, I was so tired, it didn't matter. I just needed to rest.

***

I woke up that morning with the sun fully raised and a dirty-looking man staring me in my face. I jumped up and screamed.

He jumped back and screamed too, then walked away like it was nothing.

My heart was racing. I started crying, checking myself out to see if I was in one piece. I was fine. I held my stomach, hyperventilating, thinking the guy was a bastard for what he had done.

I calmed myself down. Then I sat on the bench, looking around cautiously, trying to see if there were any other psychos around me. The coast looked clear. All that was left was for me to figure out was what the heck I was going to do, or what my next move was. Hell, I never knew what my next move was.

I needed guidance. I needed to be rescued. I needed immediate help, but I had nothing. I was all alone, homeless and lost, because no one cared.

I blended in with the homeless well. I had my bags and dirty clothes on. I was pretty much a hot mess. I had on an oversized, striped hooded sweatshirt that hung below my old school windbreaker jacket. My sweat pants were white, baggy, and dirty, dragging the ground as I walked. My once-white sneakers had turned a dingy black from wear and tear. I'd only had them since forever. They were run-down with holes in them, and too small, since my feet were swollen from being pregnant. Huh, I had to wear them as slippers. What do you know? I was "America's Next Hot Mess."

No money, no home, and no one in the world to care. Not even God. That's how I felt. I only had myself to blame though. From all the stripping and fast money I was getting, I should have never left so fast and not grab what I had left of the money I'd made. I was shook though. I didn't want a beat-down from Chuck because, as mad as he looked, he was bound to do something to me. He probably would have blocked me from taking the money anyway.

Damn. Thinking about it makes me mad all over again. I was really on some bummed-out status, with more ignorant situations to come my way.

Chapter 16

I sat on the park bench for hours. I watched people as they walked by in business suits, some thugged-out, others lost just like me. Yeah, I was sitting looking dumbfounded, confused and scared. I thought, and thought, and thought, but came up with no solution. Then it hit me. My right brain kicked in and lent a hand to the left. I remembered the card my uncle had given me and how he'd laid it out that I should contact my father if I wanted to.

There wasn't a better time to make that contact. Of course, you know, I got happy thinking I had just come up with the most brilliant idea. Puh-lease. I couldn't even find the damn card after I had thought of the solution. I searched my bag like there was no tomorrow and had no luck. I searched my pockets and drew dust. I almost cried looking for that thing, but lo and behold, it surfaced. I didn't find the card, but I remembered my daddy's name.

I searched for the nearest pay phone with a White Pages. I found one after passing what felt like a thousand broken-down pay phones. I turned to the *T* section and looked up the last name Taylor. I got to the *J*'s and followed the first name James all the way down. I counted each one, and there were about nineteen of them, if I'm not mistaken.

Like five were James Taylor, and the rest read J. Taylor with different middle initials. I tried to remember the middle initial on the card, but I ran a blank. Frustrated yet determined, I searched for my card again with, of course, no luck. It bugged me out because I knew I had the card somewhere among my stuff. *I remember glancing at it the other day.* Oh well, all I had left to do was call the numbers.

I ripped out the page with the entire listing of James Taylors. I stuffed it in my pocket and walked away like I didn't just sabotage the White Pages. I walked about a block to get away from my misdemeanor, picked up a dirty cup off the ground, and pushed that right hand out to work. Yup, I was on the corner begging for change.

I stood at the bus stop for a while collecting from the people coming off and on. Then, once it slowed down, I moved in front of a Dunkin' Donuts. Within three and a half hours, I had six dollars and fifty-two cents in quarters, dimes, nickels, and pennies. Figuring that should do, I went to a pay phone and pulled out my list of James Taylors.

I chose my first number, dialed it, and then quickly hung up. I had no clue what to say. I had no game plan whatsoever. I had to figure out how the hell I was going to know that I had the right James Taylor. I stood at a dead end trying to figure out the not-so-brilliant-anymore idea. Then it hit me. *He owns a company,* I thought. *Yes, that's how I'll know.* What were the odds of every James Taylor on the list owning a company?

I got through about the first seven of the J. Taylors, only to find out their first names weren't James. The *J* stood for something else. I continued to call and got a few people with accents. I wanted to rule them out, seeing that they were foreigners, but I had to remember that I had never met my father a day in my life. He could have been any nationality, for all I knew.

Therefore, the key thing was to get info about owning a company.

I got down to the last five Taylors and prayed it was one of them. Another time I was counting on the Lord, hoping my prayers got answered.

"Hello!"

"Hi!"

"Hello!"

"Ah, yes, I'm looking for a James Taylor."

"I told you to stop calling. James has been dead almost thirteen years now."

"Oh I'm—"

Click.

I dialed the next person.

"Hello, Taylor residence."

"Ah, hi, is a . . . James Taylor there?"

"He's out of town."

I sat on the phone silent, not knowing what to say next. "Oh, okay," I answered and just hung up.

I called the next number, and there was no answer. The one after that was disconnected.

Then listening to the so-called right mind I had, I called the other number back for the James Taylor who was out of town. I had this gut feeling to just call back and ask more questions. I felt like the call was unfinished. So I used my last fifty cents and dialed the number.

"Hello, Taylor residence."

"Hi, ah . . . does the James Taylor that lives there own a company?" I asked.

The guy laughed. "Is this his daughter?"

I paused for a second. You know I was smiling from ear to ear. I was stunned. "Huh?"

"Is that you? He said you might be calling. Come on over."

"Okay!"

I was ecstatic. I jumped for joy. I had found him. I had found my daddy. I was too happy. I didn't know what to do with myself.

I threw away the list after I memorized the address. There was no need to call the remaining numbers. I had succeeded in my search. I was going home to Papa. Until I thought about how the hell I was going to get there. The skimpy change I had collected was gone. I'd solved one problem, only to be faced with another.

Why was it always like that for me? I never got past having a problem. It made me even more upset too because I kept thinking about the money I did have that I didn't save. And I swear I refused to stand and collect more change. I had to get grimy with it. Hey, a girl had to do what a girl had to do.

I flagged down a cab with no intentions of paying. Yeah, I was dipping on the driver, little did he know. I got in and directed the driver to go toward Mattapan Square. I didn't want to give him an exact address because, for one, I didn't know where I was exactly going. I knew where the street was, but it being so long, I didn't know what end I was going to. There was a Mattapan side, a Hyde Park side, and a Dorchester side. I was going to have to check the numbers on the street to see what direction would be correct. For two, I had to jump out ahead of my destination, 'cause you know I was dipping on him.

The ride was long as ever 'cause there were dumb loads of traffic. By the time we got out of downtown, the sun was down, and a quarter moon was glowing in the sky. With the ride being so long, I lost all enthusiasm of meeting my father. I started thinking, What was he going to say? Was he going to be happy? Was I going to be happy? Then, all in one swoop, as we were approaching Mattapan Square, my spirits got a lift. I was ecstatic again. I almost couldn't control my emotions.

"You getting off in the square?"

"No. I'll tell you when to turn."

"I need to know now. Where am I exactly going?"

The street I was trying to get to was River Street. "Take a right at the light."

He made the turn. "Am I going on River or Cummings?"

"River. Keep straight. The house is on this street."

The number I was looking for was six sixty-three. I looked to see if the numbers were increasing or decreasing. The numbers looked to be increasing, so I was on the right side. My eyes lit up as I spotted the house. Oh, I just knew I was about to be rescued.

I prepped myself for the run by changing the use of my footwear from slippers back to sneakers. I jammed my swollen feet inside my too-small sneakers. I strung them tight and prepared for the aches and pains I was about to experience.

I made the cab driver pull over farther down the street by some brick buildings. He read the price off the meter. I pretended like I was looking for my money, and in the midst of my search, I opened the door, put one foot out, and then asked, "Do you have change for a fifty?"

As soon as he put his head down to look, I hopped out of the car and made a dash for it. The driver got out of the car and started chasing me. That wasn't in the script. I kept running without looking back, repeating the same thing over and over to myself. *Don't let him catch you. Don't let him catch you. You better not let him catch you.*

I felt him gaining on me. Then I felt a tug at my bag, and it ripped. Oh, man, I couldn't let that stop me.

I kept running while stuff was falling out of my bag. The Lord was on my side that night because that man should have caught my pregnant ass. I wasn't running nearly as fast as I could, especially since my sneakers were a half-size too small. I had outrun him though, and I made it to 663 River Street safe and sound.

Before I rang the doorbell, I tried to pull myself together. It wasn't much to do, but I had to straighten up, at least look a little decent. I had to change my sneakers back to slippers because the pain was unbearable. I had to carry my bag in my hand because it was ripped. I had inspected it first to see what fell out, and it turned out to be some underwear, like I could have afforded to lose that.

Anyway, I did what I could to look presentable. I tried to rehearse what to say, but nothing sounded good. I was feeling stupid when I heard myself talk, so I decided to play it by ear. I rang the doorbell quickly then stood stiff as the door opened.

A tall, hefty-looking white man greeted me at the door. I made a face at his appearance like, *Uh-oh, wrong house.* I had to make sure though.

"Hi, I'm looking for James Taylor."

"You must be the daughter. I talked to you on the phone, remember?"

"Ah . . . yeah."

"Well, come on in. Make yourself at home."

I walked in the house and followed the guy down a long hallway that led to the living room.

"By the way, I'm your daddy's friend, Bubba. I noticed you were looking at me like, *'Who the hell is he?'* I'm house-sitting for him." He laughed.

I smiled back, not knowing what to say.

"I would have done the same thing. Don't be embarrassed."

I smiled again then pranced around the living room glancing at everything in sight. I just knew I was home. The house was decent. The living room was carpeted. It had a love seat and a roundabout couch. I thought there would have been some photos, but the walls were bare. I had no idea what my father looked like, which was sad.

"So your dad is away on business, and I'm house-sitting. He'll back some time in the morning. Are you here on break?"

"Break from what?"

"You know, school."

I had no idea what he was talking about, but I went with the flow. "Ah, yeah."

"You hungry?"

"No. No, thanks."

I really was, but I didn't want to seem greedy on my first visit.

"Don't be shy now. I got some hot dogs cooking up, and I got some cheese and chili to top it with."

"Okay." I left the answer open-ended so, when I did decide to get my grub on, I wouldn't seem desperate.

"You can sit down if you like. Take your jacket off and stay awhile. You're in good hands, trust me. Make yourself at home."

I took my jacket off and got comfortable on the couch. Surprisingly, I wasn't even scared in this stranger's presence. I don't know if it had something to do with being pregnant, the fact that I had found my father, or that I just didn't care anymore. It's funny to me though, now that I think about it. I was in the presence of some 280-pound guy that I didn't know, and I wasn't scared. It must have been that I was overwhelmed with the anticipation of meeting my father. Yeah, that's what it was. I just knew I was in good hands.

Bubba showed me to the shower after I dug into that bomb chili cheese dog. That dog was out of this world. The bathroom was set up with a separate tub and shower. That was a new sight for me, and I was loving it. My pregnant, smelly behind couldn't wait to utilize the shower. I took a long, hot one too. I was well overdue for it. I couldn't believe I had gone a day without bathing.

I stayed in that sauna for almost an hour. After that, my eyes grew heavy, and it was bedtime. I was in no mood to talk to anyone except a bed. Bubba showed me to the couch, which let out into a bed. He let me see where he was sleeping at too, which was in the spare room two doors down the hall from the living room. The couch bed with no pillow was cool. It didn't bother me none. As long as I had a place to lay my head, I was good to go.

I woke up the next morning to the smell of scrambled eggs and pancakes. Bubba was up bright and early cooking breakfast for himself. My stomach immediately turned sour.

"You can help yourself to some breakfast. There is pancake mix and sausages. I ate the last egg."

"Thank you, but no thanks."

I got up and went to the bathroom, where I hurled. My morning sickness was a killer, and the smell of eggs didn't make it any better. On top of that, I didn't really have an appetite in the morning.

I came out of the bathroom refreshed, and I overheard another male voice in the kitchen with Bubba. I walked in slowly, not knowing what to expect, but having in mind that it was possibly my father. The unfamiliar face looked at me, and I gave him a strange look.

"Bubba, who's this?" the man asked, pointing to me.

Bubba laughed. "You don't know what your own daughter looks like?"

"My daughter?"

"Yeah, your daughter. The one you told me to be expecting."

"Bubba, are you fuckin' drunk? This ain't my daughter."

"You're not James Taylor?" I asked.

"Yeah, I'm James Taylor."

"You own a company?"

"Yeah, I own a dry cleaner's down on Washington Street? Why?"

"I don't know. If you're James Taylor and you own a company, then you're my father."

He had to be my father, and for the shock of my life, he was a white man. I stood there for a second trying to think clearly. I wanted to know how in the world my father managed to be a tall, skinny redhead.

"Your father? No, not me. Not this James Taylor."

"But my uncle gave me this card that said James Taylor. I can't remember the name of the company but—"

"What's your uncle's name?"

"Frank Jones."

"Frank Jones . . . Frank Jones. No, I don't know a Frank Jones. How'd you get this address?"

"I got it out of the phone book when I looked up your number. When I called, Bubba told me you were expecting me. So I got in a cab and found my way here, which is apparently the wrong place. Sorry."

I walked away and began to gather my things. I refolded my clothes and put them in my ripped bag.

"I take it you never met your father."

"No, I haven't."

"I'm sorry."

"It's okay. It's not the first time I've been abandoned," I whispered.

"What's that?"

"Nothing."

"Here, let me get you another bag. Do you need a ride somewhere?"

"Oh no. No, I'm fine. I was just looking to meet my father for the first time, but I guess not." I didn't know what else to say. I was happy he didn't notice I was pregnant. That may have led to more questions.

He handed me the bag, and I switched my belongings over to it. I folded my last pair of pants, and *voilà*, the card fell out. I picked it up and looked at it.

James Taylor WoodSteel Stock Inc.
4743 Truman Hwy
Hyde Park, MA 02136

"Do you know where you're going? Do you have somewhere to go?" James asked.

I handed him the card.

"Oh, you're looking for Jimmy Steel. I know him. I can take you by his place."

I didn't bother to get my hopes up because I didn't know what to expect. I was already at the wrong house. Who knew? I could have been going to another wrong address.

Chapter 17

Both Jameses greeted each other as they met up in the driveway. The James that was supposed to be my father looked familiar. I couldn't make out where I knew him from, but I knew I had seen him before.

"You know this young lady?" the white James asked.

He looked at me. "No. Am I supposed to?"

"I would hope so. I gotta run though."

Then, just like that, my fifteen-minute white dad was gone. He didn't even give the other James a chance to get more info. I guess it didn't matter though 'cause I was the one who had to do the explaining.

"So how can I help you, young lady?"

"I am looking for my father, James Taylor."

"Me? James Taylor?"

"I guess so."

"Noooooo. You must be mistaken. I had one child, and that was my boy Greg who was killed last year in October."

"Greg Little," I called out in amazement.

"Yeah."

"I know him. I mean, I knew him. He . . . wait, you're—I'm, I'm sorry. I read a poem at his funeral."

"Desire, right?"

"Yes," I responded, surprised he remembered.

You know I was floating inside, right? I couldn't believe he remembered me. All I kept thinking was, *Greg's father. He knows me. Wow!*

On the flip side though, I was still curdled inside, knowing that I was again at a dead end. With no more to say, I stood there silently looking around, dumbfounded.

I had to take a monstrous piss. "Can I use your bathroom please?" I wiggled.

"Oh, sure. Follow me."

I followed him into his house, and he showed me to the bathroom.

I came out of the bathroom refreshed and walked into the living room, where he was waiting on me. I glanced around at pictures galore of Greg. I took it upon myself to view each one individually.

As I glanced around, James walked out of the living room area into the kitchen next door.

"Would you like something to drink?"

"No, thank you."

I continued to surf the portraits. Then I spotted a familiar face. I picked up the framed picture, being careful not to drop it, and examined it closely. *This man looks like Uncle Frank.* I couldn't make out if it was or not, so I just asked.

"Excuse me. Who's the guy in this picture right here?"

He looked over at the photo. "Oh, that's a guy I used to work with."

Duh, I see that. "What's his name?"

"Ah, Frank, I believe."

I stared at the picture.

"Frank Jones."

"Yeah."

"This is my uncle."

"Frank Jones is your uncle? Really? Wow! Small world."

"Actually, my great uncle. He's my mother's uncle."

"Oh, okay."

"You know my mother?"

"Your mother who?"

"Never mind. You wouldn't know her."

"Yeah, I just know Frank from work."

"Oh."

I kept looking at the same pictures over and over. I didn't know what else to do. I knew I was at the wrong house again, but I didn't know how to make the getaway. *Am I supposed to say thank you and ask for help? Do I continue my journey of homelessness?*

"Are you all set?" he asked me as I was steady looking at the pictures like an idiot.

"Oh, yeah. Thanks for letting me use the bathroom."

"Oh, no problem." He showed me to the door.

I waved bye to him as I walked down the stairs. I was about to cry, y'all. I had no idea what to do next. The "daddy idea" was gone with the wind. Neither my right brain nor left brain was functioning at that point.

I heard the house door close behind me, and that was it. At that moment, I lost the feeling in my legs and fell to the ground. I landed on my side, barely hitting my stomach. I grabbed a hold of it though, as if I had fallen directly on it.

That was the first time ever that I'd emotionally attached myself to my pregnancy. I became conscious of how real it was. I felt around on my stomach as if I was calming the baby's nerves.

The house door opened, and James noticed me on the ground. I quickly stopped caressing and pretended to just have a regular non-life-threatening fall.

"Are you okay?"

I leaned forward to get off of my side. Regular fall, my ass! I didn't realize how bad it was until I actually tried to get up. I was breathing heavy to the point where I got dizzy. I had to just sit there for a bit.

James came down beside me. "You all right? Let me help you up."

"No, I'm all right. I just need to catch my breath." I did want help up, but I was so worried about him seeing that I was pregnant, my dumb ass refused.

"Did you hurt yourself?"

"No, I don't think so," I quickly answered. I looked down at my stomach. I was hoping he couldn't tell I was pregnant. I don't know why I was so stuck on him not knowing.

He stood up beside me as I put my head down between my knees, prepping myself to get up. I took a deep breath. Then I felt his hands on me. He assisted me up like I didn't want him to. Once I was on my feet, I wiped the dirt off my freshly scraped hands. While I'm doing that, I heard Mr. Taylor yell out something that sounded like profanity. I looked over at him to see what the fuss was about.

"I know you know, okay. Just cut the shit, Desire. You're my daughter, yes! What do you want from me? Why are you here? What? You need money? Here, let me give you what you want." He rummaged in his pockets.

I watched him like, *What? Wait, what did you say?*

A twenty-dollar bill came sailing my way. The money hit the ground, and I just stood there like it was invisible. Did he just throw money at me? Was I on stage dancing?

"What? Is that not enough?"

I looked down at the twenty, and then it all hit me. This was my father. This was my father, y'all! All this time, Greg and I were blood brother and sister. Tears streamed immediately. I looked back down at the twenty. I was insulted. The first visit with my father, and he made me feel like that. I was better off homeless, right?

I wiped my eyes and began walking away, leaving the twenty on the ground.

"Wait. Desire, I'm sorry."

I stopped walking but didn't turn around.

"I didn't mean that."

I wiped my eyes again from the tears that kept coming.

He came up behind me and reached for my bag. "Come inside, please."

I wanted to smile so bad, you just don't know. As quickly as he had ruined my day, he made the sun shine again. I followed him into the house and sat on the couch.

He sat down beside me holding his head in the palm of his hands. "I knew this day would come. I'm not mad at you. I can only be mad at myself." He lifted his head up and turned to me. "I'm sorry, okay. I'm sorry. I'm just unprepared."

I shook my head up and down as if I understood.

"That boy of mine would have killed for this moment. He never knew you ever existed, but that man upstairs made it happen. He brought y'all together, and neither one of you knew."

I had a flashback of Greg as I focused on one of his pictures. Tears fell. "I wish I knew he was my brother . . . not like he treated me as if I wasn't anyway."

"I know. He was that kind of person."

"Yeah, he used to stick up for me all the time. That's how I met him. My first day at school, these kids were teasing me, and he came to my rescue."

"That was my boy. He was always there to help somebody."

"Yeah, he was always there for me." I touched my face. "This scar could have been a lot worse if Greg didn't again come to my rescue."

"Yeah, he was a true saint. Every time he mentioned you, I couldn't bring myself to tell him the truth. My son was never really a worrier, but when it came to you, he was always worried. But even with his worries about you, I still couldn't bring myself to tell him the truth."

I sat silent without a word to say. I was stumped and hurt. I couldn't believe he knew about me all that time and said nothing. I was shocked he didn't at least try to swear Greg to secrecy or something.

"If you didn't want anything to do with me, then why didn't you at least tell Greg?"

"It wasn't that I didn't want anything to do with you. I just . . . I didn't want him to know because I knew he would press me about it. He would have tried to bring you here, and I wasn't ready for all that yet."

So what does that mean now? It was official. I was an outcast to both my parents. Neither one of them wanted me. I picked up my bag to leave, feeling like I was going to be a burden to my father too.

"Well, I won't waste your time. At least now I know neither of my parents wanted me."

"Wait. What do you mean? Where's your mother?"

"I don't know. I haven't seen her in like two years."

"Two years? Wait. You're the one whose mother left her after her fifth-grade graduation?"

I took a deep breath and looked up at the ceiling. "Yup, that's me."

"I can't believe that was you Greg was talking about. So you live with Frank?"

"I did but" I stopped talking. Tears rolled from my eyes. "I'm sorry," I cried.

He took a deep breath, leaned me into his shoulder, and embraced me.

I let it all out then. I had the hiccup-cry going on. It was like everything sour about my life hit me at one time. I thought about being pregnant, running away, missing school, taking my aunt's money, Malik giving me HIV, Greg not being around forever. Everything.

"Everything's going to be all right!"

"Yeah, I wish. Nothing's ever all right for me."

"Don't say that."

"It's the truth. I don't have a place to live, I don't have any money, and I'm pregnant."

"You're pregnant?"

"Yes," I answered, ashamed. "I didn't mean to get pregnant though. I was"—I started boohooing.

"Okay, okay, we can get through this. Don't cry. How many months are you?"

"Four, five months, I don't know."

"You don't know?"

"No, I mean yes . . . well not really."

"Desire, why? What are you doing? What's going on?"

"I don't know."

"What's Frank's phone number?" He picked up the phone.

"No, don't call them, please."

"Desire, you have to go back home."

"No, I can't. My aunt, she won't let me back since I ran away."

"You ran away?"

"Yes, I told you I'm pregnant."

"But what does that have to do with you running away?"

"Because my aunt told me don't ever step foot in her house pregnant."

"I'm pretty sure they are worried sick about you."

"Believe me, they're not. I called them already."

"What's the number?"

"They don't know I'm pregnant."

"I kind of figured that."

He paced the floor like he had just heard the worst news of his life. He picked up Greg's picture and stared at it.

"Give me the number, Desire. I promise I won't mention that you're pregnant, okay. I just need to let them know you're with me. You may think they don't care about where you are, but they do."

He thought he knew, y'all, but he didn't know the half. Since he was promising not to mention my pregnancy, I went ahead and decided to trust him. After all, he was my father, and he did seem to be genuine.

He dialed and got through. I was sure it was about to be "bad-mouthing Desire time." I knew they weren't going to have anything good to say about me.

While he talked, I settled in. I had calmed my nerves a bit but not too much because I knew the phone conversation was going to throw salt in my game.

After my father got off the phone after a long conversation with Uncle Frank and Auntie Linda, he laid the law down. He told me every detail about my behavior. He mentioned everything from punishment, to whuppin's, to stealing my aunt's money. And he was not a happy camper. I was the bad person from that point on.

He didn't even know my full side of the story. He didn't bother to ask, and I didn't bother to tell either. I figured it was a battle I'd never win. I had to remember, he was the parent and I was the child. Come on now y'all. He didn't know why I did the things I did. I had good reason for most of it. For the other half, I was still trying to figure out why. Shit, some things were for attention, others were "just because."

"When is the last time you've been to school?"

"I don't know."

"Listen to me and listen to me good. Don't think you're going to get over here and do what you want 'cause I can't deal with that buckwild stuff. I am going to get you a tutor so you can catch up with your school-work. You're not allowed to go anywhere without my permission. You cannot have friends over without my permission. All I ask is that you be respectful and re-sponsible. I don't know what you call yourself doing at Frank's house, but you won't get away with it here. The decision is yours. You can reside in my home and fol-low these simple rules, or go back to what you may feel was a hellhole and snake it out."

James was serious, and since I had a little bit of sense, I decided to stay with him. A part of me wanted to leave, but I had nowhere to go. I definitely wasn't going back to the dungeon house or the streets. I was staying where I was. I had to follow rules some way or another.

He didn't have to take me in. Then again, yeah, he did. I was his only daughter. The one he didn't care to father in the early years or even mention to his son, my deceased best friend. It was only right he took me in.

Chapter 18

I got home tutoring for the remainder of the school year. I progressed well too. I made it to the ninth grade, thank God. It was looking like summer school, but I got the job done. So for the summer, I was school-free. I was indoors all day every day. My father didn't want me to go anywhere as my due date was slowly but surely approaching.

Jen and I kept in touch. He allowed her to visit here and there. I didn't speak to my aunt or uncle. It was like they never existed. Oh well. At that time, that's what it needed to be, I guess. I was a little disappointed that my uncle didn't call and check up on me.

Now that I think about it, it was probably a good idea that he didn't. He would have asked what I had been up to. Then what was I going to say? Oh nothing, just sitting around waiting to have my baby. Yeah, right. He didn't know I was pregnant, and he wasn't going to know.

Staying with my dad was like hideout season for me. No school, a tutor, no friends except Jen. No family except him. I'm grateful he took me in and all, but that's all it was. He provided me with food, shelter, and an education. We hardly talked. Shoot, we barely uttered a word to each other, unless necessary. So much for building a relationship with him.

By my eighth month in July, he got rid of me. He shipped me down South in the care of other family, his sister to be exact. He wanted her to deliver the baby at what he claimed was the best hospital in South Carolina. I couldn't complain or say no.

The day before I left for Greenville, South Carolina, I snuck out and decided to pay my baby's daddy, Malik, a visit. I hadn't heard, spoke to or even mentioned him since the day I had gone to confess my pregnancy to him. I'd heard through the grapevine that he had been accepted to Alabama State down in Montgomery, Alabama. He was due to leave for school in the next month or so, and I wanted to catch him before he left.

I should have probably not even bothered though. The thought of visiting him should have remained just that, a thought. My girl Jen tagged along with me over to his house.

"Well, if it isn't Prego and Flo-Jo!"

"Well, if it isn't the already deadbeat baby daddy," Jen responded.

"I don't recall having any kids," he said.

Jen pointed to my stomach to remind him.

"Man, I don't have time for this bullshit."

"You created the problem," I said.

"You let me."

"Actually, she's too young to let you. You took advantage of her. There is something called statutory rape."

"Bitch, please!"

"Who you calling a bitch? You disease-infested muthafucka! I ain't Desire. I don't bite my tongue for nobody. I'll—"

I put my hand over Jen's mouth. "I just want to know if you're going to have something to do with the baby."

"No."

Jen blurted removing my hand from covering her mouth. "What the fuck you mean, no?"

"Just what I said, bitch!" He violated in Jen's face.

I balled up my fist and muscled up the nerve to hit Malik with a powerful blow to his left eye. He swung his fist to hit me back, but Jen stepped in the way. He jabbed her in the shoulder as she threw a kick to his stomach. He caught her leg and held it, and she struggled to get loose. I tried to shake him off without getting hit in my stomach.

Then, out of nowhere, my father appeared and sent Malik flying to the ground.

"Damn, Uncle Jim! I didn't mean to hit her."

"I ain't your uncle, you little punk. And, you, what are you doing here? You didn't have permission to leave the house, and I follow you and find you here chasing behind a boy, this boy at that."

The attention was all on me now. I just looked at my father speechless 'cause I knew I was in trouble. He had asked the right question too. What the hell was I doing at Malik's house? I had unfinished business, but of course, he didn't know that. How would he know? We never discussed who I was pregnant by. He'd never asked, and I had never volunteered the information. He was about to know now though, with the help of Jen, since I couldn't find the words to tell the story myself.

"Malik's her baby daddy," Jen blurted.

My father gave me this odd look and then extended his focus to Malik, who put his head down.

"Plain and simple, do you plan on being in this baby's life?"

"I don't know if it's mine."

"What?" Jen blurted.

"You were the only nasty dog she was sleeping with." Malik lashed out at Jen. "Shut up!"

My father moved closer to Malik, snatched him up by his shirt, and got all up in his grill.

"I'm sure you can't give a damn about this baby right now and that's all right because that's how you operate. One thing I won't allow is you lying to my face. I've known you for too long, and there is no doubt in my mind that you are the father of this child. Therefore, I expect you to do the right thing whether you want to or not. There is no choice to be made because I made the decision for you. You will be notified as well as your mother when the baby is born. Got it?"

"Yeah, man, I got it."

My father released him, and we went on our merry way. I walked away with no looking back at Malik. Me, Jen, and my dad got in his car and drove off. I felt a bit relieved that my father took a stand for me. The moment kind of reminded me of the first time I'd met Greg.

"So, Desire, I hope you don't think that just because I stuck up for you back there, you're let off the hook. You just earned yourself a school year in South Carolina. Boston is not for you. You have too much drama here."

I didn't say anything. I was stuck on why I let myself get involved with the son of a bitch Malik anyway, despite Greg's advice. I was told to stay away, but my hardheaded ass didn't listen.

"This is the bed you made, and guess what? You're lying in it alone."

Chapter 19

It was South Carolina here I come. I rode on that Amtrak train for hours and can surely say never again. I had butt sores from sitting so long. Luckily, I didn't go into labor from being stressed out during the ride.

For the long, boring ride it was, it gave me time to think. At a young age, it's sad to say, but I had tons of shit to think about. I was still juggling with the pain of being abandoned and wondering why my mother never bothered to check up on me. It hurt not knowing why. Shit, it hurt not knowing why to a lot of things in my life. Why was I pregnant at thirteen? Why did I act out for attention? Why did I yearn for love outside of where it was being given?

I sailed through that train ride in deep thought, on the verge of tears, but I was strong enough to hold them back. As I thought about my life though, I could think of nothing good. The only moment worthwhile at the time was finding my father.

When I arrived at the train station, my father's brother Jarret, aka Juggie, greeted me on the platform. He was a character. As soon as I stepped off the train, this guy with silver fronts came running toward me smiling, a tilted yellow Kangol on his head. Of course, I had no idea this was going to be my uncle. But I caught on after he grabbed a hold of me, hugging me. He hugged me so tight, I felt like I was being flattened.

"I'm yo' Uncle Jarret, but call me Juggie, Uncle Juggie."

"Okay," I whispered, suffering from the pressure of his hug.

He let go when he heard me speak. I guess he figured out that I was two seconds away from being breathless.

"I'm sorry, kid. I'm 'bout to kill yah befo' yah meet yah kin folk."

I laughed at his comment, while pointing to my bags. He grabbed all three of them, and we made our way to his pickup truck.

His ride was a character too. He was styling in a gray, pint-sized Ford Ranger with silver spinning rims. Not bad for an older man. I got the hint that silver was his color, and that he clearly wasn't a broke uncle.

"You like my ride?"

"It's nice."

"Nice?" he screeched, jerking his head back. "Girl, you see dem silva twennies?"

I laughed.

"Ya betta ask somebody," he joked.

He helped me in the truck, and we made our way down the road. We had little conversation while listening to the radio play the latest hits. It took about twenty minutes or so to get to my Aunt Millie's house, which was where I was gonna stay.

Boy, was she the aunt from Comedy Central. That lady was hilarious. She was a trip with her alcoholic behind. She greeted me with open arms, sipping her Hennessy the entire time. She was a functioning alcoholic, I tell you. And she was supposed to be delivering my baby?

I had my first visit with a midwife at one of the local clinics, and all went well. She was the last doctor I had to see before my due date. She was also the backup deliverer to my Aunt Millie 'cause if my aunt was drunk, she was delivering no baby of mine. I made sure of that.

I had enough to worry about anyway, especially since that HIV thing was worrying the hell out of me.

I had blocked it out of my mind, but my visit to the midwife rekindled the issue. She was pressing me to take a test, but I kept declining. I told her I had already taken one, the results were negative, and there was no need for another. Besides, it was optional anyway. She was pissing me off 'cause she was nagging me about it. I didn't want it. What about that didn't she get? I told the bitch point-blank to back off, and she left it alone. But she sure resurrected some old wounds.

I thought heavily about having HIV and passing it to my child. I thought about Greg dying, and my mother being gone. And I was missing Uncle Frank. My mind was just cluttered. I could hardly sleep at night. I was so bothered that every night, at the same time, I got up and paced the floor. It got so bad that my cousins started calling me the pregnant zombie.

The stress and the late nights lasted for about a week and a half. Then my baby boy was kicking to come out. This was when I experienced the live definition of *contractions*. Oh, that pain was excruciating. Talk about a new form of cramps. I was in so much pain, I couldn't even cry.

My aunt was too drunk to deliver the baby, so the midwife had to step in. Good thing, 'cause my aunt ended up passing out. She missed my entire delivery of a seven-pound chocolate drop baby boy.

I was scared half to death when I first saw my son. I almost told the nurse I didn't want to hold him, but I held him anyway. As she placed him in my arms, I got this cold chill that ran up my spine. It was real. It had happened. I had given birth to a baby boy.

He was the spittin' image of his father, who I grew to hate with a passion. I started thinking heavy about

how naïve I was when it came to Malik. Then it hit me,
the HIV thing. I looked at my newborn son and a chill
ran through my spine again. He looked so innocent
with his green eyes, but he wasn't. He was infected
with something deadly, and his father was to blame.
That low-down, dirty bastard. He had me wanting to
toss my newborn. I had a bad feeling my baby boy was
going to follow in his daddy's footsteps, and it scared
me. The chances of it happening were so high. Every
time I looked at him, fear settled. I just kept thinking,
*My baby boy is doomed. He's done for life. He's his
father's child.*

As I stared into his eyes, tears began to surface. The
nurse must have been watching me because she immediately interrupted my teary-eyed moment.

"Aw, it's all right, sugar. Lemme get 'im cleaned fo'
ya. Whatcha gon' name 'im?"

"I don't know. I'll have a name when you bring him
back."

"A'ight now, you gon' an' make a good pick, an' I'ma
bring 'im right back."

The nurse brought him back within the next twenty
minutes. I still hadn't figured out a name yet, but that
was far from my mind. She handed him back to me,
and my ill feelings toward him resurfaced. I couldn't
shake the fear for anything. It was as if bad news was
sitting at the base of my spine and slowly rising to the
top. Then, once it reached its peak, it burst into flames,
leaving me scared to want my baby.

I started to think about not being able to care for my
boy, especially with his disease. How would I explain
to him that he had something deadly? I couldn't do it. I
wouldn't do it. I held him in my arms and stared at him
for a long time. I cried when I thought about what I had
made up my mind to do. I kissed him repeatedly and

told the nurse to take him, while I got myself cleaned up.

My aunt and the rest of the family had gone for the night, leaving me with congratulation cards full of money. I received over two hundred dollars for having a baby I didn't want and had no intentions of keeping.

Around 3:00 A.M., the morning after I had my baby, I got my things, took my money out of each card, and snuck out of the hospital. I wanted nothing to do with my newborn son or my newfound family. They were good to me, which was great, but Boston was my home. That's where I belonged.

Once I left the hospital, I erased from my mind that I had just given birth to a baby boy. I got me a bus ticket, and I was on my way back home. I paid a homeless man twenty dollars to buy me a ticket, since I was too young to purchase it on my own.

I was excited about going back to my hellhole, the place I had run away from in the beginning, but things were different now. Time had passed. I wasn't pregnant anymore and had no evidence to show that I ever was. I was good to go. I was ready to renew my relationship with my aunt and uncle. I wanted to see if I could make things right somehow. She was mean, but maybe she'd changed. I was hoping this would be my chance for a new beginning.

I boarded the Greyhound and began my journey back home. It was an okay ride, until the bus got all the way to New York City and broke down. I was four hours away from home and look what had to happen. I was ready to get off that damn bus. I had taken enough abuse, shacked up with drunks, homeless people, and fake Hollywood stars.

The bus had been broken down for about three hours, and that was it. I couldn't sit still anymore. I decided to give it a thumb up and hitch a ride home. Yes, y'all, I did it. I hitchhiked like a fool.

I walked up alongside the road with my thumbs out. Within a few minutes, a black two-door Lexus with tinted windows pulled over. I ran alongside the car.

The driver rolled down the windows. "What you treatin'?"

"What?" I asked, confused, bending over with my head in the window.

"You got some money?"

"How much you talking?"

"'Pends on where you going?"

"Boston."

"I'm headed that way too. We can work something out."

I got in the car anxious about the fact that I had a ride home. I was too ready to get there.

"How old are you?"

"Nineteen."

"Cool. Long as you ain't under eighteen."

"Oh, never that!"

"A'ight, shawty. So what's in Beantown?"

"Oh, I'm going back home."

"Where you coming from?"

"South Carolina."

"Oh word? Who you was seeing?"

"Just fam, you know."

"A'ight, a'ight."

"Yeah, I was on that broke down bus back there. I couldn't wait any longer for it to get fixed though."

"I hear dat."

"I'm surprised they didn't send another bus."

"Yeah, I don't know, but I wasn't waiting."

"I don't blame you."

We were silent for about a half an hour, and I fell asleep. Then, well into my nap, I heard these police sirens. I woke up and looked out the back window. Yup, it was the damn police right behind us.

"Are they chasing us?" I inquired.

"Yeah, I think so."

"They want you to pull over? Why they want you to pull over?"

"Chill out. I got this."

He sped the car up zooming through traffic, and I held on for dear life. Homeboy was not trying to pull over, and I just knew we were going to crash.

I went into prayer mode yet again. I was like, *Please, Lord, please don't let us crash.* I vowed to never hitch-hike again if He just let me get out in one piece.

My prayers were answered 'cause homeboy pulled over almost instantly. You don't know how much of a relief I felt.

I grabbed my chest and took a deep breath as the sirens continued to sound. I turned around to look out the back window and saw two officers standing outside their cruiser with their weapons drawn, yelling for us to get out of the car with our hands up.

"Here, put this in your bra." Homeboy handed me two clear bags of white stuff.

I looked at him confused.

"Here, take it before they start shooting. And hurry up."

I looked behind us again. I did not want to get shot, nor did I want to go to jail. Shoot, I didn't want to take the white stuff either. I panicked and wanted to forget all about taking what homeboy was trying to give me.

"You don't want to go to jail, right?"

What kind of question was that? Who ever wants to go to jail? Ugh, I had to do it. I snatched the bags from him and quickly stashed them in my bra.

"They won't check you, but if you wanna get home, it gotta go down like this. Say you're my girl if they ask, but don't volunteer any other information. Let them ask the questions. And if they ask you who I am, my name is Mike. Come on, let's get out."

I thought, *Okay, that shouldn't be so hard,* but at the same time, I was like, *Aw, man. What the hell did I get myself into?*

"Step out of the car with your hands up now!"

We both stepped out of the car, hands up and all.

"Is there a problem, officer?" Mike asked.

"Keep your mouth closed, and keep your hands where I can see them."

We were instructed to get on our knees. Holding us at gunpoint, one officer stood and watched us while the other searched the car. I was shitting bricks, y'all. I didn't know what to expect.

"Whose car is this?"

"It's my car, officer," Mike answered.

"Let me see your license."

Mike reached in his back pocket and pulled out his wallet.

"And an ID from you, miss."

"I don't have one," I answered.

"Why not?"

"I lost it," I lied.

"Stand up, young lady."

After I stood up, the officer walked me over to the cruiser, reaching for his handcuffs in the process. My legs trembled, and all I kept thinking was, *My black ass should have waited on that bus.*

"What's your name?"

I wanted to give the wrong name, but I remembered the last time I got caught up. "Desire."

"Desire what?"

"Jones."

"Desire Jones, what's your relationship to that man over there?"

"He's my boyfriend."

"Is he really?"

"Yes."

"You wouldn't be lying to me, right, Miss Jones?"

"No, sir," I answered, frightened.

"Wait right here."

The officer walked over toward Mike and the other officer. He stood with them, talked for a while, then made his way back over to me.

"What's your boyfriend's name, Miss Jones?"

"Mike."

"Mike what?"

Cat had my tongue then. That was it. I was screwed.

"Miss Jones, do I look stupid to you?"

"No, sir."

"Are you holding anything?"

"No."

"Are you sure?"

"Yes."

"I'm going to ask you one more time. Are you holding anything?"

"I swear I don't have anything," I replied, nearly in tears, scared as hell.

He opened up the back door of the cruiser. "Here, sit tight for a second."

Another cruiser pulled up with two more officers, one male and one female. The officers got out of the vehicle.

"Hey, Paula, I need you to search this young lady right here for me. I think she's holding. Mr. Baker tipped us off. She said she doesn't have anything though."

Of course, two seconds later, it was confirmed that I did. Officer Paula checked my bra and found the mini bags of cocaine. Yeah, you heard right, cocaine. She patted the rest of my body down but found nothing.

The handcuffs followed.

Oh, I boohooed. I boohooed. I boohooed.

"No, no those bags weren't mine. He gave them to me. I don't even know the man. He told me to hold them. I swear."

"Just like you swore you didn't have anything on you."

"No, I was lying then. I was scared, but I'm not lying now. I promise you that."

"We're going to the station. Watch your head."

Over my dead body. I wasn't getting back in that cruiser. I started acting a fool.

"Miss Jones, stop resisting and calm down!"

"No, I'm not going to jail. I told you he told me to hold that for him. I don't know that guy."

"You heard the word *jail*, and now you're scared. You should have thought about that before you decided to transport drugs and get Mr. Baker in trouble."

"Those drugs are not mine. I'm not lying," I cried.

The lady continued to restrain me. I wanted to make a run for it, but where was I running to on the side of the highway?

I looked over at homeboy. That bastard had set me up. He was leaning against his car with a smirk on his face when I looked over at him.

"Where's your proof of identification, Miss Jones?"

"I'm only thirteen years old. I don't have an ID. I was on the broken-down Greyhound. I got my ticket in my pocket."

The lady officer searched my pockets and found my bus ticket receipt. It had my name on it, and it indicated that it was purchased for a child.

"So, Miss Jones, you were telling part of the truth. But help me understand how you got in the car with this young man and not on the bus you're supposed to be on, 'cause this ticket says Boston."

"I was in a rush to get home. I didn't want to wait anymore for the bus to get fixed. So I hitched for a ride, and he was nice enough to stop."

"You know hitchhiking is illegal."

"Yeah, I guess," I answered, unsure.

"You should have known better. Hitchhiking is dangerous, especially for a young girl like you."

I was silent waiting for the rest of the lecture 'cause I knew it was coming.

"That man is a well-known drug dealer from Providence, Rhode Island. He exploits young girls too, and you were about to be his next victim. You know he had no plans of taking you to Boston, right? Had he not been speeding, you may not have been so lucky. It is very dangerous to hitchhike—Drill that in your head. I'm pretty sure you have family back at home expecting you, right?"

"Yes."

"Imagine how they would feel if you didn't show up."

I imagined and thought, *They wouldn't feel shit 'cause they didn't know I was coming.*

"Think about it. You almost got in some serious trouble for making a bad decision."

She was right on the money with that one. I definitely needed to be making better decisions. I was on the verge of tears from the lecture. My mind surely shifted to staying on the bus. That bastard boy tried to set me up. Could anyone ever be on my side?

The police arrested the driver, Jeremiah Baker. He had several warrants, and he was wanted in another state. They didn't pull him over knowing this though.

They'd pulled him over because he was speeding. Then when they ran his license plate, it was a different story.

As far as with me, I give the Lord all my praises. He bailed me out on this one. The lady officer felt sorry for me and decided to just put me on another bus home. There was no song and dance about contacting my parents or anything of the sort. She told me it was a lesson to be learned and she was giving me my one and only get-out-of-jail-free card. Somebody was finally on my side. Yes!

I got dropped off at the nearest bus station. The officers watched me get on the bus and didn't leave until they saw the bus pull off. I waved to them, appreciating the fact that I was not going to jail and they weren't going to call home. I was saved by the bell, and hell yeah, I was very thankful.

When the bus arrived in South Station I smiled, happy to be back in Boston. I felt like a new person. Shoot, I felt like I had just gotten out of prison. This was going to be a new start for me, and this time, it was going to be for the better. I had no setbacks, no baby, no worries, no nothing. All bad memories and drama suppressed. I wasn't dealing with it. I was pushing it back, way to the back of mind.

I arrived at my old domain in no time. The moment I stepped onto the porch, I got jitters walking to the door. I started thinking about the length of time it had been since I had seen or even talked to my aunt and uncle. It was well over six months. Woo! Time flew by.

The cold feet definitely began to settle in, but I pushed it aside and motioned to ring the bell. I laid my finger on the buzzer and waited patiently.

The door opened, and my heart dropped. I was speechless. My happiness had escaped and hurt filled the space. In one swoop, her appearance killed every high spirit I had conjured up. My mind went into a time warp, and I was back to square one. The feeling of being released from prison changed to knocking on prison's door.

Chapter 20

I stumbled in the house stunned to see the lady in front of me. The lady that threw me out as if I was a chunk of spoiled milk in her fridge. She pulled me forward for a hug, and I stood unreceptive while she embraced me. I nearly melted from disgust, like a vampire chewing garlic. I'm surprised I had let her touch me. I'm getting the chills thinking about it. It was as if the devil had embraced me.

How could she? How could she have thought everything was okay between us? She was showing me love, y'all. Why? Why was it okay on her time? I hated her. She'd lied to me. She'd never come back for me. She'd abandoned me.

I walked in the living room unenthused and emotionally shut down. It was no longer a delight to see my uncle, since he didn't notice me walk in the room anyway. My aunt looked up at me surprised like she saw a ghost. That's when he saw me.

He wheeled around to face me. "Desire, oh . . . oh God, Desire! Come here. Come hug my neck. Oh my goodness, girl."

I hugged my uncle without any emotion until his high spirits took over and uplifted mine. Then I had no other choice but to hug him as if there was no tomorrow. I had missed him dearly.

"Your father let you come visit us?"

"Ah, yeah."

My mother walked over and put her hand on my shoulder. I nudged her off by giving my uncle another hug.

"When did you get up here?" Uncle Frank inquired.

"Huh?"

"When did you get up here? You were down South, right?"

"Oh . . . yeah, I got in about an hour ago," I answered confused that he knew I was down South.

"Who told you I went down South?"

"Your mother told us."

I gave her a dirty look and wondered how she knew what was going on in my life.

"When do you go back?" Uncle Frank asked.

"I'm not going back."

"So where's the baby?" my mother asked.

"Yeah, where's the baby?" Uncle Frank followed up.

My mind paused, and my body screamed. I was lost for the moment. My entire plan was shattered. When did they find out? I had to think quickly now. I didn't know they knew I had a baby. My father wasn't supposed to tell.

"Ah . . . he's at my father's house."

"What's his name? How much did he weigh? When was he born?"

I was unable to answer any questions because of how quickly they were coming at me.

"Sorry for all the questions but give us some kind of info," my uncle commented, excited.

"Yeah, sit down and tell us how it was down there. You finished school, right?"

I sat down next to my aunt, who was mute since I'd walked through the door.

"Yeah, I'm going to be a freshman this year," I answered.

My aunt got up, sucking her teeth. I knew she still hated me, and the feeling was mutual. I wasn't there for her though. I was there for Uncle Frank, but some part of me hoped that she had missed me a little.

"My girl has grown up so fast," my mother exclaimed.

I wanted to say, "Shut up, bitch!" but I was trying to show that I was a different person, you know, a bit more mature.

"Your mother just told us last month that you were pregnant. I must admit, I was a bit disappointed, but I had to get over it. I was especially upset your father told your mother but not me, but I guess he figured your mother was the best person. I'm happy to see you alive and well though. I've missed you. Your father took very good care of you, I see."

I didn't know what to say. I do know I was mad that my big-mouth mother had the nerve to tell my business. How dare she? Where did she even come from? She'd been communicating with my father. What the hell? Then my father had said he wouldn't tell. He lied. It baffled me though. When did he speak to my mother? Because he never told me. He got a hold of her, and I couldn't. She knew about my situation and didn't reach out to me. Wow! She was really here in my face with knowledge of what I was going through and never tried to reach me. Something was wrong with this picture.

Anyway, it was a bad idea to go back to the place I called home. I had left my baby for nothing. If I knew my uncle was aware of my pregnancy, I would have brought the baby with me. Hell, I would have gone back home way back when. Damn, my life was a mess.

"So when do we get to see the baby?"

"Maybe I'll bring him by later."

"So your father is babysitting already?" Uncle Frank asked.

"Ah yeah. He said I needed a break."

The telephone rang. I was about to get up and answer it, until I realized no one would be calling for me.

"So is your father letting you stay here, or are you going back to South Carolina?"

"I want to come back home, here."

Silence fell through the room. My hope for a happy welcome was answered in a nutshell. They didn't want me back. I don't know why they bothered to make me think they did. The silence didn't last long though. Auntie Linda made sure of that.

"Desire, where is your baby?"

Her intimidating voice made me stutter even more. "At, um, my father's."

"You lying little heiffa. Your father just called and said you left the baby at the hospital and they're looking for you."

All eyes were on me.

"Desire, don't start this again please," Uncle Frank cried.

Tears welled in my eyes. "I don't want him, okay. I don't want him. I'm too young to have a baby. I don't know what to do with a baby. So I left the hospital, left him there and came back home. I wanna come back home."

"You left your baby? How can you leave your baby?" my mother pleaded.

"Bitch, you left me here and never came back. I never got that so-called big surprise. You just up and left me, so don't you dare fix your lips to tell me shit about leaving my baby."

"Don't talk to me like that, young lady! I may not have raised you from eleven on, but I did put in some work. And I'm still your mother, so don't you dare dis-respect me!"

"You ain't shit to me, Christine. You walk up in here like you never left me, trying to be all friendly. You left me! You left me! You left me! Remember that. 'I'll be back, baby. I'm going to get your surprise ready.' Where's the fucking surprise? Did you just finish put-ting it together?"

She charged at me, but my aunt blocked her path.

"Not in my house! Both of you, stop it. Just stop it!"

"Desire, the surprise I had for you fell through, and then I had to rush to this meeting. I got a job offer. I gladly accepted, and I had to leave town. It was always my dream to be a writer for a magazine, you know. The opportunity arose, so I didn't let it pass me by."

"Am I supposed to feel sorry because you fucked your child over for a dream? Huh? You had your priori-ties straight."

"It was only temporary, and I was coming back for you."

"Yeah? Well, when? And when were you ever going to let me in on the secret?"

She didn't respond. The heiffa couldn't say anything then. She just stared at me.

"I didn't think so. You're full of shit!"

Uncle Frank said, "Desire, cut it with the profanity. You may have had a baby, but you are not grown."

"I'm outta here," I announced.

"Desire, wait. I'm sorry, okay. Is that what you want to hear? I'm sorry. I didn't want the responsibility of taking care of you anymore. Okay, there, I said it. I just didn't want to deal with a kid anymore, and the guy I was dating didn't want kids. He was the one that got me the job of my dreams. I did what I did, but I'm here. If you want me to, I will take care of your baby for you, so you don't have to. It's the least I can do."

"You think taking care of my baby is going to make up for you throwing me away like a piece of trash? All I had was you. No, no! You stay the hell away from me and my baby. He doesn't need anyone like you. What you going to do? Pawn him off when he turns eleven like you did me?"

"Desire, I'm trying to make things right, and you're acting inconsiderate."

"Me inconsiderate? Hmm, let me see—What would be an appropriate name for you? Oh, how about *deadbeat*? Yeah, that fits."

"Why are you acting crazy?"

"I *am* crazy. I'm a terror that you created. If you didn't desert me, then I wouldn't be like this. I hate you!"

I ran out of the living room and out the front door. Who the hell did Christine think she was? She wasn't getting her hands on my baby. No way, no how! I was putting him up for adoption with zero contact from anyone in the family.

Chapter 21

My father and his side of the family were furious with me. They cursed me out for an entire week, and they still couldn't change my mind about not wanting to keep my baby. I was content with my decision. I did not want him. I couldn't do anything for him. I wouldn't do anything for him. He was another male born in this world to bring me down, and I couldn't and wouldn't let that happen.

He looked so much like his no-good daddy. That's what really set me off to give him up. Looking like his father led me to believe that he was going to be just like him. Plus, he had the shit that I had, and I definitely couldn't deal with a sick baby.

All in all, my Aunt Millie made plans to care for him until someone wanted to adopt. It bothered me though that none of my father's family wanted to raise him, as bad as they told me off. They should have agreed to more than a measly temporary custody. My mom, on the other hand, wanted him, but she knew that was not an option for her to pursue. If I wasn't keeping him, then she wasn't going to get the privilege.

It hurt though, not that I wasn't keeping my baby, but that my father decided to disown me. He said I was resistant to him shaping and molding me, and he was done trying. He gave up on me just like that. I wondered how he could give up on his only child left in this world. He told me to never ever call him again, even if my life depended on it. How coldhearted! I couldn't understand how he could give up on me so easily.

He didn't get a chance to know me, the real Desire. The one that had emotional problems, that was confused and lost, and yearning for love. It wasn't fair. I needed my father. Hell, I needed someone, and I had someone. My Uncle Frank.

Uncle Frank welcomed me back home with open arms. Auntie Linda wasn't on the same page, but it didn't matter what she wanted. Uncle Frank, out of nowhere, took a firm stand and said his home was where I needed to be. Not my mom's home, wherever that was, not with my dad, and not down South. He wanted me with him.

For the few weeks left of the summer, I was cool, calm and collected, enjoying the remainder of the hot days.

I heard no more about my son and didn't attempt to make an effort to find out about him either. To my knowledge he was still with my Aunt Millie. It was sad because I didn't even know what they had named him.

I actually spent a lot of time with my uncle, and he was happy to have his old Desire back. I put more hours into writing. I made sure I kept journals of my days, nights and feelings on any and everything. The writing kept me sane.

On top of that, I was allowed to hang out with Jen on certain days of the week, but that all changed when school started.

My first day back to school starting the ninth grade was a reminder of my first day of school in seventh grade, except this time, Jen was not my enemy. She was the replacement filler for Greg.

Drama settled in as soon as I stepped foot into the school. I thought I was in rumor city. People were bold enough to approach me with their crazy questions. I was walking to my first period class when the first nosy heiffa approached.

"I heard you had a baby. What did you have?"

"A boy," I answered.

"That's cool. Are you going to bring him to the school one day?"

"Yeah, maybe," I lied, wanting to get rid of her.

Then I get into the classroom, and the teacher pulls the same shit in front of the entire class.

"So, class, I want to congratulate Desire on her baby boy."

The class looked at me like I was an alien coming to abduct them. I was embarrassed. Mad that I couldn't hide my face. You know I was calling that teacher all kinds of bitches under my breath, right? What if I didn't want anybody to know that I had a baby? Why would she make an announcement about my personal business like that? What kid was going to be happy about their thirteen-year-old classmate having a damn baby?

"How is the baby, Desire?" Ms. Drimmer asked.

I swear she had it out for me. First, it was assigning my seat next to Jen when we were enemies, and now she was putting me on the spot.

"The baby died. He was stillborn when I had him," I announced nonchalantly, without any remorse whatsoever.

"Oh my! I am so sorry."

"No problem. I'm over it."

Yeah, I burst her bubble. You should have seen the look on her face. You would have thought she had a still-born baby. Maybe next time she'll think twice about announcing someone's personal business.

The kids, on the other hand, didn't care. They kept coming at me like wildfire. By the end of the school day, I was the topic of discussion. If it wasn't this, it was that. I told different stories to get people off my back, and it backfired. I couldn't wait to leave school.

Jen suggested that we leave early, but it was the first day and I wasn't trying to get in trouble. I told my uncle I was going to do better and I meant it. Nothing or no one was going to hold me back. She understood where I was coming from and took the lead by telling everyone to back off. Homegirl had my back.

By the end of the day though, I had heard it all. The rumor that struck me the most was that I was a ho, who didn't know who my baby's father was, and that's why Malik dissed me. Get this, "He tried to work things out with me, but I was being a bitch." Can you believe that bull?

I ain't going to lie though. Those rumors tore me apart. I was in tears walking home from school. I wasn't a ho. I didn't sleep around like that. I was just sexually active.

Malik was the ho. He'd caused the problem. He left me hanging, and the bastard gave me HIV. The disease I had blocked out of my mind. After thinking so hard that I had deleted it altogether, I realized it was just my imagination. I thought so much about not having it, that was what remained in my head.

But those damn kids and the rumors brought me back to reality. They made me remember that I did have a disease for life. And no matter how much I ignored it or tried to blank it out, it wasn't going away.

That was it. I was a straw short of going over the edge, and I went back to my old ways. I was skipping school. I started smoking weed. It helped me think less, so yeah, I did it. I was coming home high and sometimes tipsy from downing a nip of vodka. No one in my household knew what was going on, but they weren't stupid.

My uncle tried talking to me about my behavior, but it was a blur to me. His words went through one ear and out the other. He didn't go to school with me. He didn't know how it felt to be the center of attention every single day. It was crazy how them kids were coming at me. I was almost on the verge of slitting my wrist. Believe me when I tell you, those kids had me cooked. So the words coming out of my uncle's mouth didn't mean squat to me.

It was a stupid move ignoring him though. I shut him out, and that shit bit me in the ass.

I came home late from school on a Friday night and got the worst news ever.

"See. Your fast ass is so busy out there running the streets, you didn't even know your uncle was sick."

"Did something happen to him?"

"Yeah, he died. That's what happened to him, and I blame you. He was so happy when you came back, and then you made him miserable again, with your late nights and drug problems."

"I didn't make him nothing. *You* were the mean one."

"Oh, chile! You are so blind to your own needs, you wouldn't notice a dead man walking."

I started marching through the house like a mad woman looking for my uncle, and there was no sign of him.

"Chile, what are you looking for?"

"I'm looking for Uncle Frank." I called out, "Uncle Frank!"

"Frankie is dead. Don't you hear me talking to you? I swear, you don't listen to nothing."

"He can't—I didn't get a chance to tell him about my day at school."

"And when is the last time you did that?"

It hit me hard. My Uncle was all I had left in the world, and he was dead. I was left to rot with my mean ol' aunt.

I missed school for the next couple of days. I didn't want to go back to school until after the funeral but my aunt changed those plans.

"I hope you know you're getting out of here tomorrow and taking your tail to school. Then right after, you come straight home."

"When is the funeral? Can I go back after the funeral?"

"No, there is no funeral. I can't afford to pay for no casket and services and a church and a pastor. It's all robbery. Your death cost more than living. I ain't having no funeral."

"You have to have a funeral."

"What'd I say? There is no more Frankie around here to save you. You are living under my roof, in my house, and things are going to change, starting today, right now. I haven't been in your shit all this time you rippin' and runnin', but things are going to change. I am putting my foot down at this very moment.

"Every day, you will come straight home from school. You are allowed to go nowhere. You cannot watch television unless you ask my permission. You cannot talk on the phone unless you ask my permission. You cannot leave this house unless you ask my permission. Don't use my stove unless I am in the kitchen with you. Every Saturday of the week I want this house cleaned from top to bottom. I want every single room swept and mopped. And don't forget, when you mop, make sure you are on your hands and knees. Make sure the kitchen is cleaned up every night after dinner. Now, if you don't want to do any of this, then there is the door. Stay your ass elsewhere."

What could I say? She got me at a time when I needed her the most, because I had no one else. I wasn't running away either. I vowed to my uncle that I was going to do better, and I didn't stick by it. She was right. Things had to change. There was no more running away, coming home late, or lying. I had to do right. I had to figure out a way to deal with those damn kids harassing me. Then maybe I could do right, and my aunt would change her mean, nasty ways.

I tried to do right, y'all, but it was just too much. My aunt was treating me like a freaking slave. The old times were back. "Do this. Do that. You missed a spot!"

I couldn't take it no more.

"Desire, did you clean today and dust these trophies?"

"Yes, and I dusted those trophies yesterday."

"Yes, what?"

"Yes, ma'am," I said with an attitude.

"Who you think you talking to like that?"

I bit my tongue to hold myself back from cursing her out.

"Don't you hear me talking to you, you little hussy?" *Whap!* She smacked me dead across my face.

I smacked her back off of instinct, and we were rumbling. She definitely overpowered me, but I hung in there. Then she made the phone call that sent me away for a week to hell and back.

The day my aunt laid the law down and we ended up getting into that big fight, she sent me on a special six-day journey to be locked up in boot camp. It was the worst. I actually wanted to go back home. I was better off being a slave there than at boot camp.

The girls there were at me hard. I got into four fights, not including when I got jumped for no reason. I guess it was because I was the new girl on the block. I had a black eye, twisted ankle, and a swollen wrist. I missed home like it was Michael Jackson's Neverland.

The food that was served tasted like hot water. It had no flavor, no taste, no nothing. Half the time, the food was uncooked, and you were lucky to get it served hot. That wasn't all though. Get this—You had to check the food before you ate it because the food could have anything, from rodents to spit, in it. Believe me, I didn't want to eat it, but I had to. It was either that or starve. I chose not to starve because if you did, there were consequences like time extension, getting a meal taken away, or bathroom duty, but only on the "shitters." I was cool! I did what I had to do. I wanted out.

I couldn't believe a place like that actually existed. The place was developed to be horrid so you would never want to go back. I can say it served its purpose because I sure enough was not going back there. That was one place I was staying away from. So when I got out, I did better. Somewhat.

School was a breeze-through, but I wasn't happy. I was still the center of attention, with all different types of rumors flying around about me, and at the same time I was losing my best friend again. I had to come straight home after school. I couldn't use the phone. Even when I asked, I couldn't use it. I only got a chance to talk to Jen at school briefly, because that year we didn't have any classes together. The only way we saw each other more than enough was by asking for a pass to the bathroom and meeting up in the hallway.

Every day I expressed to Jen how my aunt's attitude didn't change, that she was treating me worse. I figured if I did right by her she would maybe loosen up, but she didn't. She beat me up almost every day for no reason. I didn't retaliate because, like I said, I didn't want to go back. I told my probation officer what she was doing to me, but being the man that he was, and being in my life, of course he did nothing about it.

Over a short period of time, I drew up so much hate and hostility. I felt like the world was on my shoulders and I could no longer carry it. Every man in my life had disowned me, betrayed me, or left me. I couldn't allow them to do it anymore. So what if I got a little out of hand? I couldn't help it. I didn't get that unconditional love. Unconditional love was all I was asking for. Why couldn't I mess up and still be loved? Something had to be done.

I wanted to be happy again. The only friend I had was Jen, but all that was going to change. I had a solution to every problem in my life. My father had helped me out before, so I figured, maybe if I reached out to him in a different manner, he would understand me.

I called him up. "Hello, Dad!"

"And this is?"

"Desire."

"You can call me James."

"Dad, my aunt is abusing me, and I'm scared to stay here."

"Desire, I don't know what to say."

"I told you I don't like it here. I'm like a slave. I feel like no one cares about me and—"

"Hold on for a minute."

I held on for more than four minutes, and he never came back on the phone. I hung up and called right back.

"Hello."

"Dad," I said, crying.

"Desire, you're more than likely getting what you deserve. You're a brat, and you don't listen. Somebody needs to give you a good whuppin'. I told you I was done, and I meant it. You're the reason Greg got killed anyway. Whoever it was that jumped you, he should have let them finish. Don't call me no more, understand?" *Click*.

That was the end. He hung up on me.

I sat with the phone in my hand in a daze. How could he? I was at a loss for words, but overall I was hurt. He blamed me for Greg dying. He blamed me for being abused. He was my last resort. My mother wasn't an option because I didn't care to be around her. I wasn't taking the chance of being abandoned again. So, all in all, I had no one else. My happiness depended on me.

I sat and I thought about my life. I almost went ballistic. I started banging on the wall. I threw myself on the bed. I knocked off everything on my dresser. I just went into a fit of rage. I wanted revenge but had no idea how to execute it.

Chapter 22

I woke up the next morning, and my room looked damn near like a hurricane went through it. I didn't care either. I stepped over broken stuff and found something to wear for school.

My aunt came in the room bitching as usual. "I know you done lost your damn mind. This room better be clean before you leave out of here and go to school."

I ignored her and continued getting my clothes, stepping over things.

"I know you hear me talking to you."

I still ignored her.

"Oh, you wanna be sassy." She charged toward me and threw me up against the wall.

I tried to push her off, but I was too weak. I kicked her, and she grabbed my leg then head-butted my cheek. She pushed me down, and I hit the floor holding my cheek.

"Don't you raise your foot at me!"

I got up and tried to leave the room, but she snatched me up by my arm and twisted it behind my back. I stumbled to the floor unable to move my arm, which felt like it had snapped out of place. I swear she had cracked a bone or something in my cheek.

"Get your ass up, and get ready for school!"

"I can't," I cried. "My arm, I can't move it."

"Yeah, good. That will teach you to get sassy with me again."

I lay there on the floor crying. My aunt had beaten me up before, but never like this. She was on some other stuff. I made attempts to get up, but my body would not allow it. I lay there unable to move for twenty minutes.

My aunt came back in the room. "You must want some more, because I know I told you to get up and get ready for school."

She lifted me up, and I almost screamed from the pain that ran through my body. As bad as I was hurting, she made me go to school. She claimed I was faking, but I definitely wasn't. I could hardly move my arm. On top of that, my ankle felt twisted again, and every time I sat down, I had a sharp pain shoot through my butt.

It took me forty-five minutes to get dressed as opposed to my seven-minute routine. By the time I was ready, I had missed the bus.

"You missed that bus purposely. It ain't never took you that long to get ready."

"It's because my arm hurts, and my ankle—"

"Save it, because I don't want to hear your boohoos. Come on here, and let me take you to school."

I was reluctant, but I didn't want to get hit anymore. I was tired.

When I got to school it took me ten minutes to get in the building. Jen met me in the hallway.

"Happy birthday!"

I looked at her dumbfounded.

"Today is your birthday, right?"

"What's today's date?"

"November tenth. What's wrong with you? And why are you walking slouched over like that with a limp?"

"Because I can't move my arm and my ankle. I think it's twisted."

"From what?"

"My aunt, this morning."

Jen took a look at my arm and touched it.

I jumped in pain. "Ouch, that hurts!"

Jen checked me out. "Your arm is swollen."

"I know. I know," I wept in pain.

"Let's go to the nurse."

"Why?"

"What you mean, why? Are you crazy? Your arm could be broken."

I wasn't really up for going to see the nurse because I didn't want to have to explain how I got my injury, but I couldn't bear the pain any longer. I had to go.

We walked to the nurse's office, and I was just gone. I had forgotten about my own birthday. I don't know how I managed to do that, but I did. It was pitiful. My life had really taken a toll on me and my thoughts. I was diminishing one day at a time.

We got to the nurse's office, and she examined me.

"I think your arm may be broken. I have to call an ambulance. How did this happen?"

"I don't know."

"You don't know?"

I hesitated to answer. I wanted to tell, but then again I didn't, because I didn't want to get in more trouble.

"Desire, it's okay. You can tell me."

I took a deep breath. "I don't wanna say."

"Listen, this is serious, and I'm only here to help you. Talk to me."

Well, if she puts it that way, maybe I can tell her and get some help. "It was my aunt."

"Your aunt did this to you?"

"Yes."

"Does she live with you?"

"Yeah."

"Who else lives with you?"

"It's just me and her."

"Okay, just lie still. Jen, we got this under control, honey. Thank you. I'm going to give you a pass for your class." The nurse walked over to her desk.

Jen proceeded behind her. "She's gonna be okay, right?"

"Yes, don't worry, sweetie."

She gave Jen the pass, and Jen walked out as the other nurse was coming in.

"What happened here?"

Nurse Moon gave Nurse Greyer the one-minute finger. She was on the phone with the ambulance. She hung up the phone a few minutes later.

"What's going on? Who's the ambulance for?"

They both walked over to me.

Nurse Moon lifted my arm, and I jumped. "Look, I think it's broken," she said.

"Can she move it? Can you move it?"

"A little, but it hurts."

"How'd it happen? In gym?"

Before I could respond, Nurse Moon pulled Nurse Greyer to the side. They were supposed to be whispering, but I heard every word of their conversation.

"I think we got a DSS case here."

"Why? She's being abused?"

"Yeah. She came to school like this."

"Wow! I'm surprised she made it. I know she's in pain."

"Yeah, I see it written all over her face. I feel so bad for her."

"Yeah, especially since we know they are going to put her into immediate foster care."

"Mmmm, yeah, that's gonna suck. Who does she live with?"

"She said she stays with her aunt."

"Where's the mother? "

"No mention."

"I ain't even going to ask about the father."

"Oh please. Let's keep this simple."

"Yes, call the social worker on duty, but first clarify what happened. Make sure we got the correct story. You know the aunt can do some time behind this. It sucks if she does too, because there goes the shelter-hopping."

"That's better than getting abused."

"Yeah, it is, but she's going to be moved all over the place."

"Well, it's for her own good. She may have to share a bathroom and eat whatever, but hey, you know."

"Yeah, tell me about it. I ain't had one of these cases in a while."

"True. It has been a while."

Both the nurses walked over to me and helped me to my feet as the paramedics had arrived.

"Now tell me again, who did this to you?"

"No one. I fell."

Nurse Moon looked at Nurse Greyer, and that was that. I fixed them. I wasn't going to nobody's foster care. That was a dead issue.

When I got to the hospital, they concluded that my arm had come out of its socket and was bruised at the bone. I had a fractured tail bone, which was why I couldn't sit down without a pain shooting through my ass. My ankle was sprained, and my left cheekbone was fractured. I was just all messed up.

Big Bad Linda arrived while I was in my hospital bed being told of my conditions. She came not too long after I had been admitted into the ER. She shocked me with her fast response, but it wasn't to see about my health. It was mainly to find out what story I had given to explain my injuries. She knew from what she had done that she could be in a heap of shit. She was lucky I'd heard the conversation between the nurses at school, because that's what got her out of jail. I was not shelter-hopping. No way! I was staying home snaking out whatever she threw my way and hope that one day things would get better.

"Desire, what you done?"

"Ah, ma'am, are you her guardian?"

"Yes. Who are you?"

"I'm Dr. Snowden."

"Oh okay, Dr. Snowden. I'm Linda Jones, her aunt. What's going on here?"

"Well, she has a sprained ankle, a fractured tailbone and cheekbone, and a dislocated shoulder that's severely bruised."

"Hmmmm." She sighed.

"Do you know how this happened?" The doctor asked.

She paused, not sure of what to say, because she knew she had done it.

I helped her out, to save my ass. "I told you I fell down the stairs."

"I'm sorry. Can we talk outside, Mrs. Jones?"

"Sure."

They walked out of the room and had a chitchat for a few. Auntie Linda waited outside the room while the doctor came back in to talk to me.

"Desire, I appreciate you trying to help me out when I was talking to your aunt, but it wasn't necessary. I had a little conversation with her to clear up a few things. Now, you say you fell down the stairs, but I'm not convinced. The type of injuries you have sustained would not come from a direct stair tumble. Anyway, I've explained this to your aunt, and I'm quite sure this won't be happening again. I informed your aunt that if you are injured again from a "mysterious fall," she will be liable. She will be in major trouble, if you get my drift. She's outside talking with your P.O. She'll be in soon. You get some rest in the meantime."

He walked toward the door.

"And, Desire, don't be afraid to tell the truth. You're the victim here. By the way, happy birthday!"

"Thanks."

The doctor walked out, and Auntie Linda walked in. She looked like she had been given the worst news ever. I couldn't recall her looking that hurt when my uncle died.

"It's always something with you. You ain't hurt that bad. Got these people talking all kind of nonsense to me. You create more trouble than necessary. I swear."

I lay there not knowing what to say.

"Whatever bull you're pulling ain't gonna work for long. I'll see to that." She opened the door to walk out. "I'll be back to get you in a couple of days." And she left.

As I lay in the bed with tears in my eyes, someone knocked on the door. Not knowing who it was, I quickly tried to dry my eyes. "Come in."

"Why did you lie?"

"Huh?"

"Why didn't you tell them that your aunt did it?"

I hunched my shoulders.

"Desire, this was your chance to say something and get help. You should have just said something. Your father is not helping you. Your uncle is dead. You don't have anybody else. Why didn't you say anything?" Jen was almost in tears.

"Because I don't want to live in no shelter."

"Who said you would have to live in a shelter? What are you talking about?"

"That's what Nurse Moon was telling Nurse Greyer."

"That's not true, Desire."

"It is true, and that's why I didn't say anything. Ain't nobody gonna help me."

"Why are you talking like that? I'm trying to help you. Why don't you fight back? Hit that bitch back for a chance. Let her see how it feels to be laid up in the hospital."

"I'm not tryin'-a get in trouble for hitting her and being disrespectful. Remember, I am still on probation."

"Forget that. You got her now. That doctor knows you didn't fall down the stairs. I heard his entire conversation with your aunt, and he had her shook. He told her he didn't believe you had fallen down the stairs and knows what's going on 'cause he dealt with situations like this before."

"Hmmm."

"That's all you can say is *hmm*? Desire, you got a chance to get back at her. You can hold this against her. She can't touch you anymore. She knows what will happen. Tell her you ain't gonna put up with her shit no more and that you want to be taken off probation. And if she hits you again, then you're going to tell the truth. Here, take the phone." Jennifer handed me the phone. She was dead serious.

I don't know what high horse she had ridden in on, but I wasn't about to call my aunt talking no craziness. "No," I refused.

"Fine. I'll do it myself and pretend to be you." She started dialing.

"Gimme, I'll do it." I attempted to grab the phone from her, but she moved away from the bed.

She threw me the phone. I held it but did not put it to my ear.

Jen ran over to me and tried to grab it, but I held on to it the best I could with one arm.

"You know what, Desire? I'm done. Forget it. Do what you want." Jen politely hung up the phone and walked out on me.

With tears welling in my eyes, I stared at the glossy ceiling. My only friend had walked out on me. The only friend I had that was trying to help me. I sat there thinking that there had to be another way out, because I couldn't lose another friend. Oh no, I had enough with this shit.

I picked up the phone and dialed home.

"Hello," she answered with an attitude.

"Aunt-Auntie Lin—"

"Are you done stuttering? I know I didn't hit you that hard." She laughed.

I pulled the phone away from my ear, ready to hang it up, and I did. Then I sat in the bed and cried. I got up to use the bathroom, and pain shot all throughout my body. It was an unpleasant feeling, but I managed. I cried harder, wishing I wasn't alive.

In the midst of my sorrowful moment, the phone rang. I picked it up and put the receiver to my ear but couldn't get a hello out.

"All right, little hussy, don't be playing on my phone. What you want?"

I paused before I spoke, afraid to give her a good lashing.

"I ain't got all day. What you want?"

I remained silent, thought for a quick, and then said what the hell, I'm going to let her have it. I was hesitant because I thought about what would happen when I went home. If she created this much damage already, then it could get worse for me. But you know what? I was going to take a leap and let her have it. I'd had enough. This had to end. I was tired of being a punching bag. This had to stop.

"Hello. I told you I ain't got all day."

I took a deep breath and just went for it. "I want you to keep your fucking hands off of me. I ain't no guinea pig or punching bag and—"

"Wait a minute. Who do—"

"No, you wait a minute. I'm talking, and if you know what's good for you, you'll be quiet. We don't want the doctor to know the truth now, do we?"

She was silent. Jen was right. I had her now, so I went for the gusto.

"Mmm-hmm, that's what I thought. I lied for your ass, but I won't do it again. When I get out of here, shit is going to change. You better call my P.O. and tell him you want me off of probation. There is going to be no more 'Desire, do this' and 'Desire, do that.' You cannot order me around anymore. I'm tired of being pushed around like I'm some toy car. I covered your ass, and this is how you repay me? No, you're just like the kids in school. I can't stand you, and I can't stand them." I hung up the phone.

"I hate 'em! I hate 'em! I hate 'em! I hate everybody," I screamed out loud.

I couldn't take it anymore. No one appreciated me. I was always being called out of my name, and I was sick of that shit. My father was a jerk. My aunt was beyond that. The kids at school were my worst enemies.

If Auntie wanted war, then she got it. Let her have put her hands on me again. She was going to be the one in the hospital. And those bastards at school, yeah, I had something for them. I fixed all the nasty rumors and mended my broken heart. They wanted to call me a ho, and that's what I became. Since my aunt always thought I was up to something, huh, I was going to be. You bet your bottom dollar.

I unofficially checked myself out of the hospital. I was supposed to wait on my aunt to check me out, but to my advantage, I had a not-so-bright nurse who left my discharge papers in the room before my aunt arrived. So, of course, I signed my aunt's name, and when the nurse came back in almost thirty minutes later, I played as if my aunt arrived in a hurry, signed the papers, and left to pull the car up. She believed me, offered that I be wheeled out. I refused the assistance and crutched it out on my own, explaining to her that I wanted to get used to using the crutches with one arm. She agreed to my decision and sent me on my way.

I went to the train station across the street from the hospital, took public transportation with my student pass that got me on for free. It was a struggle with the crutches and all, but I knew I would be good once I got to the train station. My student pass allowed me eight free taxi miles from the train station nearest my home. I got to my destined train station and got a cab with no problem.

The cab pulled on to my street. I noticed my P.O. pulling off. *Hmph, I wonder what that was about.* As I was getting out, my aunt was coming out the door.

"Desire, honey, I was just on my way to pick you up from the hospital. They put you in a cab?"

I looked at my aunt like she was crazy. Who was she calling honey? I may have put my foot down, but what was up with the sweet talk?

"Let me help you inside and get you something to eat."

"I'm not hungry. What was my P.O. doing here?"

"He dropped off the papers for me to sign to take you off of probation."

"Did you sign them?"

"Yes, I did."

"Cool."

I hopped in the house with my crutches and scrambled my way upstairs to my room. I limped in tired, noticing it was rearranged and spotlessly cleaned. I was impressed. My talk really worked. I had to thank Jen. She was my rock that made me realize that I was being a damn fool. Huh, I wasn't going to be a fool any longer. Not at home or school. I had my mind made up.

I let my aunt play the nice role until it got on my nerves. I had to get out of the house. I had some research to do.

I gathered my things to leave. My body was aching, but that wasn't stopping me. My doctor gave me some pills strong enough to knock the pain out for hours. I wasn't supposed to be involved with any activity after taking them, but I liked the way they made me feel. I swallowed two OxyContin and hopped my way to the front door.

"Desire, where you going?"

"To the library. I need to do some research for class."

"You need to rest."

"I need to do my work. I'm going to the library."

"Let me drop you off."

"I'm fine. I can ride the bus."

"Not while you're on crutches."

"I got home on crutches."

"I'm taking you. Come on."

I let Aunt Linda have her way and take me to the library. I sat the entire ride in a daze. I was high in a zone, and my mind was racing a mile a minute. I had so many mischievous scenes replaying in my mind, I had to laugh out loud.

"You okay over there?"

"Yup," I answered, smiling.

"Did you take any more of them painkillers?"

"No, not if I'm about to read and stuff. Those pills make me sleepy."

"Mmmmm. Well, what time you want me to come back and get you?"

"I need like two hours."

"All right."

I got into the library and found a nice comfy spot. I did a full two-hour research on HIV—how it could be contracted, symptoms, treatment, etc. I wanted to figure out what would be the most effective way for me to pass it around. As I already knew, vaginal was one way, but as I read up on the topic, I found out vaginal wasn't the most assuring way. See, I needed to make sure these people were definitely going to get what I had to dish out. I had to be on top of my game.

I found out it was harder for a female to give the virus to a male than the other way around. I pondered how I could make sure my victims, after one visit, were left with my semi-deadly disease. I thought maybe through oral sex, but nah, there was no chance. It had not been known that HIV could be passed through saliva. The only method that would make sure a person was going to be infected after one sexual encounter was anal sex.

I researched some more and found out the particulars about the medicine that needed to be taken to control the virus. I didn't want to take anything though because I didn't want it to stabilize the amount of the virus and decrease my chances of spreading the infection. I wanted everyone to be infected with what I had, even if it meant taking it in the rear.

Chapter 23

In a week's time, I had gathered enough information to be able to send people to the clinic wishing they should have wrapped it up. I was officially off crutches, and my shoulder was so-so, but not bad enough to stop me from beginning my mission.

The library was my landing spot, and my aunt was content with dropping me there all the time. In her eyes, it was a good thing, but in my eyes, it was the home base to start my mission. I packed my bags and had my aunt drop me off, leading her to believe that I was into my studies. Yup, I sure was.

This particular time, I pretended like I had to do some research for a school project due within the next few days. I told her it would take me about three hours because I had to finish make-up work as well.

When I walked in the library, I headed straight to the bathroom to set up shop. I parked my things inside of the stall for the handicapped and unpacked a mini makeup bag, a wig, a skimpy outfit and some hooker pumps. After I got all dolled up, looking grown and sexy, I found a corner in the library to hide my stuff. Then it was "go get 'em Johnny" to my first victim. Yeah, I was ready to execute the plan for the day.

I walked into Walgreens plastered in makeup, wearing a leopard-print miniskirt, a too-small shirt showing all of my cleavage, a brown curly wig, and some knockoff red pumps from Payless. I was looking like a grown-ass woman, and that was the idea. I searched for my victim, hoping he still worked here, and indeed he did. I spotted him standing by the photo center talking to some guy.

I walked up on him and leaned into him like we were acquaintances. "Mmmm, what's your name?" I flirted.

He licked his lips. "Derrick. What's yours?"

"You don't remember me?"

He stepped back and took a glimpse. "No. From where?"

"Why don't we go back in that room back there, you know, where you take the people who steal?"

He did a double take. "What? You tryin'a set me up or something?"

"Hell no. I'm just ready now." I grabbed the bulge between his legs and massaged him. He pushed me back. "Hold on, hold on." He motioned me toward the back room.

As we walked through swinging doors, he said to me, "Are you for real?"

"You think I'm playing." I lifted my dress to show him I had no panties on, and that was all she wrote.

We went in the back room, where he lifted up my dress and pulled his pants down. He reached in his wallet and pulled out a condom.

"Do we really need that?" I asked.

"I ain't tryin'a have no kids."

I turned around. "I can't get pregnant through my asshole."

"You want me to put it, put it in your—"

"Are you with it or not?"

I didn't know what I was in for when we did the do. Anything bigger than a toothpick is definitely not meant for the asshole. I almost gave up on letting him put it in. He had to pull out some ChapStick to make it go in a little easier. It helped a little, but it hurt a lot.

I wanted to back down, but I couldn't cop out. I kept thinking about the way I was treated by my father, my aunt, and especially what the Walgreens man himself had done to me. He deserved what he was getting. I had a pretty good feeling he was going to hear some disturbing news on my behalf in the next six months or so, if he got himself checked out.

"When can I see you again?"
"I don't know."
"You got a number?"
"Nope."
"You ain't got no cell or nothing."
"Nope. You can buy me one though."
"Yeah, I can. Actually, hold up. I got an extra one you can use. Hold on, let me get it."
I walked out of Walgreens popping two OxyContin in my mouth while stuffing the prepaid calling card phone in my purse. I left him sprung already and left myself with a burning asshole. I had a sharp pain shooting through it. Whoa! Anal ain't no joke! I bled a little from him stretching my booty-hole, and I had an open cut that was throbbing. Next time, I figured I probably should take the OxyContin beforehand. Huh, 'cause with the number of people I was trying to infect, I had to get used to this.

I did an unnoticeable change back at the library and waited for my aunt to pick me up. When I reached home, I made the bathroom my first stop. I had to take a monstrous shit, and you know it was not the best time to do it either, but I couldn't hold it.

I plopped down on the toilet, and Lord have mercy on my soul, my asshole was on fire. The pain sparked up water in my eyes. My hole throbbed with its own beat. That damn research I did failed to mention the pain during and after. Something had to give. I had to get something that was going to make this anal job a smooth process. I knew there had to be something too, because I knew porn stars was definitely getting down with a substance. I needed to find out what it was, get a hold of it, and combine it with my OxyContin.

I soaked in the tub that night thinking about more research I had to do. Then, after relaxing and soaking, I put my night clothes on and made way to my computer to do some more searching. My newly adjusted aunt had hooked me up with a computer, the desk, a printer, and high-speed Internet access. I got it when I came back from my first library visit. Talk about trying to get on my good side.

She claimed she got it because my teachers said it would be easier for them to e-mail assignments to me. That was bullshit though because school wasn't that far away where I couldn't grab my assignments every day until I was due back at school. They allowed me to be out for a period of time for an excused medical reason. It was actually mandatory. You had to be cleared to go back when you were hospitalized. Whatever, though, the computer came in handy.

I went to the Yahoo! search engine and typed in the words *anal sex*. I clicked on what looked like a helpful link. Some naked women appeared on the screen. Then my aunt walked in. I quickly minimized the screen.

"What you doing?"

"Homework."

She walked over to me at the computer. "Oh. What homework you doing?"

Not fast on my feet with a reply, I hesitated. "Ah . . . "

Just then, the phone rang, and she turned around to answer the phone. At that moment, a window popped up on the screen with two females and a guy pleasing each other. What a relief that was. I was big boss in the house, but there was still a little discipline in her that I wasn't trying to release.

I exited out of the pornographic pop-up window. In less than five seconds, other stuff kept popping up out of nowhere. I kept clicking out of them. And then there was this one pop-up that read: YOU WANT TO HAVE BETTER ANAL SEX WITHOUT THE PAIN-CLICK HERE. I clicked on the icon.

There was all this information about something called Anal Eaze, a numbing substance that you apply to the butthole and slightly inside before having anal sex. This was definitely what I needed. The problem now was, How do I get it? I couldn't order it off the 'Net. I didn't have a credit card. I may have been doing grown things, but I was still only fourteen. I had to figure out a way.

I lay down to think and dozed off.

My cell phone vibrated at about one thirty in the morning. I was sitting on my bed zoned out from the OxyContin I had taken, wishing I had something stronger.

I answered the phone. "Hello."

"Yo, what's up, girl?"

"Who's this?"

"Derrick."

"From."

"Walgreens. Damn! You got other dudes ringing you on this line already?"

"Oh, nah. I was just out of it for a second. What's up?"

"I don't know. You tell me."

"Tell you what?"

"A'ight, since you want to play hard ball, when am I going to see you again?"

"I don't know."

"Okay. What you doin' now?"

"I'm chillin'."

"You wanna get up right now?"

"Oh, nah. I'm in the bed."

"That's cool. I'll come get in the bed with you."

"Nah, I live with my man."

"Shorty, you got a man and you—"

"Shhh. Let me call you back." I hung up the phone and laughed out loud. *What a dummy!* I was already getting a kick out of the shit I was doing, and I was just getting started.

Chapter 24

I made plans to get up with Derrick again. He had one more round to go. I even conned him into buying the Anal Eaze, seeing I was too young to go into the adult-only store. Amazing. I made up some lie about possibly getting caught because my boyfriend's cousin worked in the store, and if he saw me, all hell would break loose.

Like an idiot, he believed the lie and purchased nine boxes of the Anal Eaze. As usual, my aunt had dropped me off at the library, and I had Derrick pick me up like around five. I did my whole "change thing," and all went well. We went to Derrick's spot, and I let him have it one more time.

This time I was golden. Anal Eaze worked wonders. I was in the money now. Anal Eaze and OxyContin combined was the master plan.

I lay beside Derrick in a daze, feeling good that I had just infected my first victim.

"Damn, girl! You can really take it up there."

"Humph."

"So you think your man is going to be mad if you stay the night with me?"

"Maybe."

"Maybe? You know he'll be screamin' on you."

"Nah. He knows I like to do this kind of stuff."

"You mean, taking it in the ass."

"No, I mean, you know, just fucking."

"He don't care?"

"Nope."

"Yeah, right. He must not know."

"Know what?"

"What you're doing."

"He does. We cool like that. He don't care."

"A'ight, so why you with him?"

"Can we stop talking about him?"

"Cool. Let's talk some real shit. I'm married, but I'm a swinger on the side. My wife, of course, doesn't know I swing."

"What are you talking about you swing?"

"I'm a swinger," he repeated, as if that was enough to answer my question.

I looked at him confused.

"You don't know what a swinger is?"

"No."

"And you like to fuck, while you got a man?"

"Just what is it?" I asked, getting aggravated.

"If you stay with me tonight, I'll show you."

"I can't."

"Why?"

"What time is it?"

"Eight-thirty. Why?"

"I gotta go." I got up and started putting my clothes on.

"Okay. You don't have to stay the night, but just let me show you what it's about."

"Why can't you just tell me what it's about?"

"Because."

"Because what?"

"Just because."

"Well, forget it then. Take me back to the library." I put my shoes on.

"A'ight, listen. It's when couples swap partners and have sex."

I almost let out a smile. My heart did a happy dance to a hip-hop beat. "You mean like a whole bunch of guys and girls?"

"Yup." He smiled.

I bit my lip in excitement. He was one down, leading me to more.

I woke up in the middle of a water bed with three guys on my right side and a female on my left. I looked at the time, and it was seven o'clock in the morning. I hopped up out of the bed and glanced at the three guys, thinking how much of a surprise they were in for. Not only them, but the other six that I let hit it last night too.

I got dressed and looked around for Derrick, but I didn't see him. I looked outside for his car, and he was gone. "Fuck!" I stood at the window, not knowing what to do. I had no money or nothing. I looked around and the house was still. Everyone was sound asleep.

I noticed coats on the sofa and took my chances by going through them. I managed to scrape up fifty dollars. This would be enough to get me to the library to get my bag, change, and go home.

Fear built up inside me again as I thought about home. I had stayed the night out. My aunt had changed, but I wasn't sure how she was going to react about me staying the night out. I definitely didn't want to resurrect her evil spirit.

Chapter 25

I went home, y'all, and my aunt didn't say too much of anything to me. I mean I played it slick. The library was open twenty-four hours, so I rushed back there, found a secluded spot in the corner, laid my head on the table with an open book like I was researching, and fell asleep. I stayed like that until somebody came to wake me up.

Finally, a librarian tapped me, and I woke up pretending not to know where I was.

"Honey, have you been here all night?"

"Um, I don't know. What time is it?"

"It's nine in the morning."

"It's nine? Oh no, my aunt's gonna kill me." I started to pack my things.

"Do you need to make a phone call or—"

"Yes, I need to. I can't believe I fell asleep."

"Just calm down."

"See, she is right there," Auntie Linda hollered, appearing out of the blue with another librarian.

"Auntie Linda, I'm sorry. I was reading and I—"

"I found her here asleep with her face buried in a book," the librarian who woke me up informed.

My aunt gave her a tired look. Then she looked at me. A little fear set in as I thought my plan hadn't worked.

"You ready?"

"Yeah," I answered, gathering my things.

We walked out of the library and got in the car. The ride was silent for a few. Then Auntie Linda broke the ice.

"You've been doing well for yourself. I didn't think I was still going to find you in the library. I thought you had pulled a fast one, but you're all right. Keep your head in those books, and next time try to not to stay the night in the library." She laughed.

I chuckled. That was my first laugh ever with my aunt. I laughed hard too. I laughed at her. I laughed at my plan working. I was in laughter land. I had it made and stretched it to the max. I didn't get stupid and pull another all-nighter, but I did stay out late.

I had my aunt thinking I was really getting my study on at the library. I went so far as to making up assignments that I had to do. I had them typed out like the teacher had assigned it. I was doing the damn thang.

I was staying out all the time with different guys, keeping my OxyContin and Anal Eaze handy. The guys weren't hard to find. I'd meet them on the Internet, through friends, or just strutting my stuff on the block. I made sure I paid everyone of them two visits, nothing less. I gained many friends in the process, especially at school. Yeah, I was no longer the center of attention in an embarrassing way, but in a way I had accepted. I became the ho I was rumored to be, and it was fine with me. I turned a lie into the truth. It took me a year and some change to become the classy ho I was today.

My girl Jen pitched in by hooking a sister up with whoever I asked to be laid up with. Then you know the drill after that. I got down and dirty with them on a double note, unprotected, and left them guessing. I ran into a few problems with dudes tryin'a wrap it up, but when I swung the booty in their face, it was "bye-bye, condom and hello, raw dog." What a bunch of idiots!

But, hey, who was I to judge? I was just supplying the goods.

I was proud of what I was doing. It shot my self-esteem sky-high. My aunt had no clue either. She thought I was a bad girl turned good. That's what she was supposed to think. I had to keep her trusting me, while on the low.

Now, although my girlie-girl Jen helped with the setups, she couldn't understand why I was doing what I was doing. It wasn't for her to understand though. This was my thing. My prerogative. The guys I slept with wasn't 'bout shit anyway. They either had a girlfriend they were cheating on, or they were looking for a quick fix. I was simply swinging the booty in their direction. I looked at it as giving back to the men in the community. Ha! I was cracking myself up.

Today was one of them days too. There was this end-of-the-year junior hooky party going on, and you know I had to be there. The seniors and juniors did it every year. Jen was rolling with me too. She stayed rolling but never got too involved. She wasn't like me, sexing and all. She was a good girl, which was cool. I didn't have a problem with it.

I'd been in this giveaway game for over a year now, and no one or nothing was going to stop me. It's a shame how stupid these guys were out here, thinking with their dick and not their head. The sad part about it too was that half of them didn't get themselves tested. Shoot, they didn't even know what a clinic looked like, unless their baby's mama was giving birth or they got shot or stabbed. You'd think with all the "wrap it up" commercials, our men would have more sense than that. But I couldn't be worried about a nucca's problem. I had an agenda to attend to, and up next on the list was my high-school friends.

I'm preparing my bag now for the mission transmitting this disease to some more gullible people. I have to stay equipped with my Anal Eaze, pain pills, and whatever other paraphernalia I needed, depending on the situation or event. I was thinking of pulling an all-nighter tonight, since I was in a very giving mood, if you feel what I'm sayin'.

All eyes were definitely on me when I stepped through the door. Eyes were stuck on me like sap on a tree. I was the "shizznit." Damn, I scared myself sometimes.

"Delicious Desire."

"Freddy Montana."

"What's up, girl? You looking tasty, Desire."

"Mmmm. Not too bad there yourself, pretty boy."

"I try," Freddy said, dusting his shoulders off.

"Oh, do you?"

"Yes, Desire. I do," he responded, licking his lips.

"You like saying my name, huh?"

"How'd you know?" He winked.

I laughed. "Holla at me later."

"You know that's the plan, baby."

"Cool. I'll be waiting," I said, as he stared back at me walking away. I laughed again.

Jen gave me a dirty look. "You're a trip."

"Why?"

"Because . . . how can you like what you're doing?"

"I'm a sex addict. It's a craving."

"Oh, please. It makes you look like a slut."

"Thanks for the compliment."

"Any time. Just make sure you stay keeping it strapped. I don't give you condoms for *my* health."

I felt bad about lying to my best friend. She thought I was really addicted to having sex, protected sex, that is. I mean, come on, let's face it. She was the very first person to start the rumors seventh grade year anyway. I'd just finally built up the courage to finish what she started. Besides, she was the dumb one for really thinking I was addicted to sex.

I kept myself healthy though, and I stayed protected in a different kind of way. I took my daily pills for this shit I had. I wasn't no fool. I had to stay alive to keep giving this shit away. Wasn't gonna be no fun if the homies couldn't have none, ya heard.

I know you're like, "But what about these dirty nuccas out here that you're sleeping with?"

Yeah. They could've given me something too, but my system was full of penicillin. I did my own examination. If I felt an itch coming on, I popped a pill.

Most of the dudes I slept with anyway were high-school students. They were the easiest. Not saying the older cats ain't too dumb either, but it was just easier to get the young ones to run up in this pussy raw. I even took penicillin after I slept with someone, just in case they had something. I was still on OxyContin. My prescribed bottle was gone, but you know me, I found a way to get whatever I wanted.

This Arab dude that I let hit it on a regular basis worked as a pharmacist at the same Walgreens where I'd met the security dude, Derrick. Anyways, he hooked me up with whatever I needed.

My legit prescribed pills for the HIV, I got those straight from the clinic on the low. The pharmacist dude had no clue either. I used the pharmacy inside of the hospital to fill those prescriptions. I laughed inside at all of this. Every time he hit it raw, he thought he was getting a free piece of ass in exchange for some doctor goodies.

***

"Yo, Jen, I'm about to go in the room with Freddy."

"Oookay, be careful."

"Yeah, yeah. Go pop a Red Bull or something."

Jen flipped me her middle finger playfully and walked away.

I followed Freddy into a back room, where there were four other dudes. I knew all of them from school. They were the "newbies" on the block, seventh grade boys celebrating going into the eighth grade. Freddy knew how to choose young, cute, fresh meat. He earned his cool points for the year.

"Freddy, I see you got company."

Freddy walked over to me and pulled me to the side. "Yeah, ah, my little brother and his friends are new to this. I told them, you know, they could get their first piece if—"

"You know I got you." I walked away from Freddy and walked over to his little brother and friends. "Who's first?" I asked loud and clear.

They all stood up, pushing each other out of the way, arguing.

"Yo, I got this first."

"No, I got this," Freddy announced.

"Y'all said I could go first," one of the boys begged.

"Nah. Ain't none of y'all going first. This is my hookup. Just sit tight. You'll get your turn."

"Yo, how we know you ain't got nothing, if we beatin' it up after you?"

"Young one, please. I take good care of my dick. I ain't got shit."

I just stood watching and listening, laughing inside. These idiots were worried about what they had and not even questioning me. Can we say *stupid*?

I hooked every last one of them up, with breaks in between, taking shots of vodka straight up.

Freddy wanted one last hit, but I was too wasted. The shots had taken a toll on me, and I was hardly aware of my surroundings.

"Yo, Dee, you all right?"

I was feeling sick to my stomach.

"I don't feel good."

Freddy rushed me out of the room, and we bumped into Jen, who was standing guard by the door.

"What happened? What you do to her?"

"I didn't do nothing to her."

Jen held me up, and Freddy let me go.

"Jen, I gotta throw up."

"Come on," she said with an attitude, and she dragged me to the bathroom.

I ran to the toilet and *Splash!* Vomit towered on the toilet seat. I fell to my knees, and more vomit came out nonstop. I lay my head on the toilet, not able to hold it up.

Jen screamed on me, "Look at you. I can't believe you. Why'd you drink so much?"

"I wanna leave you so bad. This is disgusting. Damn, Desire! You really know how to—"

"J—just l—leave. I'm . . . fine . . . 'kay. Bye."

"You can't even talk."

"I said that."

"What?"

"Yeah, 'kay," I slurred, not knowing what the hell I was talking about.

What I wanted to say was, "Help me up," but I couldn't get the words out. My head slid off the toilet seat, and I hit the floor. I was out for the count.

I woke up with a pounding headache. I felt like shit lying in some bed. *Where am I?* I looked around to see where I was. I had my night clothes on. I realized I was in my bed. *How'd I get home?*

I sat up then lay back down. The throbbing was too much to bear. I lay on my side with my back to the door. I heard my door open. My head was throbbing so badly, I couldn't even turn around to see who was coming in. It couldn't be anybody but my aunt though.

I felt hands on me. I turned over, forgetting about my booming headache, interested in finding out who was touching me. I came face to face with my probation officer, who forced me on my stomach and placed me in handcuffs.

"What are you doing? Get off of me!"

"Yeah, get her out of here," my aunt yelled.

"Where am I going?" I asked, not really able to resist.

Auntie Linda stood there with a smirk on her face.

This bitch done snitched on me. Muthafucka! She couldn't wait for this day. *Damn! This wasn't supposed to go down like this.*

"Where am I going?" I repeated.

Auntie yelled, "I want you out of my house! You think you slick. You ain't slick. Out there sleeping around."

My P.O. pulled me off the bed.

I moaned, feeling pathetic and nauseous. "What are you talking about?"

"You know what I'm talking about. Don't play stupid with me. What? You still drunk?"

"No," I answered, a bit agitated from being interrogated in handcuffs, like I was some kind of criminal.

"Do you even know how you got home?"

"It doesn't matter. I got here."

"'It doesn't matter. I got here,'" she repeated in my face. "Huh. Your ass was laid out on the porch. Yeah. Your little chicken-shit friends brought you home, laid you on the porch, and rang the door bell. Now you tell me if that ain't straight-up disrespectful or what."

"Is what disrespectful?"

"Desire, you are not twenty-one and not even eighteen. What the hell do you think you're doing? You out there being nasty and having sex." She picked up my open book bag and began throwing the contents at me. She hit me with the condom packets in the bag. "Glad to know you were protected. And look here. You on drugs too?" She threw the bottle at me.

"That ain't mine. That ain't my bag," I lied.

"Like hell, it ain't. I trusted your lying ass, Desire. I knew you were too good to be true."

"You never believe me. That's the problem."

"I gave you the benefit of the doubt, and you blew it. I want you out of my house. Take her out of my house!" she screamed. "I'm tired of looking at her!"

"No, I ain't going nowhere!"

"Oh, you getting out of here, heiffa!"

"No! Get off of me!" I began to go wild with the little strength I had.

"Desire, settle down and—"

"No, fuck off! Get off of me! Get off me," I screamed, feeling dizzy.

"Desire, calm down."

"No, fuck you! Get the hell off of me!"

"Hey, chill out! Calm down. Let's make this an easy process."

"No, no, nooooooooooooooooooooooo!"

"Hold her still. I got something to calm her down."

"Noooooooooo, you bitches! Get the fuck off!"

When I opened my eyes, I was in an unfamiliar bed, and my body felt weary. I lay still as I looked around the dark, enclosed room that had a night light that barely shined bright enough for me to see. I looked for a door to find my way out, but the walls looked the same, showing no sign of an exit.

Suddenly an opening appeared across the room, and this heavyset, charcoal-toned woman barged in the door and made her way to me. "Get up, wild child! You hard of hearing?"

I got up and put on the dusty sneakers by my bed, and she led me to a hallway where there was a line of girls. Every one of them had on the same blue T-shirt that read DYS. I glanced down at myself and noticed I had on the same attire. It was definitely not what I'd left the house in. My aunt, that bitch, committed me to DYS lockup.

From the look of things, I wasn't going to like it here. I wanted to break loose, but I knew that wasn't about to happen. I took my place in line and followed the leader. We were ushered to a spacious room with about fifteen twin-sized beds that sat side by side.

"Good morning, ladies. My name is Miss Sheila, and I will be going over a few things with you today. First off, I want you to locate your bed. You can do this by looking on the wall and finding your first initial with your last name above your bed. Once you locate your name, please walk to your space."

I waltzed over to my bed with an attitude, as every girl in there did. I viewed my surroundings once again. I scoped every girl in there and tried to figure out why they were here. I tried to conclude what their purpose was. None of them looked as hard-core and rough as most problem teenage girls did, but who was I to judge? I didn't look like it either. And we were probably in here on the same status—bullshit!

"Now that everyone has gotten acquainted with their space, it is time to get down to business. Some of you may have awakened in a different area, which is what we call the black hole, not really a fun place to be for a young lady. But when you don't follow the rules, that's where you'll be."

Some girl blurted, "Can we just get to the rules? Damn!"

"Hey, Margie, can we get Miss Veronica here some soap? Because she obviously has not learned her lesson, and she already knows the rules."

Veronica mumbled, "Whatever."

Everyone stood around quiet anticipating some type of action because although Veronica whispered, she was heard loud and clear.

Miss Sheila gave her a dead stare for about thirty seconds. Surprisingly, Veronica stood timid. I thought with her smart mouth she'd remain bold. She stood with her head down like she hadn't spoken a word.

Miss Sheila walked over to her, lifted her chin, and smiled in her face. "I'll deal with you later," she whispered in her face and walked away.

"Let's stay focused, ladies. Cut the shit. And I'm not asking, I'm telling you—Cut the shit! We are on a schedule here. I know you don't want this to run into your lunchtime. Ooooh, no, you don't want that, especially since you haven't had any breakfast this morning. I know you're hungry right now too 'cause I can hear your stomachs growling. I can miss lunch though because I had my big breakfast this morning: scrambled eggs, bacon, grits, and pancakes. I'm cool. I don't need a lunch, but y'all do.

"We made a special lunch too—fried chicken, macaroni and cheese, mash potatoes, green beans, yams, and for dessert, sweet potato pie. I'd hate for you all to miss out on a meal like that because I'm telling you, you won't see nothing like that for a while. A good while. Therefore, there will be no more interruptions. If you gotta piss, then hold it. If you got a question, don't ask. Remain attentive and listen carefully because I'm not going to repeat myself. Now, with that out of the way, we shall continue.

"There are simple rules that must be followed. I will say them once and only once. They are too simple and self-explanatory to repeat." She paced the room for a second, just looking around at the group of girls before she continued to speak.

"Okay, number one: Be respectful to others and, most of all, yourselves. Number two: No talking allowed unless you are in this area, but only before seven P.M. After seven P.M., the talking ceases until your rise-and-shine time, which is six o'clock every morning, no questions asked. You are permitted to talk in the mess hall, but that is the only other place. Number three: There will be no gossiping allowed whatsoever. If I hear any she said-she said, you will be disciplined accordingly. Number four, ladies: No fighting, plain and simple. Number five: No profanity. If I hear so much as a—"

Whispers interrupted her speaking. Apparently, it seemed that some people had no idea what profanity meant.

"Is there a problem, ladies?"

No one answered, while a few people snickered.

I was getting agitated from the silly interruptions. I sucked my teeth and rolled my eyes as people stood around like we had time to waste. I was ready to eat. Shit!

"A question requires an answer, ladies."

Still no one uttered a word.

I wanted to say something, but I knew what profanity meant. I wasn't about to look like the idiot and get yelled at. Besides, I knew this Miss Sheila lady was trying to trick someone into talking. It damn sure was not going to be me. I looked around, waiting for the person who didn't know what profanity meant to speak up.

Miss Sheila looked at her watch. "Lunch is in fifteen minutes, and we still have not gotten halfway through the tour."

I sucked my teeth, upset that I might miss lunch.

"Do we have a problem, Miss Jones?"

I rolled my eyes and answered with an attitude.

"What?" she asked as she walked over to me.

I tensed up.

She yelled in my face. "Are you hard of hearing?"

"No!"

She continued to yell in my face. "No what?"

"What?" I was mad that she was yelling in my face, invading my territory. I knew she was trying to get me to say *ma'am*, but I was in a stubborn mood. She needed to back the fuck up. I didn't have time for the bullshit.

"We got another smart-ass I see."

I rolled my eyes and fluttered them.

"Don't roll them too hard, honey. You might get them caught in the back of your head."

I rolled them again.

"I see you like to roll them eyes there."

I rolled them again.

"You know you just broke a rule, right?"

I stood there and directed my attention to the corner of the room.

"Look at me when I'm talking to you."

I huffed, rolled my eyes, and positioned them in her direction. I wanted to sock her a quick blow to the noggin, but I kept my composure.

"What's the attitude for?"

I stood there not answering.

"My questions require an answer."

Some girl blurted out, "Bitch, can you answer her so we can hurry up and eat. Damn."

Miss Sheila turned her attention to the voice. While she turned around, I flipped the little ignorant broad the bird.

"Fuck you too!"

Miss Sheila looked back and forth at me and the girl.

"Whatever, stupid," I responded.

"Ya moth—"

"Hold up, ladies. Not here, not now, not in my presence. Oh no."

"I don't like being called stupid."

"And I don't like being rudely interrupted. Furthermore, I don't care about what you don't like. You are in my house, and you will follow my rules. You got it?"

The girl stood there quiet, and Sheila walked over to her. "You got it?"

"Yeah, I got it."

"Yes, I got it what?"

"Yes, ma'am."

"Thank you, Miss Henderson."

Sheila stepped away and went back to the center of the floor. She continued with the rules and regulations, and everyone cooperated so that we didn't miss lunch.

After lunch, we were allowed five minutes to arrange things at our beds. Each person had a cubby to put away the few hospital-looking clothes they gave us. We didn't have our own toiletries, we had to share. I definitely was not feeling that.

Once our five minutes was up, we were given a tour of the shower area. The bathroom only allowed six occupants at a time, and there was no privacy. The bathroom stalls had no doors, and the showers had no curtains.

Before bedtime, we were allowed ten minutes to do whatever at our area before lights went out at nine. I lay there missing home, where there were no rules and less stress. My aunt really hit a hate button this time. She had this up her sleeve all along. She knew I was going to slip up. This was really some extreme bullshit. She was cutting into my "free pussy" giveaway. How the hell was I going to pass this virus around, locked up with some bitches? *I can't sex no chick. Damn, I need to get up out of here.*

I looked at the clock. I had seven minutes left before lights went out. I grabbed a notebook and pen and began writing. I started jotting down everything that crossed my mind, from the guys I slept with to my first day here.

Forget this. I needed to strategize on how I could get the hell out of this joint to finish my mission. I closed my notebook and slid it under my mattress.

This girl Torrey came over to me. "Yo, ya first name Desi or something like that?"

"Why?"

"'Cause my homegirl Tameka wanna know."

"Well, tell your homegirl Tameka to come ask me herself."

The girl smirked at me and then walked away.

Whatever. I don't have time for the bullshit. I got comfortable on my bed as I watched homegirl go over to, I guess, Tameka's bed, and tell her what I said. She didn't come back over and say anything to me, so I wasn't worried. I just knew that these girls in here were already hatin'. They knew what the deal was though. Anyway, I lay my head down on my pillow and closed my eyes.

Deep into my sleep, I turned over because I got uncomfortable lying on my stomach. I lay flat on my back, and out of nowhere, I became a punching bag. Someone was pounding the shit out of me. I opened my eyes and I saw nothing. I tried to lift myself up, but somebody was holding me down.

I screamed for help, and the lights came on. Tameka, Ginger, and Torrey were standing over me. Security ran in, along with other staff, and grabbed a hold of the three girls. I guess they didn't like me. They got me good. If the supervisor didn't turn the lights on just now, then I probably would have caught a worse whupping.

One of the guards reached out to help me up, but I got up on my own and made a break for it to the bathroom. I was embarrassed. Everyone had awakened, and of course, they saw that I had just gotten my ass beat. The blood coming from my mouth was a dead giveaway.

I examined myself in the bathroom mirror. My lip was split down the middle, my eye was swollen, the inside of my mouth was bleeding, and I had welts and scratches all across my face. My shirt was torn too, and I had scratches on my chest and arms.

Chapter 26

My second night here and these girls got me on fear mode. I was trying to fight being scared, but it was impossible, knowing that I was going to be in this hellhole for a month. I took a good look again at myself in the mirror. Tears start to stream and sting the wounds on my face.

Embarrassed, I ran into a stall, sat on my ass, and balled up into a knot. I wanted out of this place. This was not the place for me.

Someone walked into the bathroom. "Honey, let me clean you up."

I looked up to see the nurse standing in front of me. I put my head back down and started sobbing. She reached over and lifted me up. I was reluctant, but I let her take control.

As she cleaned me up, a staff member on duty, Gina, came in.

"Are you almost finished, Aileen?"

"Oh yeah, just a few more spots and she's done."

"How you feeling, Jones?" Gina asked.

I didn't answer. She got closer to me and put her hand on my shoulder. I flinched.

"Jones, it's cool. I won't hurt you. I know you're a little shaken up, but don't let these girls get the best of you. You just got here."

"I wanna leave."

"You know that's not an option."

"All done," the nurse announced. She gathered her things and walked out of the bathroom.

I watched her leave, wishing she wasn't done just yet.

"You ready, Jones?"

I was mute.

"Jones, you can't sleep in here."

"Then let me go home," I whispered.

"Look, you need to suck it up. You were tough enough to get your ass in here, so toughen up to stick it out. Let's go!"

I got into one of my stubborn modes. I wasn't going anywhere.

She began to walk ahead of me, and I didn't follow. She looked back at me and noticed I wasn't behind her. "Let's go, Jones!" Gina yelled.

I didn't want to break the rules. I didn't, but I wanted to go home. My heart started to race. I wanted out of this place. I was about to pull a nutty. She walked toward me, and I sat down, determined not to go anywhere. She grabbed me by the arm.

"No, get off of me!" I screamed, resisting.

She gripped me tighter. "I was trying to be nice, but you one of them feisty ones. I gotta get down and dirty with you." She forcefully lifted me to my feet.

"No, get . . . get off . . . I wanna go home. Just let me go home!"

"You need to calm down."

"No! Get off me!" I yelled, kicking in the air.

"Not until you calm down."

There was no calm muscle in my body. I tried to wild out to the point where she would let me go, but it didn't work. She gripped me tighter.

"Get off me! Let me go!"

She loosened up on her grip, and I broke free. I made a run for it, but got outside of the bathroom and ran into Alexis, another worker.

"Jones, calm down. You're not going anywhere."

I tried to break free, but it was no use. She had me on lock.

Gina ran out behind me to find me hemmed up. "Thanks, Lex."

"No problem."

Next thing you know, I was being dragged from the bathroom, down the corridor to the black hole.

They threw me inside as if I was a dirty rag. My arms were screaming. They really manhandled me. My shoulder was feeling dislocated again, and my muscles were aching. I tried to soothe the pain, by massaging it and rotating it. It was working a little, but it wasn't completely doing the job. *I need to sleep it off.*

I made my way to the twin-sized bed that had an aroma of piss. Disgusted, I tore the sheets off and just parked by the wall on the concrete floor. I balled up into a knot, lay my head in my chest, and closed my eyes, boohooing.

"Jones, you got breakfast," someone yelled.

I lifted up my head out of my lap, and my neck ached. I noticed a light shining through the door. Then a tray of food came sliding under it.

I stood to my feet quickly, and my body felt like it was about to break into pieces. Sitting still for hours in a fetal position is no joke.

"Aw! Ouch!" My back was stiff, my legs sore, and my shoulders felt like I had been carrying stacks of bricks.

I waltzed over to the tasty-smelling tray of food. I picked the tray up to examine it closer, and it looked disgusting. The scrambled eggs with cheese looked dirty, as if it had been dropped on the floor a couple of times. The toast was burnt and hard as a rock. The one strip of bacon, my last bit of hope, looked raw. I threw the tray down and walked back over to my corner, where I sat down, pissed. I was starving, but I refused to eat that food, which meant I had to wait until lunchtime.

I tried to position myself comfortably, but my body wasn't allowing it. Every way I moved, my body was crying out for relief. I couldn't take it. I had to lie down on the bed. I walked over to the dump of a bed, and the piss whiff hit me strong. I put my nose inside my shirt and lay down. That didn't alleviate the stench all the way, but at least it wasn't as strong.

I laid down for, I didn't know how long, but all I knew was, I was up now and feeling a breeze. I was shivering in place, and then I heard this loud, roaring noise. I looked up at the ceiling and noticed the vents. I looked over at the blanket on the floor that I had tossed off the bed earlier. I was hesitant about wrapping it around me, but I was cold.

I got off the bed and picked it up off the floor. The stench on this thing was unbelievable. I thought I was going to pass out. I threw the blanket back down in disgust. I lay back down on the bed and curled up into a ball, trying not to inhale. The damn bed smelled just like the blanket. I needed that blanket though. I was cold as hell. It was already bad enough that I had to deal with this shithole. And now I had to be cold.

Tears streamed from my eyes as I got off the bed, exhaling through my mouth, and grabbed the blanket. I walked back over to the bed and lay down with the blanket. I cried as I inhaled double whiffs of piss.

I woke up when I heard the door open. I knew my eyes were red because I was feeling high from all this

piss funk I was inhaling. I couldn't even smell it anymore.

I glanced at Gina walking over to me with lunch in
her hand. I sat up on the bed.

"How's it going, Jones?" she asked, examining the
room. "How was breakfast?" She laughed.

"I wasn't hungry."

"I can see that. You were nice enough to let the floor
get a taste too."

I looked down at the floor where the food was. *Yeah,
I did myself a job there.*

"You hungry now?"

I looked up at the tray of food she had in her hand,
trying to pick up an aroma, but my nose was so clogged
with piss funk, I couldn't get a whiff.

"You don't have to answer, 'cause I know you are. I
can see it in your face. I can hear your stomach barking
for bits too," she joked.

I watched as she held the tray at her waist. I glanced
at the chicken fingers and the crispy French fries on the
plate and reached out for the tray.

Gina took a step back. "Ah-ah, you know the rules.
You can't eat the second meal until you eat the first."

I looked at her puzzled. I had never heard that rule
before. In fact, I didn't even think it was a rule. I thought
she was making up her own shit now.

"Don't give me that I-didn't-know look. You need to
eat your breakfast before you can eat this lunch."

I looked down at the floor. "There's nothing to eat."

"Oh, there's something to eat. You better get on your
hands and knees and start chowing down, baby."

"I'm not about to get on my hands and knees and eat
that expired food. I'm going to stay right here and not
move a lick."

"I wasn't asking a question, I was giving an order."

Before I could say or do anything, she put the tray on the bed next to me, snatched me off of the bed by my arm, and tossed me to the floor. I landed on my ass near scraps of the scrambled eggs.

"Pick it up and eat it!"

I refused. I didn't even care about lunch now.

"You better move. Pick up them eggs and eat them."

When I didn't move, she smacked me on the back of my head, and my neck jerked forward out of control. I began to cry.

"Crying ain't gonna get you out of this. If you ever want to get out of here and have a decent meal and a decent night's sleep, then you better eat up. And I ain't got all day."

About five minutes passed, and I remained seated. I was serious. I wasn't eating anything that had made face with the floor.

Gina got down on the floor in front of me and went bananas. She grabbed me by my hair, picked up the eggs, and shoved them in my mouth. I resisted as she kept trying to push loads of dirty eggs in my mouth. The bit that slipped in made me gag. Then it was vomit time.

As soon as the vomit fell, Gina pulled her hand back, let my hair go, and jumped to her feet. I stayed on my knees, coughing, feeling choked up.

Gina, all huffy and puffy, grabbed my good-looking lunch and tossed it to the floor. "Clean all this shit up! And if it ain't cleaned up in time for dinner, then you better get real used to this place," she yelled, walking out the door.

I propped down on my butt and just sat there crying.

The door opened back up, and Gina wheeled in a mop and bucket. "And all that food better be gone when I come back in here. I don't mean mopped up either. If I see any food inside that water, you best believe that dinner will be out of the question. Oh yeah, and it will be another night in this shithole too."

This is some bull. I'll be damned if I'm going to eat any bit of it. Wait, let me think about this again. I do want to get out of here. And she did seem pretty clear about it having to be cleaned up. I gotta do what I gotta do.

I cried and gagged as I went from spot to spot eating the food off the floor. I didn't vomit again, which was a good thing. Once I was done though, it was all she wrote. In a matter of minutes, chunks of food came hurling up. It splashed inside of the bucket.

Gina came in just in time to see me in action. She smiled then grabbed a hold of the bucket. "Let's go, Jones. You're out of here."

I can't be out just like that? She didn't even check to see if I did what I was told. I'm mad at that. I tortured myself for nothing. What the hell?

I walked toward the door, wiping the corners of my mouth with my T-shirt. I was too ready for a shower and a mouth scrub. *Forget a meal. I wanna wash my ass.*

"Go straight to the mess hall."

"Can I shower first?"

Gina stared me down without answering.

I glanced at her and put my head down, knowing exactly what that look meant. I got to the mess hall, walked in, and all eyes were on me. I noticed everyone had been well into their meals, but I swear, forks went down when I walked in.

I ignored the stares and proceeded to get my food. I filled my plate with the remaining leftovers. I wasn't too hungry, but I needed to put a little something in my stomach. I slid my tray off the counter and turned around to a crowd of girls, who all looked like they had hate in their eyes for me.

I hesitantly walked down the aisle between the tables looking for a seat. There were a few seats available but not any that I had cause to sit at. I stood for a moment scoping out a seat, and then, just like that, dinner was over.

I made eye contact with one of the staff, who walked over to me.

"I know you just walked in," she said. "But dinner is over. I'll give you five minutes to eat. Hurry up."

I took the seat closest to me and picked at the burnt garlic bread, the dry, rubber chicken, and the sticky, overcooked rice. When I couldn't take any more of just staring at my plate, I threw it away and proceeded to the bunk area.

I gathered my things, preparing for a nice, cool shower. And, of course, falling asleep came with no sweat.

Tameka and her crew were out of the hole too, but I had no reason to be scared. The facility put a night guard on duty to sit in the bunk area, so no one had a chance to do anything.

My days at the center didn't get any better. If one group of girls wasn't tryin'a jump me, then another crew was. Their excuse was, I had an "eye problem." *They're my eyes, and I can stare at whoever I want.* I didn't think there was any harm in that.

I made little to no friends. I wasn't really trying to become acquainted with anyone anyway. Their attitudes were wishy-washy, and I was good with the fakeness. I mean, I taunted them sometimes, and they tried their hardest to get at me. I ain't gonna front, most of the time they succeeded. It got so bad that staff had to alternate patrolling near my bed to make sure no one came near me.

I was handling mine though, but when you got five overgrown females jumping on you, it's not so easy. These girls were ruthless, and I was getting tired of having to protect myself, especially since the damn staff weren't doing all they could. Forget guarding my bed at night. How about during the day when everyone, especially Tameka, wanted to beat me?

I did run away a couple of times, but every time I managed to escape, I got caught. And each time they dragged my stupid behind right back to the hole. Shoot, I saw the hole so much, it became my new get-away spot. I mean, I wasn't able to write, play games, or what have you, but I was able to be alone. And I was starting to be more at peace with my situation being in the hole. I didn't have to worry about anyone bothering me, I didn't have to wake up early to do clean up, and my days in this hellhole will go by quicker. All I had to do was keep getting in trouble.

I woke up the next morning ready to execute my plan. We were doing our morning run, and I had my eye on Cindy. I was about to make her fall to her face. I waited for her to get closer to me, and I stuck my leg out.

Bam!

She fell on her face, and I kicked her while she was down. She didn't even fight back. What a waste!

A worker intervened and hemmed me up. She brought me straight to the hole.

See, this is a piece of cake. I go inside and uncomfortably fell asleep.

"Hey, hey, Miss Jones, wake up. Your hour is up."

I hold my head up. "My hour?"

"Yeah, your hour. We're being nice today."

They picked a fine time to be nice. Dang! Now I have to do something else to stay in the joint? I got up as if I was following instructions and spat in the worker's face.

She hauled off and smacked me.

Damn! That stung like a bitch!

The worker then hemmed me up and threw me into the wall. "Ain't no being nice to you. Good luck!"

I watched her as she walked out. Now I was good, and it was back to sleep.

I was laid up in the hole for three days straight. My body was stiff. My stomach was growling, as I didn't bother to eat any meals served. And I needed a shower badly, but believe it or not, I was contented with being funky because no one bothered me. I can't express enough how much I was at peace. I didn't feel the need to want to hurt anyone.

But I was supposed to be on a mission. *No, this can't be happening. Being in the hole is making me feel like there is no outside world, as if I'm all alone. How 'bout that? I don't need to hurt anyone because no one's hurting me. There is a God.*

I smiled, deep in thought, while the doors to the dungeon opened. Gina walked in. I knew that meant it was time to leave.

"Can I just stay in here?"

Gina closed the door behind her. "What person in their right mind would want to stay in here after already being in here for three days?"

"Me."

"Ooh, I get it. You don't wanna be bothered. You think if you keep it low-profile in here all day and night that you can't be touched. The staff can't bother you, the girls won't be at you, and you won't have to get up early and participate in activities. Huh, I got your number."

"No, I just like being by myself."

"Oh, do you?"

"Yeah."

"We'll see about that."

"I find peace here," I whispered.

"This is not a place for peace. It's a place of discipline for knuckleheads like you."

"Well, I like it."

"Hmm, I'm sure you do," Gina said as she caresses my face. "I'm on to you, Desire. You ain't fooling nobody. You think you gonna miss out on getting up early, cleaning, and running by sitting in here running your time down. Huh, clever, but I'm on to you."

I grew timid, feeling a bit violated in my comfort zone.

"Play your game. You'll learn sooner or later. Come on, let's go. You got seven minutes to shower."

I made my way to the shower, and the entire time Gina watched me. I felt uncomfortable, but I had no other choice. I had to do the do in front of the boss.

Once I was finished, I was ushered to my bed. After I threw on some clothes, Gina ushered me out of the room to separate sleeping quarters. The room was filled with spare beds, a bookshelf, and wooden cabins.

"You'll be sleeping in here alone tonight," she said.

Not really caring as long as I was alone, I went along with it. I lay down on my back and closed my eyes.

Deep into a sleep, I feel myself being carried. I opened to discover I was being carried by three people. I couldn't see well, but from what I heard, I knew Gina was one of them. Then they just dropped me on the floor like a hot potato, and my elbow slammed into the cement floor. "Ow!"

"Yeah, that's just the beginning of your love for the hole," Gina yelled.

As my vision improved, I spotted three unknown women with Gina. They rushed over to me, scooped me up by my arms and legs, and threw me up on the bed.

"Hold that bitch down."

I struggled to get loose. "Get off me!" I cried, fearing for my life.

"Nah, nah. Ain't this where you wanna be, baby girl? Huh? Didn't you say you like it here? Your exact words were 'I find peace here.' Ain't that right, shawty? I'm just tryin'a spice it up for you." Gina pulled a knife out of her pocket.

Noticing the blade, my face lit up, and I screamed.

"Hey, shut that noise up! Cover her mouth. Here, take this. I don't wanna hear that shit." Gina took off one of her socks, and one of the girls jammed it in my mouth, causing me to gag. "You scared, baby girl? Aw-www, don't be scared. I'm just going to proceed with cutting your clothes off."

"Mmmmm! Mmmmm!"

One of the girls laughed. "Damn! She still tryin'-a be heard."

Gina began to cut my shirt off. "Hope I don't slice a nipple," she joked.

I cried, scared for my life, while Gina cut until she could cut no more. Then she ripped the rest of my clothes off, leaving me naked.

"Oh, look at that body," she chanted. "I'm ready to get me some."

I panicked and began to fight harder, but the harder I fought, the more energy I lost. I cried, helpless, as Gina fondled me.

She even went so far as to take off her own pants and underwear, jump on top of the twin-sized bed with her legs spread open, and rub her genitals in my face. "Take that, take that, yeah, yeah!"

I moved my head from side to side, trying to avoid coming in contact with Gina's raunchy-smelling private parts.

"Keep this bitch's head still!" she commanded.

One girl let go of one of my legs, while the other took over both.

Tracey grabbed a hold of my face and positioned it still by gripping my jaws. I cried hysterically while Gina sat her coochie in my face.

"Y'all ready for the magic trick?" she said.

"Yeah," they all answered in unison.

I wondered what the hell the magic trick was, and lo and behold, Gina shoved a bottle with a condom on it into my vagina.

I screamed for dear life with no one to hear my cry.

The gang rape went on for about another twenty minutes, but it seemed like forever. Each girl took turns rubbing their privates against mine. I thought I was on the verge of dying. I lost control of myself, and after an endless struggle, I fell into a daze, damn near passing out.

"Desire, ooh, Desire," Gina called pleasantly. "Desire."

She got no answer.

"Desire!" she yelled, slapping me.

"She dead?" Tracey asked.

"I don't know."

"Desire, Desire!" Gina screamed. "Oh shit!"

"What? What?"

"She's bleeding."

"Damn! What are we going to do?"

"Let's dump her outside."

"And then do what?"

"Get her in the morning and make it seem like she ran away or something. I don't know. Just help me get her up."

"Wait. How we gonna take her out? Ms. Tanner is guarding tonight, and you ain't even supposed to be in the building, Gina," Sheila said.

"I know. I know. Shit. Okay, wait, I'm thinking. I'm thinking."

"Well, hurry up. Shit!"

"You the third head bitch in charge. You should be thinking too," Gina told Sheila.

"Let's all just put our heads together," Alex suggested.

"I got an idea," Gina announced. "Just gimme a second."

"Ah, Gina," Tracey called out.

"What? What? I'm tryin'a get it together here."

Tracey told her, "I think we have a bigger problem."

"What?"

"I think she's dead. I don't feel a pulse."

Chapter 27

I tried to open my eyes, but I couldn't. I saw nothing but darkness from the back of my eyelids. How can a female be raped by another female? I didn't think it was possible. Being hit by my aunt or even being teased by the kids at school couldn't compare to the abuse I had just endured.

I woke up to find myself fully clothed on a nice, neatly made up twin bed, the same bed I had originally started my night in. I looked around and noticed I was alone. I lay there with blank patches in my mind as to how I got back in this room, and wondered if I had ever left. Since I had been barely conscious, I couldn't remember much of what happened after being raped. I closed my eyes and instantly got a flashback of being held down against my will. *Am I dreaming?*

I sat up slowly, trying to come to my senses, and wanted to scream. My entire body was aching as if I had lifted weights three times my own. I wasn't dreaming. Something did happen to me. I moved to put my feet on the floor, and my vagina throbbed. I felt myself down there, and instantly another flashback hit me. I was gang-raped by four women, four grown-ass women.

I sat there in a daze again, and tears flowed down my cheeks. *Why is this happening to me?* Oh, the pain! *I don't deserve this*. I cried even harder, catching more flashbacks.

Suddenly, I lost it and became hysterical. My legs started shaking, and my mouth quivered. Then I stood up and continuously pounded my fist on the bed. I started ransacking the room, tearing the sheets off and kicking the bed. It was like my pain just disappeared, because I couldn't feel it. It was gone, hopefully never to return. Then instantly it did.

She walked in the door, the Tracey girl. I remembered her, but by the look on her face, she thought I didn't. Oh, I remembered her, and I saw the images very clearly now.

I held my head in the palm of my hand. "No, no! Go away! Go away! Nooooooo! Stoppppppppppp!" I yelled, seeing vivid pictures of that night's vile episode.

Tracey came over to me and snatched me up by the arms. "Calm down, kid!"

Her touch was evil. She triggered something inside of me, and I went haywire on her.

"Hey, hey, we got a loose one in here," Tracey yelled, unable to restrain me.

The security guard along with Gina and other staff rushed in.

"Take her out. Take her to the hole."

When I heard *hole*, I went berserk. I kicked, scratched, spat, and punched. The hole was a place of bad memories. Memories I wanted to forget and leave behind.

"I ain't going to that place. No, not anymore. I hate you! I hate you, Gina!"

The director, Ms. Tanner, rushed in to the call for help.

"Get these fuckers off of me! I don't want to go back in that place. She'll do it again. I know she will."

Tracey tried to cover my mouth to prevent me from talking, but I bit the hell out of her palm.

"Wait, hold on here. Hold on just a minute," Ms. Tanner said.

Tracey tried to keep a hold on me while the other staff listened to Ms. Tanner's command.

"Tracey, did you hear me? I said cool it."

Tracey released her grip on me, and I hit the floor.

Ms. Tanner bent down to my level with a concerned look on her face. "Please remain calm. We are not here to hurt you."

I stared at this lady like she was crazy. I wanted to say, "Too late," but I couldn't get the words out. I just lost energy instantly. My mouth wouldn't move, my voice wouldn't speak, and my body said it didn't want me to fight anymore.

"Are you all right?"

I didn't answer. I sat on my ass like a mental patient medicated with a sedative, staring at the floor.

"That's fine. You don't have to talk. Here, let me help you up."

I let her assist me to my feet.

Tracey watched with an evil warning stare. "You want me to take her now?" Tracey persisted.

"No, no. Go ahead and attend to the cafeteria. I got this."

Ms. Tanner took me to her office and ordered lunch for the both of us. She ordered me some slammin' whole fried chicken wings, onion rings, and French fries. I was in heaven with this meal. I chomped it down like a junkie getting a quick fix after being sober for two years. She watched me as I ate. I had no shame in my game. I was hungry, and furthermore, it kept my mind off the terrible abuse I'd suffered.

"You are very hungry, I see."

"Mmm-hmm," I answered, unable to talk with a full mouth.

"Well, eat up. That's what it's here for."

I nodded in agreement.

"While I have you in a good mood, I'm going to talk to you, ask you a few questions."

I slowed down with the eating, and my face grew weary.

"No, please continue eating. I'm only here to help you. For now, I'll ask yes or no questions. If you don't feel like answering the questions, you can just ignore me and say nothing."

"Your full name is Desire Jones, correct?"

I nodded my head up and down.

"You will be turning sixteen years old soon, correct?"

Having forgotten my age, I had to think about it, then acknowledged by nodding my head again.

"Do you have many friends here?"

I shook my head no.

"Do you like it here?"

Again, I shook my head from side to side and stopped eating. I froze for a moment knowing these questions were leading to an event I wanted to forget. I no longer had the urge to pig out, and my hunger pangs came to an end.

"No need to stop enjoying your meal. Eat up."

I ignored her comment and wiped my greasy hands on a napkin.

"Have you ever gotten into a fight here before?"

I nodded my head yes.

"Have you ever started a fight before?"

Again, I nodded my head yes.

"Are there any people here you want to be friends with?"

Unsure, I shrugged my shoulders.

"Do you get along with the staff here?"

I ignored the question.

"Are you on medication?"

I shook my head no.

"Do you like the staff?"

I began to tremble, and my eyes teared up. I thought about it again. The pain struck me all over.

"Desire, what is it?"

I closed my eyes and wished the memory would go away.

"Desire, please talk to me."

I wanted to do what she asked, but I couldn't bring myself to talk about it. Then, when I opened my eyes, I saw Gina. I jumped back in my chair, and it tilted backwards.

"Desire, oh!" Ms. Tanner yelled as she tried to save me from falling backwards in the chair.

I hit the floor, fell on my elbow, and just lay there for a second in pain.

"Desire, are you all right? Oh goodness!" Ms. Tanner lifted me to my feet.

"Ow! Ouch!"

"What? What's wrong?" Ms. Tanner brought me to my feet and sat me back in the chair. "Your arm hurts too?"

Before I could answer, she rolled up my sleeve. She noticed the rings around my wrists. She examined my other arm and noticed the same thing.

"What is this from? Did somebody—"

"Ms. Tanner, yo, they need you. Lisa said two girls ran away," Tracey blurted out, bursting into the office.

"Okay, but I'd appreciate it if you knock on my door and not just barge in."

"Sorry, it was an emergency."

"Indeed it is, but you still need to knock. I'll be with you all in a moment."

Tracey stood there and stared at me for a good five seconds before she walked out.

"Excuse me, Desire. I'm sorry for the interruption. Did somebody—"

"Gina did it."

"Gina . . . Gina from here?"

I nodded my head up and down.

"Okay, Desire, now I have had situations where people were accidentally mishandled, or even roughed up more than they should have been, but that's it, nothing more than that. Furthermore, no one here has ever lied to me."

I put my head down.

"She picked me up in the middle of the night, she took all my clothes off, and she touched me while she had the other people hold me down." I stopped and wiped my tears, wanting to get it all out. I was not going to be made out a liar.

"It's okay. Take your time."

I replayed the scene from beginning to end in my mind, but giving full details was just too painful. I just wished she could see the picture in my mind.

"Gina raped me. They all raped me. And Tracey was one. She helped."

"Desire, now, understand what you're saying to me. This is serious."

"I understand clearly," I shouted, finally finding my voice.

"They tortured me. They put their stuff in my face, and they put a sock in my mouth. I was on that nasty bed in the hole, and when they cut my clothes off, I thought I was—"

There was a knock at the door.

"Stop. It's okay. You don't have to tell me any more."

I sat there, both hands covering my face, catching every tear that fell. "I want to go home. Anywhere but here. This place is . . . I hate it here."

"Desire, I can only imagine how you feel right now. And no, of course this place is not supposed to be Disney World, but it shouldn't be the combat zone either. I need to look into this right now. I want you to remain here in my office for a while. Feel free to get acquainted with the couch over there. I need to run out for a second, but I'll be back. I will be locking my office, so if someone knocks, don't worry. They'll just go away. I'm the only one with a key, so if you hear the door opening, don't be startled. It will only be me."

"Okay."

"Are you going to be all right?"

"Yes," I answered sadly.

"Fine. I'll be back in a bit. And, just to let you know, I don't usually let detainees stay in my office, but I sympathize with you. Try to get some rest."

After she walked out of the door, I wasted no time getting comfortable on the sofa. There was a blanket and pillow there waiting too. I stretched out on my back and stared at the ceiling. I couldn't believe I had just told the director what had happened to me. What was going to happen to me now that I'd dimed out Tracey and Gina?

Fear set in, and tears rolled from the corners of my eyes. I closed my eyes, and vivid pictures appeared. This time it wasn't Gina's face, but Jay's, Jen's brother. I grabbed a hold of my private area and tossed and turned while seeing his face. I could feel him breathing on me. Then I got a whiff of Gina's polluted-smelling coochie.

I sat up, beating my head, trying to get the thought out of my mind, but I couldn't. I fell to my knees and prayed for a new brain, a new vision, and a new me. Then *poof!* and the memory was gone. Just like that.

I sat there repositioning myself to sit on my butt with my back against the couch. I laid my head back and dozed off right there.

"Sleeping your life away?" someone yelled.

I woke up as I felt a pillow hit my face. I lifted my head to an upright position and saw Tracey and Ms. Tanner standing in front of me. Something didn't feel right.

"I don't like liars, Miss Jones, and I don't like you because you're a liar."

I looked at Ms. Tanner like she had lost her mind.

"How dare you lie to my face about something so explicit and raw? Mmm-hmm, I investigated your so-called rape."

I looked at Tracey, who had a smirk on her face.

"I believed that you were raped, bruised up, and mistreated by my staff, but before I jumped the gun, Tracey informed me that you're one of our frequent self-destructors. You tend to abuse yourself and blame other people."

I looked at her confused.

"It's all in your file. I don't know how I missed it. Frankly, it doesn't matter at this point because I know now, and that's that. Get your things. Tracey will escort you out. It's up to her what disciplinary action will be taken."

I sat there not able to move, trying to understand what the hell she was talking about. *My file? Self-destruction?*

"Oh, and by the way, Gina was off last night. Funny how she was a part of your lie too."

An alarm rang in my head. I shook my head no. "No, no. What are you talking about?"

As Tracey neared me, I said, "And, you, don't touch me! Get away from me!"

"I dictate, and you take the orders." Tracey reached for my arm.

Ms. Tanner stopped her. "Wait a minute. Let her talk."

"Ms. Tanner, it would be a waste of time. She's a—"

"Let her talk."

I sat there. I didn't really have anything to say. Well, I did, but I didn't think it would've made a difference. I was in a "lose-lose" situation here. Tracey had filled this lady's mind with all kinds of lies, and now she didn't believe me. No one ever believed me. *They got me! I'm trapped in this muthafucka.*

"I'm giving you the floor. Speak."

They both stood, staring at me, and I said nothing. My mouth formed no words whatsoever. I was speechless. My lips were stapled shut. There was no need for me to beg, plead, or ramble on with any of that "help me, help me" garbage. I had to face the facts. Their shit was planned, and planned well. All I was left with was a swollen pussy, a gruesome memory, and more time in lockup.

"Tracey, she's all yours."

I didn't even put up a fight. I went with the flow of things.

Tracey didn't utter a word to me either as she took me to the regular bunk area. Her silence scared me though.

"Eat your dinner right there and then lights out."

I looked over at my bed, and there was what looked like a frozen dinner waiting for me. The tray was filled with a quarter-sized Salisbury steak, potatoes, and sweet peas. I removed the plastic covering and jammed the plastic fork into the Salisbury steak, and the damn thing was half frozen. *Is this supposed to be a joke?*

I tossed the half-microwaved frozen dinner in the garbage and lay down on my bed. Not before long, the rest of the detention center girls entered in silence. They shuffled to their beds to get their last-minute whatever in before lights out. Everyone was present too. Not one person was in the hole. Something was definitely wrong with this picture.

Enemies were amongst one another like cat and mouse. Lights went out, bedtime set in, and I lay awake in the dark alert. My fear increasingly heightened as I lay motionless, unable to close my eyes. I sat up in my bed and just stared into the pitch-black darkness.

In the wee hours of the morning, I heard movement. I listened harder, and the noise seemed like it was getting closer.

Before you know it, I was hemmed up by Tameka, who had a knife to my throat. "You gonna die tonight, bitch!"

For some reason now, I was unafraid. In no way did I fear for my life, which was weird. The reason I didn't go to sleep in the first place was because I was scared shitless, but now this bitch had a knife to my throat and I was fearless.

"You hear me? You gonna die tonight. Shine the light on her."

Someone flicked up some flames from a torch-lighter, and Tracey's face appeared.

I thought, *I'm tired of this bitch. I know this is all her doing.*

"A'ight, you got the green light. Get yours."

"Yeah, go ahead. Slice my throat. Make sure you cut deep too. I want blood to be everywhere."

Tameka loosened up her grip on my neck. "What? I mean, yeah, I'm slicing from left to right."

"I'm ready when you are," I announced.

As Tameka pushed the knife into my skin, the lights shot on. She quickly dropped the blade, and it landed on my bed.

Ms. Tanner appeared, and Tracey, out of nowhere, bum-rushed Tameka, saying, "Hey, I need help over here."

Ms. Tanner quickly radioed for security, and I sat there as if nothing was happening while Tameka and Tracey tussled.

Tameka was wilding out. "No! Let me at her. I want that bitch. Let me at her. You said I can get her."

Security rushed in and ushered Tameka out.

Ms. Tanner walked over to me as I lay down. Before she could get a word out, I said, "I'm good."

"Did she—"

"I'm good. Ain't nothing happen."

I laughed inside as she walked away. That old scaredy Desire was out the door. Being fearless meant I was back. That was what that feeling of being unafraid was about. Oh, and make no mistake, I was back on the grind. I had some blood I wanted to give away. *Ha, ha, ha!*

Chapter 28

My time got extended for the trouble I had gotten into, so I had to deal with this place for the whole damn summer.

The whimpering, hollering, scared-of-life Desire was no more. I needed to fuck. Yeah, that's right. I needed to give away this virus I was carrying. Being in here should not have made me lose my edge. Damn! I was mad I let that happen. It was only going to take me a couple of days though to come up with something.

At night, I thought about what I could do to get me back in the groove of things. I knew, for one, that I needed to get that bitch Tameka back for sure 'cause I'd had it up to here with her and her two disciples. Two, I had to weigh the option of risking sneaking out, hitting the corner, and getting with people against linking up with the night guards. I didn't know how easy either was going to be. Then there was the complex problem of passing this shit to these females in here, 'cause I wanted to get at them too.

But my first priority was Tameka.

I had a weapon at reach, so that was a start. Yeah, I forgot to mention that when she'd dropped her knife on my bed, I'd scooped it up and stashed it before anybody could think about retrieving it. To cover her own ass, Tracey had lied, saying Tameka didn't have a weapon, but after Tameka had bragged about almost slicing my throat, Ms. Tanner came looking for the weapon. I told her Tracey must have taken it, because all I did was feel it leave my neck, and that was it. She took my word for it and then tried to apologize to me about the incident, but I brushed her off, so she could keep it moving. I didn't need her in my face trying check up on me while I was trying to do me.

It was a new morning, and I was ready to get at Tameka. My plan was to get her at breakfast time. I reached underneath my mattress for the hidden blade. I became startled when I heard my name being called along with some other girls' over the loudspeaker. I left the blade in its hiding place and went to see why I was being called out.

"If you have just heard your name, please report to Ms. Tanner's office."

"What?"

"There is no question about what I said. You heard me," one of the staff said.

One of the other staff escorted us to Ms. Tanner's office. There were seven of us. I guess we were all in trouble. Why? I had no clue.

We reached her office and saw a table outside of it with donuts and bagels.

"Help yourself, ladies, to anything you see on the table then kindly take a seat in my office."

These hungry bitches ran to the table before she could even get the full sentence out. Me, I wasn't up for a donut express meal. I made my way to the room and sat and waited to see what bullshit was about to go down now. The scavengers came in with plates filled to the ceiling with different kinds of donuts and shit, with Ms. Tanner behind them.

"Please take a seat anywhere—the floor, the couch, or the rug."

Everyone pretty much sat wherever.

"I know you're all wondering why you're here. You're not in trouble or anything, so you can set your minds at ease."

A collective sigh of relief went around the room.

"Wow! That took a load off, huh?" Ms. Tanner joked.

A few girls laughed.

"But on a serious note, this meeting, which I'd like to call 'a session,' can either be harmful or helpful. You make the choice. I'm asking for everyone's coopera- tion. Today, I have low tolerance for the silent treat- ment, and that means I'm going to ask you some ques- tions that require answers."

I thought to myself, *Here we go again with the question-and-answer gig.*

"There are different cliques here that don't like each other, individuals that don't like each other, and groups of people who don't like a particular person. I'm going to ask everyone individually who they have, as you all call it, beef with. I want an honest response, and I want a reason why. If you can't give a reason why, then keep the name to yourself. I'm going to start from left to right. Please give your last name, the first name of the person you have an issue with, and the reason you have an issue with them. And please don't be afraid to say someone who is in this very room. That's what this mediation session is all about. This disliking each other for whatever reasons has to stop, because there WILL be no blood on these floors."

I looked around the room to see if I had beef with anybody. Although I didn't care for anyone of these girls, and I was sure they didn't care for me, I had no beef with any one of them.

"We'll start with you first, Desire."

I knew she was going to put me on the spot. *Dang! I wanted to hear what the other girls had to say first.* "I don't—"

"Last name please."

"Jones, and I don't have a valid reason."

"Does that mean there is someone, but you don't know why you have a problem?"

"I guess."

"Understandable. Next."

"I'm Holmes, and I have a problem with that bitch Ta—"

"No swearing, please."

"Okay. I have a problem with the broad Tameka."

Everyone giggled.

Ms. Tanner just shook her head. "What's your reason?"

"Before I got locked up, she and this other girl jumped my cousin Nikki, and I wasn't feelin' dat."

"Good. Next."

"Amesbury, and I, hmmmm, I don't know. I don't wanna say."

"Is the person in this room?"

She put her head down. "Yeah."

"Speak your mind then. It's all right. Nothing violent can go down in this room."

"Okay, whatever. I got a problem with Desire."

I looked up, shocked. I had forgotten all about Cindy.

"And why?"

"She jumped on me for no reason when we were running one morning."

"Understandable. Next."

Ms. Tanner went down the line and concluded that I was one person's problem and Tameka was everyone else's. I knew Tameka had enemies, but I didn't think almost everyone was an enemy of hers.

"Ladies, I thank you for your honesty, and we are now one step ahead in a positive direction. Everyone seems to have a problem with the biggest troublemaker we have in here. The question now is, How do we resolve that?"

"Kick her out," I blurted.

"Ha! Good answer but not an option."

Another girl followed up with, "Why not?"

"Because it doesn't work like that around here. Think about it. Why is each of you here? Because you did something wrong, and being here is supposed to be punishment."

"And it sure is. I hate this place," Cindy blurted.

We all laughed.

"That's good. You're not supposed to like it. I don't want you back here after your first visit either. One should be enough. You get in and get out, but while you are here, you have to learn to get along with each other, no matter what the circumstances. In here, you are sisters, you are a family, and family sticks together. I know you're not sisters by blood, but you should be by bond. This bickering and fighting because of the . . . "

I blanked out from the conversation and fell into "mission mode." I had solved the riddle that long awaited a solution. I knew just how to pass out this virus to these bitches in here. *Damn, I love Ms. Tanner!*

When the meeting was over, I began my rounds of talking to Tameka's enemies. To get Cindy on the team too, I apologized to her.

"Yo, Desire, you said it right when you said that bitch needed to be out of here. There's mad girls in here that want to get at her."

"Not as bad as me," I answered.

"Nah, not as bad as me," Aja cut in.

"No, no," Malika Holmes said. "Nobody wants her like I do."

"Shit. Enough of us don't like her. Let's just get together and stick the bitch."

"I'm *d*," Malika said. "She jumped my cousin anyway. She needs to get hers."

"Let's do what it do," Aja added.

Everyone else gave the go-ahead of being down, while I remained silent.

"Desire, you down?"

"I don't know. How I know y'all ain't gonna turn on me and shit?"

"Nah, I'm with this. I want her," Cindy assured.

Everyone else gave head gestures of feeling the same way.

"We need to do some type of promise or something."

"Let's do pinky-swear," this girl Kristen said.

"Nah. Y'all ever hear of blood sisters?"

"Hell yeah! Me and my best friends used to do it all the time," Aja said.

"Well, that's how we all in. We gotta become blood sisters. I already got a plan for Tameka, and I got the steel too."

"You're already packing?"

"We haven't sworn in yet," I said. "Chill out."

Cindy asked, "So we gotta cut ourselves or something, right?"

"You down or what?" I was trying to avoid questions altogether.

"I'm *d*. Anything to get at Tameka."

"A'ight then. In the morning on the field, during our break, we'll meet up."

"Cool," everyone responded in unison.

The initiation process was a success. I brought my blade to the track, and everybody, every single one of them bitches, sliced their thumb, and we swapped blood. It was a beautiful thing. Everyone came up to me and pressed their thumbs against mine. Then we sucked the blood off in unison as we chanted the words, "Blood sisters for life."

We came up with an exclusive name for our crew and a secret handshake, like the fraternities have. It was sweet. I had these chicks. I had 'em right where I wanted, with a plan to keep 'em coming. We were to repeat initiation at least once a week. This way I knew the blood was really getting into their streams, giving them the virus. I planned to infect every girl I can.

It was one task down and one more to go.

Next on the list was Tameka. Me and the girls came up with a plan on how to get at her. She hadn't really been at any of us in a few days, since we looked like we were ten strong. She and her girls kept giving me the eye, letting it be known that they still wanted a piece of me. It was all good. I had something for that ass.

I had the knife strapped to my waist, armed and ready for battle. My girls gave me the heads-up when Tameka and her crew were coming in my direction.

I got my cereal and started walking to my seat, making sure to cross her path. I knew they would try to fuck with me, which was why I made it a point to put myself in their presence. She did just as I expected her to.

Big bad Tameka and her girls pushed past me, making my tray of food fall to the floor. One of my girls stood up, and while I discretely pulled my blade out, she pushed her way through Tameka's girls as I simultaneously grabbed Tameka by the arm. She flung my hand away, and I swung toward her stomach with the blade in my hand. She jumped back and Torrey, one of her girls, jumped toward the blade, and it sliced her on the arm.

Then Ginger tried to snatch the blade from me and ended up slicing her hand.

Tameka tried the same move, but I let her take it as I quickly pushed away from her, and Malika knocked her to the floor.

By now, a crowd had formed.

A staff person came over, pushing through the crowd of girls hovering over us. She attempted to break up the rumble but couldn't get a grip on anyone as multiple people, mostly my girls, were taking cheap shots at Tameka and her followers.

It ended quickly though, when backup arrived. And I'll be damned! I succeeded in my plan. Tameka was caught red-handed with the blade, and she was the one that caught hell.

"She was tryin'a stab me," I yelled as one of the staff members held me back.

"Fuck you, bitch!" Tameka tossed the blade to the floor. "You had this fucking blade."

Security guard Sharon wagged a finger at Tameka. "Watch your mouth."

"Fuck you, play cop! I ain't going down for her."

I just stood there not saying anything. My girls started butting in, saying Tameka had the knife and they were just trying to break up the commotion.

Sharon jumped on top of Tameka while she was still on the ground and twisted her arm behind her back. "Did you say something to me?"

"Get the fuck off of me!"

I stood there watching; laughing inside, a smirk on my face.

"Something funny, Ms. Jones?" Miss Tanner said out of nowhere.

I didn't answer.

"I didn't think so! What the hell happened here?" She noticed Tameka on the ground. "Get her out of here," she commanded.

"What? I didn't do nothing. She came at me. That bitch came at me!"

"No, you were bothering her," one of my girls yelled out.

Sharon lifted Tameka to her feet and began escorting her out.

"This is—what the fuck! I ain't coming back here! I'm tired of this place! I didn't do shit! I'ma get you, bitch! You hear me? I'ma get you good!"

Tameka didn't put fear in my heart. If her girls weren't standing right here, all cut up might I add, she would not be talking that shit.

"I'm not gonna even entertain stories right now. Get these ladies out. Breakfast is over. Tameka's a goner. Ginger, you need to see the nurse and then see the hole. You too, Torrey. The rest of you girls, move it out. The show is over."

"She started it," Ginger yelled as we all shuffled out of the way.

"Yeah, and I'm finishing it." Ms. Tanner smirked.

To my relief, it was *adiós*, Tameka, and hello freedom. She was kicked out of the detention center for good. No doubt she cursed me saying I was going to get mine, but I wasn't worried. By the time she tries to come back here, I will be long gone. I only had three more weeks left in this joint, and I could care less about Tameka.

I was on to my next task—sexing. I had a chance to continue my mission. With the help of my girls, I was able to sneak out on a regular basis. On their end, I was hooking them up with Vicodin. Yeah, I had Jen make a

few phone calls for me, and we got a little street pharmacy going here. I got the girls hooked on it too. They
were doing anything for me and still pressing thumbs.

Along with the sneaking out, I was, of course, hooking up with any dudes on the block, from wherever.
Inside the center, I was building up a relationship with
the security guard. He would be a guaranteed help for
looking out when I snuck out, and I could give him a
taste to make him keep quiet.

I waltzed pass the security station every day around
5:00 P.M. when the shifts changed. I had my eye on this
dude Jerry. He wasn't a hot shot, but he had the goods
to become a victim. I knew I could get him easy. He had
that I-wanna-piece-of-young-meat look in his eyes.

"Hey, Jerry!"

"What's going on?"

"You."

"Oh yeah!"

"Yeah. You look good in that security uniform."

"Girl, you better watch yourself."

"Why? You gonna tell on me?"

"Nah, I ain't no snitch."

"How old are you?"

"Too old for you!"

"Age ain't nothin' but a number."

"Not to the law!"

"I thought you said you ain't no snitch."

"I ain't, but I don't mess with minors either."

"Hmmm. Who said I was tryin'a mess with you?"

"Okay, continue your route, young'un."

He nudged me off, and I laughed as I walked away
swaying my apple-bottom booty from left to right. I
turned around to see if he was watching and he was. He
knew he wanted this. Their eyes never lie. The booty
gets them every time.

Jerry may have said I was a young'un, but guess what young pussy he was tearing up? Desire's. Almost every other night he wanted some.

At first, he wanted to use condoms, and I refused, saying I was on the shot, but he still wouldn't let up. So he got his way.

But not for long. I guess it was so good to him, he wanted to raw-dog it. And, by golly, wow! He got what he wanted. We had a little barter going on too. Every time I gave him some, he would let me go out at night for a few.

I was mainly meeting up with dudes, sexing them after we drank and puffed on some trees. I was continuing my mission as planned. I had to have had sex with about forty guys this summer, and no telling who they slept with. I was doing the damn thing accomplishing my goal. I was getting out of this place in about a week, and the number was definitely going to multiply.

The night before my departure, me and Jerry planned to meet up and get our last groove on. I met him downstairs on the late night in the basement. This time he had his brother with him. It was his first night on the job. Jerry thought I was going to pull a fit about his brother tagging along, but of course I didn't. The more, the merrier.

I got down and dirty with both of them, and while his brother Andrew was taking his turn, the supervisor Diane walked in on us. She was the fill-in for Ms. Tanner, who was on vacation. I was in some deep shit now.

I fumbled to put my clothes on and ran up the stairs.

"What the hell were you doing down there?"

I stood there unresponsive. What did she expect me to say—having sex? Duh, she saw me.

"Do you know you just violated all ethical codes, rules, and regulations?"

Andrew walked up the stairs as she said this.

"And, you, your shift is complete for the night. Report to my office first thing in the morning for a termination hearing. Where's Jerry?"

Luckily Jerry had gone to the bathroom. He was saved. She had no clue he was in on it.

"Come to my office now, Desire."

I walked to Diane's office as if I was on stilts. I knew I was going home tomorrow and there was nothing she could do to me, but in the back of my mind I was thinking maybe she could prolong my stay.

"Sit your ass down right there. I am so disgusted at what I just saw."

She pulled out my file.

"Oh, I see. You're going home tomorrow, and you thought you could get away with anything, huh. Sorry, baby, it doesn't work like that around here. I'm a tough one to come by, especially when a young lady like you is doing something so disrespectful like this. It's not only disrespectful to me, but it's disrespectful to you and your body."

She had to be the one to preach. She had me so caught up in her words that I really began to think that what I did was wrong, but it wasn't though. It wasn't! She didn't know what I had been through. She didn't know me.

"I'm fine with what I was doing. I'm not stupid. I know what I'm doing."

"Oh, so I got a conscious person who knows it all. Did you know that you just got an employee a statutory rape case, huh? Did you know that this place can be shut down within a heartbeat if something like this gets reported? And guess where you would spend the rest of your time? Prison. It wouldn't matter if you were a minor or not."

She didn't scare me, and I could give two shits about a damn statutory rape case. I ain't taking nobody to court.

"Oh, you're quiet now, huh?"

"What you want me to say?" I smirked. *Why is she wasting my time? I'm out of here in like nine hours.*

"Okay, smart-ass. Since this is all a big joke to you, laugh at this. Go unpack. Because guess what? You're snaking this joint out for another month, and I better not catch you so much as talking to any males in this facility or else."

"You can't do that! I'm leaving tomorrow."

"I can do whatever I please. Try me if you want to."

I stormed out of her office and headed to my bed.

Jerry tried to get my attention on the way, but I ignored him. I was so furious inside, he might have gotten a chronic curse-out that he didn't deserve.

I got to my bed and couldn't sleep the entire night. I couldn't do another month in this hellhole. This was ludicrous.

I did my extra month, and it was torture. Diane was clocking me like white on rice. Every move I made she was there. She had me doing all kinds of labor. If I wasn't washing dishes for all three meals, then I was scrubbing tables. And if I wasn't doing that, then I was sweeping, mopping, washing down the walls, or getting together loads of trash barehanded. I was working like a slave. No different from my years at home.

I needed to get out. I was starting to feel too confined. I needed to infect someone. I'd been off track for a few weeks now, and I wasn't feeling like myself. I was fienin' to give someone HIV.

Jerry even stopped letting me go out, let alone talk to me. The new security guard, Shane, was trying to get at me, but he was just disgusting. He had what we young people call a yuck mouth—inflamed gums, yellow stains between the teeth, and breath you can smell from a mile away. As much as I was craving for my next prey, I was not about to jeopardize it on stankin' Shane. He had a skunky body odor too, and the closer you got to him, the more awful he smelled.

I was too anxious the night before I was scheduled to leave. I went to sleep way before the lights went out.

I rolled over in the middle of my sleep to find a light shining in my face.

"Desire, you 'sleep?"

I look up, and it was Shane. "What?"

"You 'sleep?"

"Mmm-hmm!"

"Come on, get up."

"For what?"

"Because you have to come with me."

"I didn't do anything."

He picked me up out of my bed and placed his hand over my mouth.

Ugh! His hands smelled like he had been playing in shit. His body odor was below zero, and he was touching me, violating me. I started kicking for him to let go of me. This was not about to happen. He got me out of the room and dragged me down to the basement, which was only one flight down from the sleeping area. He pushed me up against the wall, held me so I couldn't move, and unbuckled his pants with one hand.

"When I say you get up, I mean what I say, trick. You know you leaving tomorrow and you ain't gonna give me none? You gave Jerry and his brother some."

His breath smelled like garlic and sour milk. I wanted to scream, but he was still covering my mouth. I began to cry. This was not about to happen again. His hand loosened up a little, and I bit into his skin, but it didn't faze him.

He got my pants down, and then Jerry opened the basement door and flashed the light for a quick second.

There is a God. My panic eased up.

"Oh, my fault, dog. Do your thang."

Can he not see what's going on? This guy is trying to rape me.

Jerry's little distraction allowed me the opportunity to knee Shane in the balls. I struck him as hard as I could. As he curled over, I bolted up the stairs and was heading out the door.

Jerry stood in my way as I tried to push the door open. "Hold up, Desire. Where you going?"

"Out of this fucking place!"

Shane came up the stairs with his clothes properly fixed.

"Get him the hell away from me. He just tried to rape me."

"Okay, calm down," Jerry insisted.

"That bitch is lying, man. You know I ain't try to rape her. Why would I try to rape somebody who already gives it up?"

"He's lying."

From all of the commotion, Diane had come downstairs. "What the hell is going on here?"

"He tried to rape me," I screamed in tears, pointing at Shane.

"What?" she exclaimed.

"Girl, I didn't try to rape you. Don't you lie on me."

"I ain't lying!"

"You are. Lying bitch!"

He tried to charge at me, but Jerry held him back. "Wait. Everybody calm down."

"Desire, come here."

I walked over to Diane. She whispered for me to go to my sleeping quarters and promised we would talk in a few, after she dealt with Shane and Jerry.

I woke up that morning tired as all hell because I didn't get any sleep. I was paranoid the entire night and afraid that someone was going to try and do something to me. So I remained wide awake until the lights came on. Diane had never come to talk to me like she said she would. I was happy to see the lights come on. I piled my stuff up and carried everything I had to the first floor.

"Desire, you have to eat breakfast first," Diane informed me.

"I don't want breakfast. I just wanna be released." I was in one of those moods. I had to get out of here.

"All right, no breakfast, but let me talk to you for a minute. Come to my office so you can be properly discharged."

I walked to her office. She had me sit and wait for her for like a half an hour. If this was going to be the case, then I would've eaten breakfast. I skipped, not wanting to delay my release.

She strolled in the room with coffee in her hand. I was so mad. I could have knocked that shit right out of her hand for having me waiting so long.

She took her seat behind her desk with a smirk on her face. "That stunt you pulled last night was clever but not good enough to get past Dynamite Diane."

"What stunt? Shane came to my bunk and pulled me out of my bed against my will."

"Desire, you know men are not allowed in the bunk area, especially the security guards, since the incident with you and Andrew."

I can't believe this shit. Here I am complaining about what was about to happen to me for the third time and this bitch doesn't believe me. And I'm wrong for doing what I do?

"I have no reason to lie."

"And I have no reason to believe you."

"Shane was trying to rape me," I yelled, almost in tears.

"You have two options. Either you tell the truth, or you are here for another month."

"I'm telling the fucking truth! He tried to fucking rape me, and I want to press charges!"

"You think somebody is going to believe your story? Especially when I've already let them know what I walked in on the first time you were supposed to be discharged?"

I sat silent knowing she was right. I could do nothing. Telling the truth and crying wasn't going to get me out of this one.

The office telephone rang.

"What? . . . Yeah . . . Okay . . . Handle that."

I stared her down for the three seconds she was on the phone. This would not have happened if she had just let me go home the first time.

"I fucking hate you!"

I grabbed my bags to get up leave, and she rushed behind me.

"You can't leave. Sit down."

"Blow me!"

She grabbed my shoulder, and I yanked her off.

"Get off of me!" I power-walked to the door.

"No, Desire, you can't go—"

I ran out of her office. She chased me, and I made sure to stay far enough ahead so she couldn't reach out and grab me.

I bolted out of the front door, and before I could get down the stairs, Tameka stood in my way. She had come back as promised. She charged at me as I stood surprised, but I quickly regained my senses and was ready to go toe to toe. I dropped my bags and everything.

She pulled out a knife.

I tried to pick up my feet and run, but my feet wouldn't move. It was too late. She got me, just like she said. I held my chest as blood seeped out. I felt the side of my face split open as she slid the blade across my cheek and through the corners of my mouth. I fell to the ground helpless.

She dropped the knife, got on top of me, and attempted to choke me, but I gained control. I started wailing on her nonstop.

I busted her lip open, and then went for the opportunity. She was right at hand to taste my blood. I pulled her closer to me and started kissing her.

Staff ran over and pulled us apart.

I started coughing up blood. Tameka had my blood all over her face. I chuckled, knowing I had just made her a new HIV patient.

"You dirty dike! You nasty bitch! Tryin'-a kiss me. I should have killed you," she yelled.

I continued to chuckle in pain. She had gotten me, but I got her ass too. I knew that her open wounds had absorbed a good portion of my blood. I knew it did, and I was laughing inside.

I started feeling woozy. I coughed up more blood, holding my chest.

"Someone call an ambulance. She's bleeding a lot. I think they're both hurt."

I lay on my side, feeling like I was choking, shaking.

"She's losing blood quickly. She might not make it. Where's that damn ambulance?"

A short time later, the paramedics rushed over, announcing, "We're here."

They put me on a stretcher in a flash, got me in the ambulance, and sped off.

"Step on it, Charley. She's losing consciousness."

A loud beeping noise sounded off.

"Ah shit! We need more pressure!"

"Nah, man, she's leaving."

"Shit! Shit! Shit! I don't have a pulse anymore!"

"Damn it, Charley. Not another one. She's just a baby."

Chapter 29

This all could have been avoided if I had just listened to Diane and sat my ass back down. But nooooooo. Desire had to be hardheaded and make a run for it. And look where it left me. Hooked up to a damn heart monitor with bandages across my face.

I was in a heap of pain. My chest hurt every move I made, and I practically had no feeling in my face. I was going to be scarred for life. Ain't nobody gonna want me to put it on them now. Shit, that bitch! Oooh wee! She got hers though. I ain't mad. She put a dent in my plans, but I got her.

I positioned my bed to lean back so I wouldn't be so upright and while in motion a visitor walked through the door. It was Christine. The lady that did nothing but give birth to me. I almost went into cardiac arrest. *Why is she here? Why is she in my presence again unexpected?*

"How are you, honey? I got here as quickly as I could."

I rolled my eyes then closed them, wishing that when I opened them back up, she'd be gone.

"Oh, look at my baby. I can't stand to see you like this," she cried.

"Then why you here?" I asked, barely moving my mouth, trying not to aggravate the stitched corners.

"You almost died, Desire, and please, baby, don't talk. I know it hurts for you to talk."

"I'm fine," I spoke through my clenched teeth.

"No. Fine is when you don't have to be admitted to the hospital and then have life-saving surgery. That's fine. I almost lost you. You wouldn't believe how fast I rushed down here. People were cursing at me, blowing their horns, and—"

"I guess I have to be on my death bed to hear from you."

"Desire, please don't start. I'm here, okay. Give me a chance."

"You had a chance."

"I made a mistake, a huge mistake. I chose my career over my child. I'm sorry baby."

"Apology not accepted."

"Desire, what else do you expect me to say?"

I lay there blinking repeatedly, trying to halt the tears. She sounded so sincere. I wanted to believe her, but in the back of my mind, I felt it was phony.

"Just leave me alone."

"No, I've done it once, and I'm not going to do it again."

"Try twice."

"Okay, two times, but I was caught up in a man and I'm not anymore. Just give me a chance."

"Don't you get it? I don't need you anymore. It's too late. As far as I'm concerned, I don't have a mother or a father. I'm my own woman—me, myself, and I."

"You're a child lost, and it's not too late. I'm still your mother."

"Oh yeah? Well, where was my mother when her daughter was being mistreated by Auntie Linda? Or when she was crying to come home because her best friend's brother raped her? Or where was she when her child was humiliated on the first day of school? Where

was she when her best friend Greg died? Or, better
yet, where was she when some man made her take off
her clothes and feel her up like a fifty-cent ho? Huh?
Where were you?" I yelled through my clenched teeth,
sounding like one of the Charlie Brown adults. I took a
deep breath, trying to keep from getting anxious. The
corners of my mouth were beginning to throb.

"I, ah, I didn't know you had to go through so much."

"Humph!"

"But, Desire, it's not like what it seems. I mean, I
tried to come."

Auntie Linda walked into the room. My mom stopped
speaking and wiped her eyes.

*Wow, I must be getting ready to die! What brings
this visit?*

"I hear you almost died," Auntie Linda commented.

"I *am* dead," I mumbled.

"Desire, don't say that," my mother interjected.

"Why not? I hate this world. I hate my life!"

"You're just full of hate. Like you're some kind of angel. You still don't appreciate nothing, and that detention center obviously didn't teach you anything either."

I sat up in my bed and leveled the height. I was gonna have to be heard right now and deal with the pain.

"What? Am I supposed to appreciate that you beat
me silly until I could take no more? You abused me
for no reason. I was trying. I tried to get right, but you
never let up."

"I went a whole year letting you do whatever the hell
you wanted, and you went wild. So don't give me that
mess. You deserved everything coming to you."

I began breathing fast. "I didn't deserve to be treated
like shit." I grabbed the pillow from behind me and
hauled it at my aunt. Then I instantly grabbed my chest
and the sides of my mouth from the excruciating pain.

My heart monitor started beeping.

Two nurses ran in as my aunt and mother just stood watching.

"Please, you all have to step out for a second," a nurse demanded.

I watched as both my aunt and mother walked out, my mother reluctantly, but my aunt, strong, tall, and proud. She was probably wishing I would die, and I was wishing the same thing.

I only had to be stabilized though. I needed to be calmed down from getting worked up. The nurses advised me to get some rest as they injected me with more morphine to ease my pain. All visits for the remainder of the day were canceled. Good. I didn't need anymore surprises anyway.

I woke up the next morning feeling refreshed but still in pain. A doctor was sitting in one of the chairs, I guess, waiting for me to awake.

"How are you feeling this morning?"

"In pain, but fine."

"Where is your pain?"

"My face is throbbing, and my chest feels caved in."

"On a scale from one to ten, how would you rate the pain?"

"Eleven," I mumbled.

"All right. That's not unusual for now. For these next couple of days, it's going to be extremely sore. You were cut very deep. At times you may feel like hyperventilating because your heart may speed up unexpectedly. The knife just missed—"

"My heart, I know."

"Yup, kiddo. You're lucky."

"Humph."

"What? You don't think so?"

I shrugged my shoulders.

"Come, on kiddo. You have much more life to live, having fun, playing games, going to college," he rambled as he checked my vitals.

He put the stethoscope to my lungs. "Take a deep breath slowly for me . . . now breathe out. That a girl. One more time. Breathe in and breathe out . . . okay, great."

"Are you having trouble breathing?"

"Not that I know of, but it hurts inhaling."

"How does it feel to talk? I notice you're talking through your teeth and not really trying to move your mouth."

"Yeah. 'Cause it hurts."

"It's okay to do what you're doing, but you should work on talking and talk regular to exercise your jaws. I'm also going to have you blow into this tube a few times a day, so I can measure how much air you are able to expel from your lungs. Eventually, I want your breathing to be effortless."

"Great. When can I get out of here?"

"Let's take it slow. First, let me give you another dose of meds to ease the pain. It will allow you to rest better."

"What about my chest pain?"

"This will take care of that too."

"So when can I leave?"

"Not sure, kiddo," he answered, smiling and pressing buttons that administered more morphine into my IV.

"Once you are more stable, we'll talk about releasing you and removing those bandages."

"Why?"

"It's procedure to ensure you are healing as expected."

"If you say so."

"Cheer up, kid. Everything's going to be all right."

"When? I've been waiting. I go from bad to worse. The story of my life."

"How old are you?"

"Sixteen."

"Oh, kiddo, you're going to have many more stories to tell and surviving this one is a start."

"Not if I don't get AIDS first."

"What was that?"

"You heard right. I got the disease."

The doctor turned beet-red. "What disease?"

"The human immunodeficiency virus, better known as—"

"HIV," he finished.

Boy, the look on his face.

"It's okay. I'm good with it, you know."

"No, no, I understand," he said taking down some notes. "How do you know you have this?"

"Because I got tested."

"Are you on medication for this? Why didn't I know about this?"

"I was on meds, but since I was locked up, I stopped taking them. And nobody knows, not even my family. So please don't say anything."

"Don't worry. Everything is confidential. Have you sought any counseling for this?"

"Why? For what? Like I said, nobody knows, and I plan on keeping it like that. I only told you because you started talking about surviving to tell stories."

"I'm not saying spread the word to the world, but I'm concerned here about your mental health. And, your mom, she seems to think the—"

"She doesn't know anything about me."

"That's fine, but from the little bit we have talked, I think it would be a good idea if you saw one of our mental health counselors. I'll send someone up later in the day."

"I'm not crazy."

"No one said you were. Seeking professional help doesn't mean you're not sane. Let's forget that for now. Get some rest and buzz the nurse if you need anything."

I couldn't wait for him to leave. He got to me. I didn't want to show it, but he agitated me. I was feeling real violated right now. Why did I tell him about what I got? What was I thinking? He thought I was crazy. I wasn't crazy, I was just living life, that's all. Ha! Yup, just living life. My mother got a nerve too, trying to be concerned about me.

"Bitch, it's too late. Ha! Ha!" I yelled out loud to myself. *Damn, I just might be borderline crazy, either that or this morphine is messing with me.*

I dozed off, and I rested for a few more hours as instructed. I tried to force myself to eat the nasty tomato soup they gave me because I was hungry, but I spat it out once I wrapped my lips around the spoon.

Jen walked in right on time to see me in action too. "Ew! I think you're supposed to eat that, not spit it out." She smiled. She greeted me with a soft hug and a tap of a kiss on the cheek. "How you feeling?"

"In a little pain, but the nurse just gave me my dosage, so I should be cool in a minute."

"I came yesterday, but they told me you couldn't have any more visitors."

"Oh yeah. My mom and aunt came unexpectedly."

"I know. I saw them. How'd that go?"

"It went. They think I'm crazy, and they want me to see a shrink."

"That's not too bad."

"Oh, here you go. You're supposed to be on my side."

"I am on your side, but I ain't gonna lie to you."

"Whatever. Just forget I told you. I ain't doing it anyway."

"Why not? I think you should. You've been through a lot."

"And what's new? You don't even know the half."

"Exactly. And this is why it is a good reason for you to get help. Talk to a professional who can help you sort out your problems and hopefully get you to living a normal life."

"I'm dealing with it on my own. Plus, I don't have major problems."

"Dee, you were taking pills. You—"

"You supplied me with them."

"Hey, wait a minute. Don't blame me, Desire. I got in on it for the money, not to use them."

"Well, I used them. So what? It made me feel good like I'm feeling right now, and you're blowing my high."

"And you're blowing your life away. Some therapy can do you good. You won't need a drug to make you feel good."

"Just leave it alone."

"Desire, you're my best friend . . . more like a sister to me. I don't like how you're living your life. I'm scared for you since this has happened."

"What's so wrong with how I'm living my life?"

"You're popping pills, sleeping around, school is a joke, you been in lockup for the entire summer. You—"

"Blah, blah, blah, blah, blah. Spare me the lecture. Okay, Jen."

"Desire, I'm serious."

"And I am too. Now let's talk about what's going to happen when I come home."

"If it's not legit or helping you, then count me out. I'm through. I can't."

"You can't what? You can't help your best friend?"

"Help my best friend do what? Run herself into the ground? You ain't in this hospital for a measly asthma attack or an annual checkup. You almost died from getting stabbed. Desire, are you not here with me? Take a look at your life."

"Yeah. My life. Don't knock the hustle."

"What is with this stupid talk? You get stabbed and now you think you're an *O.G.*?"

I grinned at her comment. "Jen, lighten up. What's with you? I come home from lockup and you're trippin'."

"Hell yeah, I'm trippin', Desire. You almost died. Doesn't that scare you?"

I thought about it for a moment. "Nah, it doesn't."

"I'm not talking to a sane person here. I gotta go."

I looked at Jen's back as she turned it on me and walked out of my room upset. I couldn't blame her for feeling the way she did, but she'd never have understood, best friend or not. I wanted to tell her the truth. Believe me, I did, but I couldn't. I just couldn't.

I needed to think. I was letting these people get to me. I didn't need help. I needed to get out of here so I could get back on track. I was losing sight of my mission. These people, they're getting in my way. I couldn't have that.

I couldn't even think right now. What was the number of people I'd infected? Damn, I didn't know. But I knew this. I was feeling like I hadn't even started yet. *Okay, okay. Let me calm down.* I was getting too excited. I needed to close my eyes for a minute. Then when I opened them, I was going to get up, get myself together, and check myself out of this joint. *I got more people to infect.*

Chapter 30

I woke up and saw a bunch of people in my room. I panicked. *Oh shit. What they found out? Who told?* I looked to see who was in here. Ms. Tanner was amongst the many, my doctor, my ex-probation officer, my damn deadbeat mother, and some lady I had never seen before a day in my life. *What the hell is going on here?* I was sure my mother had something to do with this. I sat myself up in the bed.

"Desire, you're up? Glad to see you alert. How'd you sleep?" the doctor asked.

"What's going on? Why y'all here? What y'all doing here?" I smelled trouble.

"I came to give you some good news," the doctor announced. "And the others have to follow up on what I have to tell you."

"What?" I asked, not really understanding him.

"Just bear with us. You're going to be discharged in a few days pending your stability level, and that's why Dr. Shuman is here. She's a psychologist."

So that's who the lady is. They still think I'm crazy. I got their number.

"Good evening, Desire," she greeted.

I didn't greet her back.

"Desire, the woman is speaking to you," my mother intervened.

"I'm not deaf."

"Desire, these people are here to help you. You need to show more respect."

"Everybody just get out! Get out! I'm not crazy! Nothing's wrong with me! Just get out!" My breathing grew heavy.

The doctor ordered everyone to follow my orders, everyone except the shrink.

"Slow down with your breathing. It's okay. Calm yourself. Breathe in and out, in and out slowwwwly," my doctor coached.

I continued to breathe heavy, wanting the shrink to leave too. I didn't want her to see me like this. She'd really think I was crazy. I wasn't though. I was just in pain. There was a pain every time I took heavy breaths.

"Ouch!"

"Yes, kiddo, it hurts. That's why I said breathe in and out slowly," the doctor reminded.

I did as I was told, trying to bear the pain. It began to ease up. The breathing techniques actually worked.

"Good girl. Your vitals are stable now," the shrink lady said.

"You have to keep your cool, kiddo. Try not to get yourself excited like that. The heavy breathing expands your lungs and leads to sharp, uncomfortable pains, which in turn raise your blood pressure. We need to keep your blood pressure stable if you ever want to get out of here."

I nodded my head to acknowledge her advice.

"Does your mother's presence bother you?" the shrink asked.

I didn't answer, but took a heavy breath, which indicated the answer was definitely yes.

"Remember, breathe slow, Desire. I need you to be comfortable."

I sat there reverting back to the good breathing techniques I had just learned. My doctor came over and did his routine checkup.

Dr. Shuman chatted with me about things other than my life, which was great, and I actually liked the conversation. She didn't question me about my feelings, or the reason why I was in the hospital at all. It was just general conversation. She talked the entire time the doctor did his thing. Then they both left together.

The doctor assured he'd be back in an hour to check up on me. The shrink mentioned nothing about coming back at all. I thought she got the impression that I was sane, and not crazy, like those other miserable people thought I was. At least I was hoping I left that impression. That was the plan.

"Hello," a nurse barged in, interrupting my thoughts.

"Hi."

"I'm here to remove your bandages."

"Completely?" I asked excitedly.

"Yup, completely. Your wounds need to breathe. I'm going to need you to bear with me because this may hurt a little. If you need a break, just give me a sign by raising your hand." She started with the bandage on the left side of my face.

Hurt a little? This joint is excruciating. "Erghhh-hhh," I groaned, raising my hand. Breathing heavy and feeling the sharp pain in my chest, I started my breathing techniques.

"Wait, let me get you another dose of pain medicine." She pressed the button calling the nurses' station. "Bring me twenty milligrams of Roxanol for patient Jones."

The nurse arrived in no time with the Roxanol.

"What's that?" I asked.

"A pain medicine equivalent to morphine. It's just a little stronger than morphine. I'm just going to recline your bed to avoid you becoming nauseated."

The nurse let me lay for a few minutes before resuming with taking off my bandages. This time the process was smooth sailing, and I was definitely high.

"You're all set. I have a mirror, if you want to take a peek at yourself. You seem to be healing pretty well."

"Yes, I'd like to see."

The nurse handed me a mirror, and I looked at my face. This wasn't me. It couldn't have been. I looked so different. I looked ugly. I looked deformed. My face looked distorted. *Who's going to want to sleep with me now? No, this can't be. I can't leave here with my face looking like this.* I threw the mirror at the wall across the room and heard the glass break on impact. The nurse backed up a bit.

"I know it looks bad now, but that's only because your wounds are still very fresh. Don't worry, sweetie. Everything will be okay."

"Fuck that! Do you see my face?" I yelled.

"Sweetie, calm down. It only looks like that now because your face is still swollen and the stitches have not dissolved."

"I look ugly," I cried.

I was crushed. I certainly didn't expect to look in the mirror and see what I saw. My face was pushed to one side like I had suffered a stroke. On top of that, my face was swollen like a balloon, and I had this long line of stitches. My lips looked like I had collagen injections, and the corners of my mouth looked like the stitching on a football. I looked just like Frankenstein.

"Calm down. Let the medicine relax you."

Again, I started my breathing techniques.

"Hey, can I talk to her for a second?"

I looked over to see who the familiar voice belonged to, and it was Ms. Tanner. I forgot she was waiting in line. I quickly turned away, so she couldn't see my horrible face.

"Go away. I don't want any visitors."

"I'm not visiting. I'm on business."

"Well, it figures. Why else would you be here?"

"Desire, you will be leaving here in about two days, and you are due to come back to lockup."

"No, I did my time," I stated firmly.

"Not quite."

"Not quite? I—"

"Listen before you get upset. That day when you told me what happened to you, well, I now know that you were telling the truth. I'm sorry I didn't believe you, and I'm sorry that you had to experience something so traumatic."

I looked up at the ceiling, not wanting to relive the horrible moment.

"Desire, I truly am sorry."

Tears welled up in my eyes and rolled down my cheeks. Me being me, of course, you know, trying to be tough, I acted nonchalant, trying to avoid the pain. I wiped my eyes.

"Yeah. Well, things happen, right?"

"Desire, no, it shouldn't have happened."

"But it did, and I'm over it."

"Listen, I'm willing to take this all the way if—"

"Forget it happened. Just forget it."

"This is too serious to just—"

"Please, just forget it."

"It's not right though."

"But it's better for me, and much better if we kill the conversation. Why are you here?"

"A week was added to your time at the center."

"What? I did my—"

"Wait, just listen. I worked it out so that you don't have to come back to the center."

"Should I be happy, or is there a catch?"

"You have to make up the time with community service."

"Figures."

"It's not that bad."

"Yeah, well, your face doesn't look like this. You don't have to go out in public looking like Franken-stein. Community service . . . that's . . . that's . . . look at my face."

"Desire, you are a beautiful girl inside, and that's what counts. Your outside appearance doesn't make you."

I was silent. She'd brought a tear to my eye. Greg had told me that. *Dang, Greg. I forgot about Greg.*

"And, plus, you made good friends before you left because of your personality."

I thought about the facility and the girls, my blood sisters. Damn! I had done them wrong for a purpose though. For a purpose. *Yeah, I gotta get out of here.*

"I'm with the community service."

"I thought you would be." Ms. Tanner smiled.

Today was my first day of community service, and I was mad that I had to report to this crappy nursing home every day after school. Yeah, I was back in school—eleventh grade.

My face was back to normal, and I wasn't trippin' no more. I had a large scar on the left side of my face, but it wasn't bad looking. It was actually kind of cute. The guys in school dug it, and that's really all that mattered. I was back in full effect, baby.

"Excuse me, Desire?"

"Yes."

"Hi. I'm Jane Malloy, your supervisor."

"Hello."

"Glad to have you."

"Glad I'm here," I lied.

"Good. First things first. I want to go over a few things with you. Your daily assignments will be right here in this basket with your name on it. For the most part, you will be checking the rooms and making sure that everyone is where they're supposed to be. Occasionally, you may have to lead a game or something, but I'll let you know when that happens.

"I see you have a cell phone. Unfortunately, we are not allowed to use them in the building. They interfere with the electronic equipment, including patient monitors. So, for this reason, you will need to turn it off before entering the building each day."

Dang! No cell phone? "A'ight."

"Soooo, you understand everything?"

"Yup."

"All right, here you go." She handed me the sheet with my assignment for the day.

I looked it over and got right on my first task. The first order of duty was to check with the fourth- and fifth-floor residents to make sure they were signed up for an activity on Thursday.

The first woman I met with talked me to death. I heard stories about her children, grandchildren, and then about her husband, who put her in this home. She drove me crazy, so I can imagine what she was doing to her husband. She was hilarious though. I had to tell Jen about her. I knew I wasn't supposed to use my cell phone, but this story was too funny to hold out on until later. I hadn't laughed this hard in a while.

I dialed her up before going into the next room.

"Bitch, please. I'm in this hellhole with these old-ass people for another hour," I said, talking real loud.

"Could you watch the cursing, miss," some old man said.

I couldn't even get in his room before he's ordering me around. *The elderly, I tell you.* I kept on with my conversation, ignoring his comment.

"Jen, this shitty ol' guy didn't just tell me to stop fucking cursing," I whispered into the phone, loudly emphasizing the curse words.

"That was two more swears I heard," he informed.

Being the smart-ass I was, I continued to curse. "Who fucking cares what you heard?"

"That would make five total."

"Well, count these. *Shit*, seven, *fuck*, eight, *muthafucka*, nine."

I laughed, and Jen laughed, telling me to stop being disrespectful.

"I see things have not changed," the old man said.

I finally directed my full attention toward the old man, getting ready to tell him off. "You don't know me to say"—I quickly lost grip of my phone, and it hit the floor. I thought I was going to faint.

I walked over toward him as he lay in the bed. He stared at me with tears in his eyes.

"I don't understand. You're supposed to be dead, but you're alive. You're here. I see you here!"

Something came over me that I couldn't control. It was like a backed-up current that released through my eyes and nose. I couldn't control it. I became very emotional. My uncle being in my life meant a lot to me, and to know that he was alive all this time was giving me a crazy feeling.

My mind was racing. *Desire, your Uncle Frank is dead. There is no funeral either because I don't have money. You are not going to that boy Greg's funeral. If you can cut school, then you can miss this. Desire,*

*you're a ho. Desire, you are no longer my daughter
from this day forth. I disown you. Greg would be disappointed. Miss, your test results came back positive
for HIV. Why do you like sleepin' around? You better
stay protected. Where's your baby, Desire? When can
I meet him? I am your mother, you listen to me.*

Before I knew it, I fainted.

"Desire, Desire!"

I felt a cold cloth on my face, and I jumped up. I
looked at my uncle as if he was a ghost. I blinked twice.
"Uncle Frank," I say, mesmerized.

"Yes, Desire. It's me." He touched me.

"Uncle Frank! It's really you!"

"Yes, Desire. It is."

"But Auntie Linda told me you were dead. She lied to
me. Why'd she lie to me?" I was getting furious, tears
streaming down my face.

"Desire, I was dead to you way before that lie."

"She lied to me! I hate her!"

"No, Desire. You hate yourself. I made her lie to you.
I wanted to leave. I couldn't take it anymore. You were
disrespecting me left and right. You couldn't even hold
a conversation with me. You stopped talking to me.
You stopped caring. Why? Desire, I gave you everything, and I protected you, yet you just continued to
lie, become more and more out of control. Whenever I
tried to talk to you, you didn't have time. You were so
caught up in the streets. You think I didn't know about
your drinking and smoking? I knew, and I got tired.
I was dead to you before Linda made the announcement."

My uncle was right. I was so caught up in the streets,
I cast him away well before Auntie Linda lied and told
me he was dead.

"What is that scar on your face?"

"I got stabbed by some girl."

"What are you getting yourself into? Desire, you are only fifteen. Your birthday is in a few months. You gonna live to see it? Why are you going through all of this drama? Why are you not taking care of yourself? Huh? Where is your son? Have you even been in touch to see how he's doing? Take a look at yourself. Take a good look. You're still young. You have such a long life ahead of you, and you're throwing it all away. These streets have got your mind corrupted. Are you back in school?"

"Yeah, I'm a junior."

"Have you been going to school?"

"Yes."

"What else are you doing for yourself?"

I didn't answer.

"You better get yourself together."

I put my head down.

"Look at me when I'm talking to you."

I put my head up, ashamed.

"Desire, all you got is you. You've burned bridges with so many people who have tried to help you. And it's hard, I know, because you're a child. I know what you been through, and right now, as God is my witness, I'm hurting for you. My wife Linda, yes, she mistreated you. Her way of disciplining wasn't great, and I wish I could have done more, but I couldn't. I did what I could, but you drained me, Desire. I couldn't bear it anymore. That's part of the reason why I left. The other is because my cancer came out of remission. I was getting too sick. I didn't tell you because you had so many other worries.

"Linda did too, which is part of the reason why she acted the way she did. It hurt her to no longer be able to care for me, and she took it out on you. She shouldn't have, but she did. The blame is not all on her though. You take part in this too. You have to start thinking about you, Desire, and taking care of your responsibilities, and stop letting people run all over you. Get yourself through school, and take care of what's yours. Go get that baby, and do what's right. Do you even know that baby's name, or how old he is?"

It was sad to say, but I didn't have a clue about my son. Not a clue.

"I know you don't know his name because you left him and never looked back. Your auntie got him down there in Greenville. He's doing well, quite well, but you better go get him."

"Is something wrong?"

"It doesn't have to be anything wrong. He's your child, and he belongs with his mother. I know you may be scared and think you're unable to take care of a baby, but you will manage. Especially if you can survive these streets. Get it together, Desire. You only live once without being able to turn back the hands of time."

Tears streamed down my face.

"What did I tell you about that crying?"

I smiled in the midst of my tears. I hadn't smiled a happy smile in a long time. Uncle Frank always had a way with words. He could change a mood quick too, good or bad. What he was saying was the truth. He was right. I had to get myself together, get my son, and make a change for good.

Chapter 31

As soon as I got out of that nursing home, I borrowed money from Jen, not telling her what it was for, and I got on the next Greyhound to South Carolina. Now that I knew my son had been staying with my father's family, I was going to get him and bring him home. Yes, I was showing up unannounced.

It took me sixteen hours to get to Greenville, North Carolina by bus. The ride seemed never-ending, but I made it. As soon as I got off the bus, I hopped in a taxi to my Aunt Millie's.

I got the jitters as we approached the house. It'd been a long time since I'd seen my boy, since birth, to be exact. I was hoping my aunt didn't give me any trouble. I just wanted to be cordial, chill a bit, get my son, grab his things, and then go home. It was time.

I rang the doorbell, and before I could take my hand off the bell, my little cousin Earl answered the door. He was smiling from ear to ear. Boy, was he happy to see me.

"Desire," he joyously yelled, jumping up on my waist.

I tried to back up before he took the leap, but it was too late. Now, he knew his big ass was well over the weight limit to be jumping all over somebody. I was almost on the floor, until he decided to jump off me.

He ran down the hall calling out to his mother. "Mama, Desire her'."

I followed behind him as he made his way to the kitchen screaming. My aunt gave me this surprised look as I walked in the kitchen, interrupting what looked like a meeting with some nasty, trailer trashy-looking white folks.

"Is this yo' daughtar?"

"Oh nah. She kinfolk. What brings you all the da way down her' from Boston?"

I answered straight to the point. "I came to get my baby."

My aunt looked across the table at the white lady. I saw that the white lady was holding a little boy. My boy. I could tell from his green eyes. *Oh my baby!*

"What?" my aunt exclaimed, surprised.

"I came to take my son home. I wanna take care of him. I'm ready." I reached across the table. "Can I see him please?"

The white lady handed over him to me. *Oh, he is so big.* I took a good look at him. He's a porker. He's a chubby, handsome, dark-chocolate little porker. I stared at him and almost cried. How did I allow myself to give up on him so easily? He was so precious and innocent. Wow! I had given birth to such a beautiful child! What was I thinking when I left him?

"He's so precious, isn't he?" the white lady asked.

"Yeah, he is!"

"You should see 'im when he tries to run."

"He can walk?"

My aunt laughed.

"I hope his big ass can walk. He two goin' on three."

I started calculating in my head. *Damn. It's been that long.*

"Okay. Well, I don't have much time. We oughta get goin'." The lady reached out to take my son back from me.

I pulled away and looked at her like she had two heads. My aunt just stood there and walked away.

"We gotta be goin' now. I'm sorry." The white lady reached out for me to hand her my child. She looked at my aunt.

With a puzzled look on my face, I looked at her too, unaware of what was actually taking place before I'd walked in the kitchen.

My aunt laughed. "Girl, stop playin' and give dat woman Shyne."

"Shyne . . . that's his name? His name is Shyne?"

"Dumb heiffa. You didn't even know yo' own boy's name? Hand 'im ova to his new mama."

She was right. I didn't know his name. Shame on me. But I'll be damned, to hand over my baby to some dirty white lady. Was she buggin'?

"Nooooo, my baby is not going anywhere. How is she his new mama? The adoption went through?"

The lady looked at my aunt. "She doesn't know?"

"I don't know what? So the adoption did go through? I didn't sign any final papers."

My aunt grabbed her lit cigarette out of the ashtray and took a long drag. That was a dead giveaway that she was trying to pull a fast one.

"Her' you go fuckin' up shit again. Gotdammit, every time I turn 'round you fuckin' up sumtin'!" She reached in her bra and pulled out a knot of money. She reluctantly dropped the stack on the table.

The white lady reached her dirty hand across the ashtray and picked up it. "So the deal's off?" She frowned.

My aunt tapped her foot nervously. "Gimme that baby," she shouted to me.

"No," I said, looking at her like she was crazy.

She aggressively reached out for Shyne, and I swung him around so she couldn't get to him. In the midst of the commotion, she bumped into me, knocking me over. As I was falling to the floor, I twisted around so that I landed on my back to prevent from hurting Shyne.

She grabbed Shyne by his waist, to take him out of my hands. "Gimme dis damn boy. You didn't want 'im no way. I been takin' care of dis boy all dis time an' now I'ma gettin' paid fo' 'im."

"You ain't selling my baby to no white trash."

I muscled full control of Shyne, got on my feet, and ran through the hallway out the front door. I pushed past my cousins, Jo-Jo and Boog, coming through the screen door.

"Hey, girl, slow down," Jo-Jo yelled.

I ignored him and kept on going. I had no idea where I was running to, but I kept it moving. I got way up the road, and then noticed that no one was chasing me. I don't think anyone had been chasing me for a while. I can't believe my aunt was trying to sell my baby. What the hell was she thinking?

I looked at Shyne, and he was crying. Poor baby probably was scared. What was I thinking for not wanting him? He was so innocent and cute. And I was so innocent and young. *Do I really want to do this? Yes . . . no . . . no. What am I doing?*

I looked at Shyne again. *Yes, I have to. I have to take him home with me. He's my responsibility now.* I wiped the tears from his eyes. "It's okay, mommy's here."

He continued to cry.

"Shhh, it's okay. I'm here to take care of you."

It took him a minute to calm down. I thought he was never going to stop crying, but he did. Our second time together and I did a mommy deed. I felt proud.

I had walked about a mile by the time I realized I only had sixteen dollars to my name. My bag that I came with was at my aunt's house. I had planned to try to get some money from her after at least chillin' for a while, but you see that didn't go down as planned. I didn't know what I was going to do.

I can't hitchhike with Shyne; it just ain't safe. And this damn sure ain't like Boston where you can get a cab anywhere or hop on public transportation. Maybe I should go knock on the door of the first house I come to and ask for a ride. Hey, what I got to lose?

As I walked along the road, people were driving by beeping their horns, being friendly. Shyne loved it too. He was waving, saying, "Hey," like he knew all these people.

"Hey car, oooooh car," Shyne yelled.

I looked at him strangely. I had no idea he could talk and, for that matter, identify things.

"Yeah, that's a car. Can you say *Mommy*?"

"Mommy," he said clearly with a big smile on his face.

"Yes, I'm your mommy," I said, excited.

"I wanna get down," he said.

As fast as the cars were speeding past, I was scared to let Shyne down, but since he was so heavy, I did. I don't know how I held him that long, with his weight.

We walked as I thought about my next moves. I thought back to my conversation with my uncle and with Jen when I got stabbed. I was a fool. I looked down at my son and got all emotional. I left him. I left this precious little boy. What possessed me to do this? What possessed me to . . . oh my God . . . infect people with this thing I got? What was I doing? Then it hit me. I was purposely giving people—guys, women, boys and girls HIV. I did that. I was wrong for that. What was I thinking? I wasn't thinking. Oh God, what have I done?

We walked for about twenty minutes on the road
while my mind raced. Out of nowhere, a truck pulled
up beside me. I kept walking, ignoring the driver honk-
ing his horn. I was not going to repeat another hitchhiking episode, especially not with Shyne in my care.

The driver pulled closer beside me and honked the
horn again. "Desire Jones, is dat you? What in the hell
you doin' down her'? And why you walkin' all tired wit'
that fat boy of yours?"

I looked up to notice my Uncle Juggie. I walked over
to his truck.

"Girl, when you get down her'?"

"About an hour ago."

"You goin' to Millie's house?"

"Well . . . no."

"Talk to me."

"I just came from over there. I went to get Shyne, and
she was tryin'a sell him or something to these white
people and—"

"Say no mo'. I gotcha. She at it again."

"At what?"

"Nothin'. Just get in. Where you headin'?"

"I was heading back home to Boston."

"Ha, ha, ha! Well, it wiz gon' take you fo'eva walking.
I'll get you an' ya boy a ride back home."

"I left my bag at her house, and I don't have any
money."

"I gotcha. C'mon."

I picked Shyne up and got in the truck.

"Hey dere, boy."

"Hi, *Jud-gee*," Shyne greeted.

I smiled, hearing him talk.

Uncle Juggie put his head down. "Desire, you gon' do
right by him?"

"Yes."

"Are yah sur'?"

"Yes, I promise."

"A'ight now. I'm trustin' you."

I nodded my head in agreement.

He put his hand on my shoulder. "Everything gon' be fine. I sees it in ya eyes dat you shole iz determin' ta git dat boy back home witchu."

I nodded my head in agreement again. He pulled off as I tried to get comfy in his dirt-filled pickup truck. I looked around like, *What happened?* The wheels he had before were way better than this. This truck was beneath him, and talk about bad decoration. He had oil-stained sheets as seat covers, pieces of quilted blankets as floor mats. I wanted to laugh my behind off when I saw pieces of plastic trash bags covering the bullet holes in his windshield.

"An' don't be jealis' of my new truck neitha," he said, proudly tapping the dashboard.

"Don't worry, Uncle Juggie. I'm not." I laughed.

"Hey dere, boy."

"Hi, *Jud-gee.*" Shyne smiled.

I looked at Shyne and was no longer scared of what lay ahead for us. I planned to love my son unconditionally, no question. And I vowed to protect him from all harm, with or without help.

Chapter 32

Shyne and I got back home safely on the bus. I had praises coming from everywhere about what I had done to get my son back. My Auntie Linda even did a 360 with her attitude. The same day I got home, she went out and bought stuff for Shyne. She bought training pants, clothes, a stroller, and a car seat. I was surprised and impressed. I think she felt bad and wanted to do right by me since she knew I had found out that my uncle was still alive. I never asked her why she didn't tell me 'cause I knew my uncle would have dug in my ass if he found out I sassed her.

My day was going great. Jen had come over to sit with us for a while. She seemed just as excited about getting him back as I was.

"He is so cute with his pretty eyes."

"I don't know where he got those green eyes from," I commented.

"His father. Did you forget he had one?" Jen reminded.

"Yup. As soon as he forgot he got me pregnant."

"He may come around now if he saw Shyne. Shoot, Shyne makes me want a baby. I know you're going to make me his godmother?"

"Of course. You already know that."

"We have to go to church to make it official though. Get the baby baptized and all of that."

"Yeah, yeah. I know."

That last month during the summer when Jen had walked out on me, she'd decided to turn her life over to God. I should have seen it coming, the way she lectured me in the hospital. She joined a church and was in attendance every Sunday, and was even going to Bible study during the week. I was sure her mother was happy that she decided to stop running the streets. I know with me gone, it was easier for her to keep Jen on track. I was heading on Jen's path too, but I wouldn't say church EVERY Sunday. Hey, at least I was trying.

"Well, girl, it's already three thirty, and I have to be back at church by four, so I need to get my behind to the bus stop," Jen said.

I let Shyne walk with Jen to the door.

"Bye, baby. See ya later," she said, letting go of his hand.

"Bye, baby," Shyne mimicked, waving.

We both fell out laughing as she opened the door to leave. Then we both stopped short as the surprise visitor greeted us at the door.

"Malik," I stammered, stunned by his presence.

Jen stood still for a good minute. I was sure she was about to give him a good cursing out, but she didn't. She smiled cordially at him, walked down the stairs, then turned around and said, "I'll see you in school tomorrow. Don't be late!"

I half-listened to her comment as I stood in a daze, staring at Malik. I wanted to know what the hell he was doing here. I stood stiff, not inviting him in.

"Can I come in?"

"For what?"

"Desire, come on. Don't be like that, baby."

"I ain't your baby. You can't sweet-talk me anymore, Malik. Remember, that was eighth grade. Then I got pregnant."

He sighed. "I just wanna talk to you."

"Talk. I'm listening."

"Desire, please can we sit down and talk?"

I was about to tell him no, but then I took one look at Shyne and changed my mind. I decided to give him a chance to be in Shyne's life, and if he screwed that up, at least I would know I didn't stand in his way.

"Come in."

We sat down in the living room in silence for a good few minutes as he just stared at Shyne. Either he was going to talk or get the hell out.

"You said you wanted to talk, so talk."

"How has everything been?"

"Good."

"Yeah, I'm holding up too."

"I didn't ask."

"What's the attitude for? I'm trying to make amends here."

"Well, you ain't trying hard enough, and I haven't heard a 'sorry' yet."

"Listen, I didn't come over here to get chewed out. My mother heard about the baby, and she wants custody of him."

"What? What baby? Not my baby."

"Yes. That is my son that you're holding."

I laughed. "Huh? Your son? You mean, the one you just saw today for the first time and haven't even really acknowledged?"

"Yeah, him. The one you just decided you wanted."

No, he didn't go there.

"My son doesn't need a ho for a mother. I hear you damn near slept with everybody in Boston—Roxbury, Mattapan, Dorchester. Did you hit Cambridge yet? I bet them nuccas in New York would love some of that HIV pussy."

I smacked Malik. "Fuck you! Get out!"

Shyne repeated after me, "*Fut u.*"

Malik surprisingly took the hit like a man and stood to his feet. "Oh, you want me to leave 'cause I'm telling the truth."

"I got the shit from you, muthafucka. You gave me this shit! This shit that I can't get rid of," I said in a fit of rage, releasing an unknown demon from its locked box. I picked up a pillow and threw it at him. Then I charged at him. "Fuck you! Go to hell! This is all your fault anyway!"

Shyne ran behind me. "*Fut u.*"

Malik grabbed me by my shoulders. "Why you think I told you I didn't want that baby? It was because I knew he would have it too. And God forbid he gives it to someone else, like I did to you."

I jerked him off of me and spat in his face.

He wiped the spit and smirked. "You better watch your back, Desire. That's all I'm saying."

He walked out the door, and I slammed it behind him. He had definitely opened up some old wounds, wounds that never healed, and now I was wondering if they ever would. *I knew I shouldn't have let him in. Damn it! I knew it.*

Chapter 33

"Yo, ma, how many hoes like you do you think I can give HIV to?"

"You can't do that, Shyne. It's not right. I've been there before."

"I don't give a fuck where you've been, bitch. You better talk to me with some respect. Remember, I'm the man of this house."

Shyne jumped at Desire and made her flinch. It wouldn't be the first time he hit her and definitely not the last. Between the mental and physical abuse, Desire had another man in her life who she let walk all over her.

"Clean up this gotdam house, and when I get back, dinner better be ready."

He sounded so much like his father Malik, not to mention being his spitting image. Shyne definitely had Desire scared for her life. She had given birth to the devil himself.

"Desire! Desire! Get up! Shyne's crying."

I woke up in a cold sweat. I gazed around the room frantically, not really understanding what was going on, until my aunt handed me Shyne, who was screaming his head off. I just looked at him.

"Rock him or something, Desire! Don't just stare at him," Auntie Linda shouted as she marched out of the room.

I became somewhat alert, rocking Shyne to quietness.

After he had calmed down, he lay there silent with his eyes wide open. My eyes locked with his, and I saw it all over again. I was in a trance. It was a picture of the devil in his eyes. Tears streamed down my face. It couldn't be true. My son was no devil. I had to be just dreaming. I pinched myself and realized this was no dream. I was wide-awake, staring at the devil in my son's eyes.

Then the devil disappeared. He faded away as Shyne closed his eyes. My fears were at ease now. He looked innocent again, like he always did.

I was able to lie back down and go to sleep. I had Shyne snuggled up right beside me too. I fell back into a deep sleep.

"Mommy, I'm going to be a ho just like you when I grow up, giving HIV to every girl in the city. Daddy told me I was going to be like you. Where is my daddy anyway? Do you remember my daddy? Do you know my daddy? How many people did you give HIV to? Was it fun?"

I tossed and turned, sweating, unable to wake up.

"Hi . . . Miss Jones . . . Your son . . . gave me . . . HIV!"

"My son didn't give you anything."

"Yes, he did. He gave it to me."

"He gave it to me too."

"And me."

"Hi . . . Miss Jones . . . I'm Lisa . . . Your son . . . gave me . . . HIV."

"Hi . . . Miss Jones . . . I'm Tasha . . . Your son . . . gave me . . . HIV."

"Hi . . . Miss Jones . . . I'm Tara . . . Your son . . . gave me . . . HIV."

"Hi . . . Miss Jones . . . I'm Keisha . . . Your son . . . gave me . . . HIV."

"Hi . . . Miss Jones . . . I'm Jessica . . . Your son . . . gave me . . . HIV. I told my father . . . He's a cop."

"That boy of yours is the devil, and he needs to get his ass out of Boston before I kill 'im."

Startled from the loudness of my alarm clock, I woke up from my nightmare, my clothes drenched from sweat. Shyne was wide-awake beside me, eyes wide open. His green eyes looked red to me.

I did give birth to the devil. I had to get rid of him. He couldn't grow up to do what I did. I saw it in his eyes. He was going to be just like me. I couldn't have that happen.

I looked at him one more time, and his eye color didn't change. They were bloodshot red. I stared and became hypnotized.

Why you think I didn't want to have this baby? I knew he would get it too. Desire, your test results came back positive. You are HIV positive. If you're pregnant, the baby will have it too. Desire, go get that boy and take care of what's yours. Your test results came back positive. You have HIV. Get rid of that boy. He is the devil. You are HIV positive. Your baby has it too. I knew he would get it too. That's why I didn't want him.

I hit my head trying to stop the voices I was hearing as I kept my eyes on Shyne. A river flowed from my eyes, and there was only one thing left to do. I contemplated on how I was going to kill Shyne without him feeling any pain.

Strangling? Nah, I couldn't stand to see his face turn purple. Maybe I could overdose him on pills, but how would he swallow? He's just a baby. I could shake him to death. Nah, 'cause I would still have to look at him. What if I suffocate him? Yeah, that could work because I wouldn't have to look at his face and he wouldn't suffer much, besides not being able to breathe. That's it!

I had to keep replaying in my mind that this was something I had to do. My son had to die. He couldn't go around giving people HIV like I did. I couldn't let him live to do that. Auntie Linda had already gone for the day, so no one could stop me from doing what I was destined to do. I didn't have those dreams and thoughts for no reason.

I took Shyne downstairs and laid him on the couch, as he had fallen back asleep. I looked at him. He wasn't innocent anymore. The bull's-eye was still there with his eyes closed.

My eyes watered as I thought about what I was going to do. I started shaking and breathing heavy. Tears hit my cheek, and my vision blurred.

Just as I grabbed the pillow next to me and placed it over Shyne's face, the phone rang, startling me. I picked up the receiver without saying a word.

"Hello"

"Hello," I answered back, sniffling.

"Desire, what's wrong? Why you ain't in school? Why's the baby crying? Is everything okay?"

"I have to do this, you know. He can't do like I did. Malik was right."

"What? What are you talking about?"

"I'm talking about me, Jen. Me . . . me and my baby. We have it. We have it . . . and I have to kill 'im before, before he—"

"Kill what? Desire, no. Wait. I'm coming over."

"No! Don't come here!"

"Is your aunt there?"

"No."

"Okay, wait. Just listen to me. Everything is going to be okay. Just tell me what's wrong."

"He's gonna be a whore like his mother."

"Desire, stop it! You know you are better than that. And Shyne is just a baby, an innocent baby."

I had to give it to Jen for trying, but she wasn't going to change my mind. She didn't even know what I knew about my son. I sat on the phone listening to her, looking at the pillow still covering the baby. Then I heard a loud boom in the house. I didn't know what it was.

"Desire, what was that?"

Then this guy appeared out of nowhere and grabbed me by my neck. "Here you are, bitch! You gave me fucking HIV!"

"Desire, what's going on?"

I dropped the phone.

I had no idea who this man was or where he had come from. I had slept with so many people, I couldn't recall his face. I couldn't really get a good glimpse at him either. He came at me so fast. I had no time to do anything but curl up into a ball.

I lay there as he punched me with his large hands that felt like brass. He battered me until I could no longer see or move, but I had enough energy to talk.

"Kill the baby. I'll take care of me."

"No! I'm taking care of you, bitch!"

He picked me up like rag doll and threw me across the room, slamming me into the glass trophy case. Glass shattered everywhere, cutting me up all over.

I was still able to talk though. I was determined to get him to finish what I'd started. "Kill my son! He has it too. Kill him! I'll take care of me!"

"You still talking?" The intruder picked up a trophy off the floor and bashed my head with it.

Just as he did that, the police rushed in. Jen followed right behind them. Then all you heard was Jen's scream.

The intruder hit me again. Jen wailed louder.

The police tackled the guy.

"Oh my God! Desire!"

"Young lady, get back," the officer yelled to Jen, while his partner was reading the assailant his rights and placing him under arrest.

The guy didn't resist, but he kept screaming, "The bitch gave me HIV! She deserved what I did to her! I can't believe that bitch gave me HIV!"

Jen, ignoring the officer, came over to me in tears. She was in "blood territory."

"Oh, Desire, why? Why is this happening to you?" Jen cried desperately.

"Kill . . . kill the baby . . . " I slurred, whispering, not fully conscious.

"I'll get the baby. Don't worry!"

"Noooo . . . he . . . "

"Miss, please get back and let the paramedics through."

"But that's my best friend. Why did he do this to her? She didn't give him anything. He's lying! He's crazy! She doesn't have HIV. He doesn't know what he's talking about. She's only sixteen. I can't lose my best friend! I can't!"

"Miss, calm down. Hey, Chris, get the baby and make sure he's not hurt."

"He's fine, and I'm calling Social Services."

"No, no! Don't call Social Services! This is my baby!"

More officers rushed in. I hear mentions of blood, young girl, baby, tried to kill her. I could no longer keep my eyes open. I fell unconscious. This was the end of my journey. I could feel it.

Chapter 34

"Desire, Desire. Are you awake?"

"Jen, is that you?"

"Yes. It's me. I'm here."

"Thanks." I struggled to speak.

"The doctor said that you'll be okay." Tears came to her eyes. "And the police, they arrested that man. He was crazy. I can't believe he did this to you," she cried. "He kept saying you gave him something. I knew he was lying though. He had to be lying because how could you possibly . . . "

Jen kept going on, and on, and on, and on. I wanted to stop her, but I was too weak, and I had the hardest time getting her attention.

"I was so scared when I saw all that blood."

"Jen."

"And he was so adamant about you giving—"

"Jen!" I managed to yell.

"Yes, yes, Desire. What's wrong? Is something wrong?"

I shook my head no.

"Oh, you scared me," she said, grabbing her chest.

"Listen to me. I have to tell you something."

"Go ahead."

I turned my head to the side. I didn't want to cry, but it hurt. It hurt that I was about to tell my best friend the truth. I looked back over at her.

"What is it?"

"The guy who beat me up . . ."

"Yes, I told you the police got him."

"No, listen." I coughed.

"What? You don't have to worry about him."

"Jen, he's not lying."

"What do you mean, he's not lying?"

"I gave him HIV, Jen. That's what I've been doing. That's why I was sleepin' around."

"What?"

"I got it from Malik. Shyne has it too. Nobody knows though."

She just stood there. "You must be overmedicated or something."

"I'm telling the truth."

"So you're telling me you were giving people HIV on purpose?"

Tears streamed down my face as I looked at her all hurt and confused.

"You put people's lives at risk with HIV?"

I closed my eyes without giving her a response.

"So he wasn't lying," she cried out.

I opened my eyes and looked at her. "You have to kill Shyne."

"What?"

"Shyne . . . he can't grow up with this disease."

"I will not kill my godchild! Are you insane? I can't believe you! You are definitely overmedicated."

"Just do it, Jen."

"No, no. I'm not like you, Desire. You can't just take people's lives and think it's okay. You played me. You played me. All this time you had me hooking you up with guys, and you were infecting them, and you infected your baby. You're sick! You're plain sick!"

"Man up, Jen. You've always been so scaredy. He's only a baby."

"He's only a baby. He's only a baby. I don't kill people, Desire. I don't fucking kill people!"

"Your brother killed me."

"You are so . . . *Ugh*! I hate you! I hate you! I hate you!"

She kept going on about hating me. Then, next thing you know a pillow was covering my face, and I was struggling to get air.

"You're the one who needs to die. Die, Desire. Die!"

I managed to push her off of me, gasping for air.

The nurse walked in. "What's going on?"

"Nothing," Jen answered. "I was just leaving."

"Jen," I yelled.

She turned around.

"Just do it."

"Yeah, you know what? I will. It's about time I man up!"

I watched her walk out hoping she was going to be true to her word, or I was going to have to do it myself. I'd have to kill Shyne and move on like nothing happened. Only now, since Jen knew everything, I may have to kill her too.

Notes